WITHDRAWN

W9-CGV-544

KILL THE INDIAN

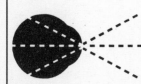

This Large Print Book carries the
Seal of Approval of N.A.V.H.

KILL THE INDIAN

A KILLSTRAIGHT STORY

JOHNNY D. BOGGS

THORNDIKE PRESS
A part of Gale, Cengage Learning

GALE
CENGAGE Learning·

Detroit • New York • San Francisco • New Haven, Conn • Waterville, Maine • London

GALE
CENGAGE Learning®

Copyright © 2012 by Johnny D. Boggs.
Thorndike Press, a part of Gale, Cengage Learning.

ALL RIGHTS RESERVED
The publisher bears no responsibility for the quality of information provided through author or third-party Web sites and does not have any control over, nor assume any responsibility for, information contained in these sites. Providing these sites should not be construed as an endorsement or approval by the publisher of these organizations or of the positions they may take on various issues.
Thorndike Press® Large Print Western.
The text of this Large Print edition is unabridged.
Other aspects of the book may vary from the original edition.
Set in 16 pt. Plantin.

LIBRARY OF CONGRESS CATALOGING-IN-PUBLICATION DATA

Boggs, Johnny D.
  Kill the Indian : a Killstraight story / by Johnny D. Boggs.
    pages ; cm. — (Thorndike Press large print western)
  ISBN 978-1-4104-5375-4 (hardcover) — ISBN 1-4104-5375-8 (hardcover) 1.
Comanche Indians—Fiction. 2. Murder—Investigation—Texas—Fiction. 3.
Large type books. I. Title.
PS3552.O4375K48 2012b
813'.54—dc23   2012032597

Published in 2012 by arrangement with Golden West Literary Agency.

Printed in the United States of America
1 2 3 4 5 6 7 16 15 14 13 12

For Lucia St. Clair Robson,
fine friend, great writer, and a
Comanche at heart

CHAPTER ONE

Sweating profusely, Daniel pushes his way through the throng crowding the boardwalks of Hell's Half Acre.

Over the silk top hats, bowlers, Stetsons, and battered slouch hats, he can just make out Rain Shower, in her doeskin dress and moccasins, fighting through the multitude. She's maybe twenty yards ahead of him. He calls out her name. Screams it louder, but she can't hear him. He can't even hear his own voice.

The people — taibos, *all of them, white men without faces — grunt like pigs, pushing him backward. He turns sideways, letting some of these men rush past him. Now he can no longer see Rain Shower. He jumps, tries to catch only a glimpse of her. A boot steps on his own moccasin. A spur's rowel grazes his calf. Angrily he slams an elbow into the side of a passer-by, but doubts if the faceless man feels anything. He curses, in the language of*

The People and in the pale-eyes tongue, forces a path through the crush, jumps again, screams Rain Shower's name.

He spots her shiny black hair, but just briefly. She's too far ahead of him. He wants her closer. Needs her to be closer. Why does she keep walking? Why doesn't she wait for me? Why doesn't she turn back toward me?

"Rain Shower!" he cries. "Wait! Stop! Wait for me!"

Fort Worth, Texas, is no place for a Nermernuh *girl. Especially not in Hell's Half Acre.*

A white man in dirty vest and bandanna shoves him, and he stumbles, catches himself on a wooden column in front of a hitching rail. No horses tethered here, he notices, so he pulls himself onto the rail, gripping the column for support, finally able to see above the mass of people. They look like buffalo now, the way the buffalo used to look on the Llano Estacado, millions of them, so thick you could not see the ground.

Again, he yells Rain Shower's name, and this time she turns. His heart races, but he can breathe again. He almost slips on the rail; in fact, he swings off briefly, but somehow he manages to get his feet back on the wood. Recovered, he looks down the boardwalk.

Rain Shower laughs at him, and he smiles back at her.

8

"Wait for me," he says. Or starts to say. Before he can finish, he sees the hand reach around the corner. It grasps Rain Shower's arm.

Fear etches into her face. She stares at the man holding her — Daniel can't see the man, just his arm and hand, and the hand is covered in a bright red glove — then Rain Shower turns back toward Daniel and screams.

Only he can't hear her scream. The hand jerks her out of sight, around the corner of a false-fronted mercantile.

"No!" Daniel yells, losing his grip on the wooden column, feeling his moccasins slip off the rail. He falls onto the boardwalk, landing on his back, hard, forcing the air out of his lungs. He rolls to his side, opens his eyes, tries to catch his breath, and sees the stampeding buffalo, feels the first hoof crush his ribs, as thunder rumbles and the skies darken. . . .

Daniel Killstraight woke with a start.

His heart pounded, and his long black hair felt as if he had just been dunked in Cache Creek. He ripped the sweat-soaked sheet off his body, and stared at the darkened ceiling, trying to recall the dream. No, he decided. It would be better to forget that nightmare. It would be better to figure out

9

where he was.

Not home. Home, for Daniel Killstraight, was a cabin the Pale Eyes had built for Ben Buffalo Bone's late father, a wooden structure his friend's father, and now his uncle, used as a stable. For the past two years, those unshod ponies shared the house with Daniel Killstraight. Ben was Rain Shower's brother, and that started Daniel thinking about the nightmare that had awakened him.

He wasn't on the reservation near Fort Sill in Indian Territory, but at the Pickwick Hotel in Fort Worth. No, that wasn't right, either. When Daniel and his Comanche Indian friends had arrived in Fort Worth to meet a few Texas cattlemen, and attend a lecture by Captain Richard Pratt, the hotel manager had smiled like a weasel and stammered that no rooms were available in the hotel.

"No rooms for Indians, you mean," Daniel had said.

The hotel manager, a balding man with a waxed mustache, ran his finger underneath his paper collar, shaking his head, saying: "No, no, young man, no. That's not it at all. It's a busy weekend, you see. Lots of guests. But I have taken liberty to arrange for you to stay in the Taylor and Barr building. It is not far from her, gentlemen, just over on Houston Street. They have five modern and quite comfortable apartments upstairs." The man's small eyes shot from Daniel to Charles Flint to Yellow Bear and, finally, to Quanah Parker.

"Indoor plumbing," the man stammered. "Gas lamps. Much quieter, too."

This wasn't his first trip to Fort Worth, and Daniel let the manager know it.

"We stayed in the Texas Hotel last year," he said.

Quanah nodded. "Treat good. No ticks in bed. Ice cream."

"There are no ticks in our beds, either, Mister Parker." The manager sounded indignant. "I assure you." He trained his eyes on Daniel. "And you, young man, I'll have you know that a noble savage . . . I mean, a dignitary like Quanah Parker and his entourage, a friend to great cattlemen Dan Waggoner and Captain Lee Hall, both friends of the Pickwick Hotel, would be most welcome in any of our suites . . . if any happened to be available. We are full up, sirs."

Quanah Parker might be welcome here, Daniel figured, but not Daniel Killstraight. Not tonight. Not ever.

So here he was in the Taylor and Barr

11

building, sweating in a room that felt like a furnace. It was August, however, so no one could do anything about the heat. Charles Flint was just down and across the hall. Next door to Daniel were Quanah and Yellow Bear, who had insisted that they share the room. Isa-tai, Charles Flint's father, bunked with Nagwee, the *puhakat* of the Kotsoteka band who had come to counsel Quanah, in the room next to Flint's. As far as Daniel knew, the fifth room, directly across from Daniel's, remained vacant.

Sighing, he reached above his head, and turned up the gas lamp, before swinging his feet over the bed. Once his heartbeat had dropped to something more reasonable, he stood, and eased his way to the open window. Putting his hands on the sill, he leaned out into the Fort Worth night, hoping to catch a breeze, but the wind did not blow, and the air felt heavy with humidity. The thermometer outside the plate-glass window in front of Taylor & Barr's store had read one hundred and four degrees, and Daniel doubted if the mercury had fallen much.

Even at night, however, even in a miserable heat wave, Fort Worth's citizens remained active. A hack's carriage clopped down the street, and he could make out the noise of a piano, a banjo, laughter. A whistle blew. A horse snorted. A woman giggled.

Fort Worth, Daniel decided, never slept.

It reminded him of the cities he had seen back East. Philadelphia, Pittsburgh, and Carlisle, and while the latter seemed even smaller than Fort Worth, Daniel figured it couldn't be. Fort Worth, however, was certainly different than those Pennsylvania cities, and a long, long way from home.

The window overlooked an empty alley running between Houston and Main. With no street lamps in the alley, he could make out the dim outline of the walls of the Fakes & Company furniture warehouse. The three-story Pickwick Hotel was northwest, at the corner of Main and Third. He couldn't see that hotel, could barely make out anything in the darkness, although light shone from the windows and door at the saloon across the street, illuminating at least a part of Houston Street. Jinglebobs started singing a song beneath him, and Daniel looked down.

No, the alley wasn't empty. A cowhand was busy muttering something as he unbuttoned his pants, and soon began spraying the wall of the Taylor & Barr mercantile with urine, soaking the white-stenciled lettering on the brick walls.

WE OFFER OUR ENTIRE LINE OF CHILDREN'S, MISSES' and LADIES' CLOAKS AND DOLMANS, BOYS', YOUTHS' and MEN'S CLOTHING AT MANUFACTURRERS' PRICES.

Daniel wondered if he were the only person in Fort Worth who realized the painter had misspelled manufacturer.

Quanah had bought a cloak and a dolman earlier that afternoon, even though Charles Flint had told the Comanche chief that he could buy something cheaper at the agency near Fort Sill once they got back home.

Daniel could still picture the look Quanah gave Charles Flint. "But I ask you what dolman and you say you no know," Quanah had said as they stood on the boardwalk, staring at the wall advertisement.

"But . . . I . . . you . . . it's . . . I. . . ." Charles Flint could not think of anything else to say, and Daniel knew that rarely happened.

"Come," Quanah had announced, speaking in broken English for the Texians accompanying the Comanche delegation. "We find dolman. If like, me buy one for Tonarcy." Tonarcy was undoubtedly Quanah's favorite of his eight wives.

"Hell's bells, this alley stinks of piss!"

Daniel looked down at the cowboy again, heard him laugh at his joke, saw him stagger, those spurs chiming while he made a wandering path back toward Houston Street. As soon as he stepped out of the alley, he stopped. A police officer had grabbed the cowhand's shoulder, spun him around, and the tall, gangling man had toppled into the dust on his backside.

"Jesus, Mother Mary, and Joseph, what in the bloody hell were you doing in that alley, you drunken waddie?" The officer pointed something — nightstick, Daniel guessed, what he remembered both coppers and miners in Pennsylvania calling a billy club — at the cowhand.

It sounded like the cowhand answered: "Waterin' my mules."

The policeman said something Daniel couldn't understand, but a shout came from up the street, probably from the Occidental Saloon, and the policeman left the cowhand in the dust, and took off running toward the shouts, yelling something, and blowing his whistle.

After three clumsily failed attempts, the cowhand managed to push himself to his feet, and weave his way across Houston Street and through the batwing doors of Herman Kussatz's Tivoli Hall.

More whistles sounded, and he could make out shouts, curses. For seven years, Daniel had lived among the Pale Eyes in Pennsylvania. First as the lone Comanche student at Carlisle Industrial School — although Charles Flint would join him during Daniel's last year learning to be a *taibo*. Then in Franklin County, working for that hard-rock German until blisters covered his hands and feet. Finally, breathing coal dust and hardly seeing the sunshine at the Castle Shannon Mine near Pittsburgh. Yet he never really understood the Pale Eyes. For two years, he had been back among his people — if they were his people anymore — wearing the badge and uniform of The People's tribal police. Metal Shirts, The People called them. His own uniform showed the chevrons of a sergeant. At least it had, until Daniel, and all the other Metal Shirts, had cut off the sleeves of those scratchy, ill-fitting gray woolen blouses. Now they wore them like the pale-eyes vests.

More whistles blew. A window smashed. A horse whinnied.

He heard something else, and bumped his head against the open window. A door had shut down the hall. He rubbed his head, and walked to the dresser to pour a glass of water.

Tepid, tasting like iron, the water didn't cool him. He could barely even swallow it, but he made himself, then mopped his face and the back of his neck with a hand towel, and wiped his long black hair, sopping wet. He stared at the door, then at the clock, wondering who would be coming to his room so late. If that cheap little Progressor kept the right time, it was 3:17 A.M.

Daniel smiled then, remembering. He and Quanah had retired shortly after supper, and Charles Flint had said he would soon join them. Yellow Bear, however, had said he wanted to see the sights, so George Briggs, a pale-eyes cowhand who worked for the big *taibo* rancher Dan Waggoner, had promised that he and old Yellow Bear would "tree the town" — whatever that meant.

The shutting door he had heard must have been Yellow Bear, finally making his way back to the room after a night on the town. He couldn't wait to hear Yellow Bear's stories over breakfast.

Outside, a cow bawled, probably from those giant shipping pens at the stockyards.

Cattle reminded him of buffalo — *cuhtz* in The People's tongue — and that brought the final image from his nightmare to his mind. Daniel shook off the thought. Instead, he settled into the cushioned parlor chair,

17

remembering what had brought him to Fort
Worth.

CHAPTER TWO

"You two are going to Texas," Joshua Biggers said with a smile.

Daniel and Charles Flint looked at each other, then stared at the young Baptist minister who had been appointed agent — the third in two years — for the Comanche, Kiowa, and Apache reservation, giving him the blank stares The People often gave Pale Eyes.

Hugh Gunter, Daniel's Cherokee friend and a member of the United States Indian Police with jurisdiction over the Five Civilized Tribes east of Comanche country, called it: "The dumb look."

The smile faded from the young agent's face. "Not permanently," he said, swallowed, and shuffled through the papers on his desk. Beads of sweat peppered his forehead. His Adam's apple bobbed, and at last he found the paper he wanted.

"This is a letter from Captain Pratt," he

said. "He's giving a talk in Fort Worth. He specifically requested that you two join him. . . ."

"Pratt." Charles Flint tested the name.

Daniel remembered Pratt. How could he ever forget him? A bluecoat, Richard Pratt had started the Carlisle Industrial School, teaching Indians to follow the white man's road. When Daniel was thirteen, he had been loaded onto a wagon with several Arapahoes and sent to the railroad station. In Pennsylvania, they had joined other frightened Indians — Lakotas, Cheyennes, Kiowas, even Pawnees, traditional enemies of The People. It was at school that School Father Pratt had given Daniel his new name.

Once, Daniel had been called His Arrows Fly Straight Into The Hearts Of His Enemies, the name his father had given him. Pale Eyes never could quite translate that name into their own tongue, so they had shortened it to Killstraight. At Carlisle, Pratt had made all the new students point to a Pale-Eyes *word* written on a blackboard — after white men and women had shorn the new students' long, black hair, forced them to bathe with smelly soap and steaming hot water, and made them wear itchy Pale-Eyes clothes. Reluctantly, almost defiantly, Daniel had pointed to one, and watched as

School Father Pratt nodded and scratched a white line through the *word,* the chalk screeching and making Daniel's skin crawl. "Now," School Father Pratt had said with a smile, "your name is Daniel."

Later, one of the School Mothers had demanded that Daniel take a new surname. Her word still rang in his ears. "Killstraight conjures simulacrums of depredations, of rapine, of the barbarous nature of these savage fiends. Strait. . . ." He could see her double chin wagging as her head bobbed with satisfaction. "Daniel Strait would fit him well. A noble Anglo-Saxon name. I knew many Straits in Hertshire."

"Perhaps," School Father Pratt had said with a smile, as he placed a hand on Daniel's shoulder and squeezed gently, "but, having taught this lad for these past few years, I think Killstraight fits him like a glove. Leave it Killstraight, Missus Hall. Daniel has earned that much, I warrant."

That might have been Daniel's only victory at Carlisle. He could remember the beatings, still feel the sharp sting of a switch against his back or one of the School Mother's rulers smashing his knuckles. Punishment for speaking his true tongue.

"You are no longer a savage!" School Mother Hall had admonished him. "You

21

must speak English!"

They had made him pray to the pale-eyes god. Taught him to speak the pale-eyes tongue, taught him to learn the pale-eyes trades, taught him to eat like Pale Eyes, think like Pale Eyes, be a Pale Eyes.

Daniel had fought. Fought against all of them at first, and he was not alone. Lakota boys and girls fought. Kiowas resisted. Cheyennes argued. Some even died, not from the whippings, but of sickness, of broken hearts. They had been buried like Pale Eyes, in wooden boxes, buried deep in the smelly Pennsylvania earth far from their homes.

"Who are you?" School Father Pratt had once asked him, when School Mother Hall had brought Daniel into Pratt's office and told the bluecoat that Daniel would be better off sent to the prison in Florida, that he would never learn to follow the white man's road, that he would always be a savage. It was in his heart.

"Who are you?" Pratt had repeated.

"Nermernuh." He had answered in the language of The People.

"Comanche, eh?" That the School Father knew enough of The People's tongue surprised Daniel. Pratt rose from his chair, and moved around the desk. Daniel's fingers balled into fists. He stared ahead, not looking at the School Father, just staring at the portrait of Abraham Lincoln hanging on the wall behind the desk. "I was commissioned a second lieutenant back in 'Sixty-Seven. My first station was at Fort Arbuckle in Indian Territory. I've been to Fort Marion, son. Three years there as a jailer. Trust me, Daniel. You don't want to go to Florida." Pratt had sighed, shaking his head. "Many white men and women would like to see your race exterminated. I don't believe that's right. It certainly isn't Christian. We must live and work together. But you're Comanche. Perhaps you think differently."

Abraham Lincoln had not moved. Daniel had not blinked.

"I wanted to bring Comanches," Pratt had continued. "More than just one. More Kiowas. More of the Indians I had gotten to know during my duty in the Territory, and there had already been schools established on the reservation. But Commissioner Hayt insisted that we start with primarily Sioux. Use the children there. They would be hostages, force the Sioux to stay on their best behavior. But you're Comanche."

Silence.

Daniel had kept staring at Abraham Lincoln.

Slowly School Father Pratt had stepped in front of him. "Wasn't your mother Mescalero?"

Daniel couldn't help it. His shoulders sagged, and he looked away from the Great White Father and into School Father Pratt's eyes. At that moment, Daniel knew the Pale Eyes had beaten him.

His father, who had taken the name Marsh Hawk, had been a Kwahadi warrior who had been shipped off to Florida. Soldiers had shot him when he had tried to escape from the train taking those prisoners to Fort Marion. Dying a fitting death for a warrior. Yet it was true. His mother was Mescalero Apache, and Daniel could remember boys his own age, some younger, and men much older often teasing him. "Your blood is not pure," they would say. "You are not whole." Or even worse: "You are not *Nermernuh*."

Years later, after Daniel had accepted the paper that said he had been graduated, School Father Pratt had smiled, shaken his head, and said: "You're one of the best students I have had, Daniel. Other Comanches, I hope, will follow the example you have set, son."

Charles Flint was one of those.

Flint had arrived the year Daniel had left

Carlisle, and had gone to work in those coal mines. After seven years of learning to be a white man, Daniel had returned to the Territory, to his home. Now he was a sergeant in the tribal police, a Metal Shirt, earning $8 a month. Charles Flint had returned from Pennsylvania a year earlier, and now worked for the Pale Eyes, George McEveety, who ran the trading post between the agency and Fort Sill.

"He's a crackerjack bookkeeper," Mr. McEveety said. "Got the best head for numbers I seen in any man, and I'm talkin' 'bout white men. Not just Injuns."

We are a lot alike, Daniel thought, *Flint and me. "White Comanches," Mr. McEveety would say.*

Glancing at Flint, Daniel realized *White Comanche* probably applied to Charles Flint more than himself. Two, maybe three, years younger than Daniel, Charles Flint kept his raven-dark hair closely shorn, and sat bolt upright in the chair in front of Agent Biggers's desk, hands folded neatly on his lap, a soft black fedora resting on his crossed knee. Despite the heat, he wore a double-breasted coat of gray wool, although he had unbuttoned it, matching trousers, and Congress gaiters that, if they weren't covered with so much dust after the walk from the trading post, would have been as dark as his hair and eyes. A red satin tie clung tightly to his neck, dangling over the plaited-front, polka-dotted shirt of fine cotton. A silver-tipped mahogany walking cane rested against the arm of his chair, and Daniel could hear the ticking of Flint's gold watch. If Flint's skin had not been so copper, he could have passed for a Pale Eyes.

Yeah, School Father Pratt would definitely be proud of Charles Flint.

But proud of Daniel? No, Pratt would likely consider Daniel . . . what was the word he had heard Agent Biggers use once after a Sunday sermon?

Backslider.

Daniel's hair had grown long, and now hung in braids over his shoulders. His shirt, a flowery calico of red, green, yellow, and blue, came from the trading post, and his gray coat-turned-vest, an artifact from the Centennial Exposition, was pale-eyes clothing. Yet the bear-claw necklace, the buckskin leggings, and his comfortable moccasins were Comanche. And his hat, stiff-brimmed, high-crowned, caked with dust and made and sold by Pale Eyes, was the kind you'd find on just about every Comanche man on the reservation these days. Daniel had dressed his up by sticking a hawk feather in the band.

A man cannot hide behind clothes, Daniel knew. Charles Flint dressed like a pale-eyes bookkeeper. Daniel wore the clothes of a Comanche Metal Shirt. After years at Carlisle, however, both struggled trying to accept who they were, what they had become. White? Comanche? Or, in Daniel's case, a pale-eyes-educated, Mescalero Apache-*Nermernuh* mongrel.

"Captain Platt thought this would be a great opportunity." Joshua Biggers was speaking again. Daniel looked up at the agent. "Captain Hall has requested that Quanah join him and the other stockmen in Fort Worth to negotiate a new lease on The Big Pasture."

Daniel only knew Captain Hall by name and reputation. For a while, Hall had commanded a Ranger company — a *taibo* Metal Shirt, Daniel mused — and before that had served as peace officer in a couple other North Texas towns, but had not worn a badge for several years now. He was president, Daniel remembered, of the Northern Texas Stock Growers' Association. Just before Daniel had returned to Indian Territory, however, Hall had served as an agent up at Anadarko, but had been removed. Daniel wasn't sure why, although he sus-

27

pected the captain had been charged with graft. Practically every agent on every reserve in the Territory had been charged with graft. He hoped Joshua Biggers would be an exception.

That tenure on the reservation, however, had led Captain Hall to meet and befriend Quanah Parker, which now came in handy since the captain operated a large ranch down in Texas.

Texas longhorns needed grass, and grass could be found aplenty on the Comanche reservation.

"Captain Platt says this would be a wonderful chance for you two young men, and Quanah, to show these Texians how much improvement has been made on the reservation," Joshua Biggers continued. "They have arranged speeches at the Wednesday Woman's Club and on the City Hall lawn. Captain Hall and Captain Pratt will pay all expenses for you. It will be a grand adventure, and an education to be sure."

To be sure. Daniel rubbed his crooked nose with two fingers. The last time — the only time — he had traveled to Fort Worth, he had damned near gotten himself beaten to death. The nose was a reminder. Well, actually, that had happened in Dallas, but Fort Worth hadn't been that much better.

28

With the exception of the Queen City Ice Cream Parlor, he remembered.

Texas cities were pretty much all the same. At least, that's what Hugh Gunter always told him. A "God-awful state" peopled with "fool Texians." On the other hand, Daniel wasn't sure his Cherokee friend and mentor had ever really set foot in Texas.

Charles Flint cleared his throat. "We would go to Fort Worth with Quanah?"

Not a trace of The People when he spoke, Daniel marveled. Half the time, Daniel still spoke in grunts and snorts, like most reservation Comanches. *What would School Father Pratt say when he hears me speak?* he wondered.

"Yes." Agent Biggers's head bobbed like a rocking horse. "Certainly."

Daniel studied Flint. He had removed the fedora from his kneecap, and was crushing the soft felt hat in his hands, staring directly at the young Baptist agent.

Daniel liked and admired Quanah, but not all of The People did. Daniel had been just a young boy, and Flint — in those years known only by the name his father had given him, Tetecae — had been even younger. Yet Daniel remembered the hunger, the pain. He could recall the cries of the young babies, the weariness everyone felt. Bluecoat Long Knives had killed their pony herds, burned their villages. Then there were the other *taibo* men, Pale Eyes who had killed buffalo by the thousands, more heartless than the bluecoat Long Knives. In the year Pale Eyes called 1875 but that The People sadly recalled as The Year The Kwahadis Quit Fighting, Quanah had been forced to lead the last of the Kwahadi band, the last of The People still resisting the Pale Eyes, to surrender at the bluecoat fort built near Cache Creek, in what not only once had been The People's homeland, but as sacred ground as The People had known.

Pale Eyes had made Quanah Parker the chief of all The People.

Some *Nermernuh* resented that.

Maybe Daniel saw much of himself in Quanah. Daniel's mother had been Mescalero; Quanah's was a white woman that had been captured on a raid in Texas. Daniel had heard some men complain that Quanah was not pure, was not truly of The People, but never to Quanah's face. As a warrior, he had been relentless in his fight to keep The People free. As the designated chief on the reservation, he now understood how hopeless fighting the Pale Eyes was.

So he took the white man's road. Lived in

a big, white-man house the Texas cattlemen had built for him. He encouraged the mothers to send their children to mission schools. He encouraged the men to eat beef, for there were no more buffalo. He wore pale-eyes clothes even better than what Charles Flint donned.

In his own way, however, Quanah resisted.

Every Indian agent assigned to the reservation — Joshua Biggers included — had tried to tell Quanah that he must have only one wife. Yet Quanah still had eight. When he spoke English, the words were broken, often butchered. Yet when he spoke the tongue of *Nermernuh,* it was pure, powerful, and forceful, and not lazy reservation talk.

Daniel waited to hear what Charles Flint would say.

"I must seek counsel with my father on this matter," he said, and rose, bowing, extending his hand to Agent Biggers. He reshaped his hat, set it atop his head, and walked outside.

Confused, Joshua Biggers turned to Daniel.

"I thought he'd jump at the chance to go to Fort Worth." Biggers's head shook slowly. "I hope he'll go. Or you. Else, I'll have to send Frank Striker to interpret, and I'd rather have Frank here to help me."

"I'll go," Daniel said. He remembered the peach ice cream at the Queen City Ice Cream Parlor, but he had also recalled hearing Deputy U.S. Marshal Harvey P. Noble say that butter pecan tasted even better.

Daniel tried to shake off this thought. Maybe he was becoming more Pale Eyes. But Charles Flint? Seeking out his father before making a decision? Tetecae was showing that he had not forgotten all the ways of The People.

CHAPTER THREE

Ration day came, as always, with much fanfare among The People. Men dressed in their best war shirts, shunning the open-crown pale-eyes hats for eagle feathers or dusty buffalo headdresses, smiles carved among the crevasses of the old women's wrinkled faces.

Toddlers stumbled. Dogs yipped, their tails wagging. Horses snorted. Young women sang, their eyes bright with joy. Boys acted like men. Men acted like boys.

By the corrals of the agency, Joshua Biggers, *taibo* cattlemen, missionaries from the schools, soldiers, and a half dozen laundresses from nearby Fort Sill watched. Daniel recognized the looks on the faces of those Pale Eyes. It was the same look he and his fellow miners had revealed when Adok Król had chided them into attending the Atkinson Dime Museum in Pittsburgh. Seeing the half-man, half-woman with the beard and arms thicker than Adok Król's had turned Daniel's eyes bulging. Watching a man swallow a sword had left Daniel's muscles tightening in his bowels. He knew those looks. Disgust. Fear. Amazement.

The corral gate swung open, and inside rode five boys, the tails of their painted ponies tied up, their small hands gripping huge lances. Spears carved from wood by old men, the way The People once hunted buffalo. No rifles. The People did not care to hunt that way, and this was as close to hunting buffalo as. . . . Daniel shook his head.

Yipping excitedly, mimicking coyotes, the boys kicked their horses into the midst of the bawling longhorns, got the beefs running, raising dust, and began thrusting lances into the sides of the cattle. Women sang louder. Older men, the fathers of these teenagers, laughed, pointed, called out encouragement.

A Negro laundress fainted. A white woman soon joined her.

When the slaughter was complete, the women came in, with skinning knives and buckets. Kneeling beside the revived laundress, Joshua Biggers mouthed a prayer, as he always did on ration day.

As a member of the tribal police, and

drawing his $8 in government script, Daniel was not eligible for rations. It was his job to keep the peace, make sure the lines moved as men and women stood in line to get their monthly rations: sugar and flour, both often not worth eating, corn that Mr. McEveety was decent enough to trade for coffee, barrels of salted pork, and sacks of bacon. Earlier that morning, Daniel and Ben Buffalo Bone, with Agent Biggers watching, had opened some of the barrels and sacks. Often, suppliers would put coal in the bottom of the barrel and fill the sacks with more rocks than rancid meat. But this time, the rations were fairly acceptable.

"My son remembers not the days of *cuhtz*," a voice said. "Do you?"

Daniel turned.

Isa-tai's shadow fell across Daniel's face. He was large, even for a man of The People, needing a neck like a bull to keep his huge head from sinking into his shoulders. A long strand of hair fell across his wide cheek. The strand was well-placed by the Kwahadi holy man. Isa-tai was just vain enough to try to hide the scar an angry Cheyenne had given him years earlier.

He had wrapped a trade blanket around his waist, and wore a calico shirt and gray woolen vest, a red silk bandanna secured

35

around his throat by a silver slide. A gold wedding band tightly gripped his left pinky, just between the fingernail and first knuckle, a ring he had taken off a pale-eyes woman killed during a raid up in Kansas, and a conch-shell hair-pipe breastplate, decorated with Russian blue beads and German silver, clung tightly to his broad chest, the buckskin neck strings wrapped with ermine skins.

"Yes, *Tsu Kuh Puah,*" Daniel answered, using the term of respect for an older man. "I remember."

Isa-tai grunted. Standing slightly behind him, his son, Charles Flint, still dressed in suit, tie, and fedora, dropped his head.

Yes, Daniel remembered when The People ate buffalo, not cattle. *Cuhtz* was indispensable. Hide and hair, blood and bones, just about everything on the buffalo would be used by The People. He pictured his mother, holding his hand, singing from the top of a mesa, pointing out her husband, Daniel's father, down below as the Kwahadis chased a thundering herd of buffalo on the Llano Estacado of the Texas Panhandle. Dust soon swallowed everything below, and the hoofs of the great herd drowned out the shouts of the men.

He pictured his father, standing before him some time later, holding a liver in his bloody hand. He could taste the liver now, after his mother had emptied the contents of the buffalo's gall bladder onto the raw meat. His mother had laughed, and gone back to work, singing as she skinned and butchered the buffalo cow.

"All gone," Isa-tai said. His face showed no emotion. "I will tell you two the story of the time before *cuhtz.*"

Charles Flint lifted his head. Daniel nodded, waiting.

Isa-tai spoke.

"The People were playing games when a strange old man approached them, saying nothing, a quiver over his shoulder but he held no bow. He watched The People play, then said it was time for him to go shit. So he removed the quiver, laid it on the ground, and went down to the creek. One of The People decided to look into the quiver, and he pulled out a large piece of fat. 'This man has plenty of meat,' he announced.

"The old man came from the creek bed and changed into a bird. He flew over the mountain.

"Naturally The People were curious. They wanted to follow him. They wanted to fly over the mountain, to see what was there. So one man changed into an owl, because an owl flies quietly, and another became a quail, because a quail walks quietly. These two flew over the mountain as well. There, they saw a lone teepee, facing east, as is the custom of The People. At sunset, Owl flew to the teepee, but the old man knew that Owl was really one of The People, so Owl flew away and told Quail. Quail then walked softly to the teepee, and returned, telling Owl . . . 'There are three people inside . . . the old man, his wife, their daughter.' Both Owl and Quail returned to the teepee, and waited, listening.

" 'Mother, I am hungry,' the daughter said.

" 'Shush,' the mother said. 'Those Indians might be here.'

"But the old man said that he was hungry, too, so the woman opened a parfleche from which she pulled out much meat. The meat smelled good. Quail wanted to go in and snatch some, but Owl would not let him, whispering wisely . . . 'We must wait.'

"When their meal was finished, the woman brushed the remnants to the back of the teepee, and then they all went to sleep. When they were asleep, Quail entered the teepee, grabbed the crumbs, the suet, a few loose chunks, and brought them outside. Owl and Quail took all the meat they could carry and flew back to The People.

"There was much excitement in the village that night. The People loved the taste of the meat, and they were hungry. So they decided to move camp. They packed their stuff on ten horses, for ten horses represented each band of The People, and they rode around the mountain.

"The old man was not happy to see The People, who said they were just visiting. The old man drew a line from a tree to a stump, telling them that they must camp on this side of the line and never cross it. The old man visited The People each day for three days, but he always said that he knew not where to find any meat. But The People did not believe him.

"On the fourth morning, Kawus arrived, but the hero of The People came in the form of a coyote. He told The People that the old man would not give them any meat, would not tell them how to find it, but he would find it for them. He told The People that they must move their camp away from the old man's teepee. Then, Kawus changed himself into a puppy.

"The People moved their camp, but the old man followed them to make sure they were indeed returning to the other side of the mountain. Satisfied, he returned to his lodge, where he found his daughter calling to the puppy, who was whimpering under a juniper. She would approach, but the puppy would back into the brush that grew near the trunk of the juniper. 'Come here,' the girl said, 'you are mine now.' The puppy just whimpered.

" 'Do not be afraid,' she said. 'I will feed you.' And she held out a chunk of meat, and the puppy crawled out of the brush. It was suspicious, but it followed the girl into the teepee. Kawus saw a hole in the floor, and in the hole he saw a hundred thousand buffalo!

" 'Take that dog out or I will kill it!' the old man shouted. 'It is not a dog, but one of The People. You can tell by its eyes.'

"The girl obeyed her father. The old man walked out of the teepee and looked at the puppy, then went off to make sure The People were not coming back.

"When her father was gone, the girl picked up the puppy and brought him right back into the teepee. 'You will never go hungry again,' she said, and scratched the little dog's ears.

"Kawus jumped out of the girl's hands, and ran around the hole, shouting like one of The People. The buffalo stampeded. They crashed out of the teepee and took to the plains.

" 'You tricked me!' the girl yelled, and she picked up a club to brain the puppy, but by then Kawus had changed into the form of a man. He leaped onto the back of the last buffalo, and escaped the girl. Kawus rode straight to the new village of The People.

"They asked him what had happened. Kawus smiled and said . . . 'Tomorrow at sunrise those buffalo will be outside our door. The People will never go hungry. There will always be buffalo to eat.'

"That is how we got buffalo." Isa-tai, his face hardening, gestured toward the corrals with contempt. "And this is how we lost them!"

He was moving now, making a beeline toward a gathering of men beside a small fire outside the corrals. Daniel glanced at Flint, and both followed Isa-tai. *Keeping the peace today,* Daniel thought, *might not be so easy.*

Quanah Parker stood in front of the fire, stumping, as the Pale Eyes would say.

His long black braids, wrapped in otter skins, fell well past his shoulders, and beaded moccasins covered his feet. Yet he also wore black-striped britches of the finest wool, a matching Prince Albert coat, silver brocade vest, and a puffy silk tie with a diamond stickpin in its center. A black

41

bowler topped his head.

Tall, lean, especially for one of The People, he towered over the men who had gathered by the fire to hear him talk. Nagwee, the grizzled Kotsoteka *puhakat,* squatted, arms folded, eyes staring into the smoke. Yellow Bear sat in a folding Army camp chair, glancing every now and then through the corral slats to watch the butchering process. Across from Yellow Bear stood Cuhtz Bávi, Ben Buffalo Bone's uncle, another Kotsoteka, who had married Ben's mother after lung sickness had sent her husband on the journey to The Land Beyond The Sun. A young Kwahadi named Eka Huutsuu, meaning Red Bird, leaned against the corral, while a gray-haired Penateka, whose name Daniel could not remember, squatted by the fire, looking up as Quanah talked.

Whatever words Quanah had now died on his tongue as Isa-tai positioned himself between Yellow Bear and Quanah.

Quanah nodded, his face hard, eyes angry.

Flint stepped behind his father, and Daniel walked to the corral, put his hand on the top rail, and turned.

He knew what this conversation was about. It had to be about one of two things, or maybe both.

A year ago sometime during the Sleet

Month, *Positsu mua,* the Congress of the United States had enacted the Dawes General Allotment Act. Daniel had met Henry L. Dawes when the Massachusetts senator had been doing some stumping of his own before Quanah Parker at the Comanche chief's Star House.

The way Daniel understood it, the new law would allow the President, whenever he so pleased, to give up their reservation. The land the government had placed The People on would be surveyed by *taibos* and divided into . . . what was that word? Yes, allotments. The land would be owned by individual Indians.

Which was foreign to Daniel as it was incomprehensible to all of The People. Land belonged to everyone, or at least everyone strong enough to hold onto it. Individuals did not own land. Land was not the same as horses, as wives.

So far, the President had not yet decided it was time for The People to relinquish their reservation. That time, Daniel knew, would come soon. He had learned that much about Pale Eyes. They wanted to own all the land on the earth.

Or, it was about the lease. Quanah had made a tidy profit, and so had The People, by leasing pastures to the *taibo* cattlemen to feed their longhorns.

At first, Quanah had opposed both Senator Dawes and Texas cattle barons, yet he had been won over by their arguments. Or maybe Quanah was wise enough to know that Pale Eyes would get whatever it was they wanted. Hadn't they already stolen the land that once belonged to The People? One had to follow the white man's road, it seemed, for at least a little bit, or be squashed like a bug. Quanah, Daniel knew in his heart, would do what he thought best for The People.

Isa-tai, on the other hand, was not so certain.

"You speak like you dress," Isa-tai said, nodding at Quanah. "Like a *taibo*."

"I speak for The People." Surprisingly Quanah spoke in a reserved voice that belied the expression etched in his face.

Isa-tai spit into the fire. "The People." He grunted, shaking his massive head. "Pale Eyes say you are our chief, but that is not our way."

"This I know," Quanah said. "But I also know we must bend. For the benefit of our loved ones, our children, our wives. If not, The People will disappear like the buffalo."

Yellow Bear grunted and nodded. That didn't surprise Daniel. After all, Yellow Bear was the father of Quanah's favorite wife.

Cuhtz Bávi looked from Quanah to Isa-tai, as if he expected a fight to commence. That didn't surprise Daniel, either.

"Hear me," Isa-tai announced, loud enough for the women and children inside the corral with the dead cattle to hear. "Quanah has his own herd of *taibo* beef. The white cattle rancher named Hall pays him in the paper money of the Pale Eyes. These same liars built Quanah that fancy pale-eyes house." Isa-tai's eyes found Cuhtz Bávi. "Quanah is not like your brother, Cuhtz Bávi."

Ben Buffalo Bone arrived, thumbs hooked in the belt that held his ancient Remington revolver, and stopped beside Daniel.

Isa-tai smiled at Ben, a fellow Metal Shirt and probably the best friend Daniel had on the reservation.

"I remember your father," he said, his head bobbing, and spoke the name Ben had known before the Pale Eyes gave him a *taibo* name. "The Pale Eyes built a home for Naro Toneetsi, too, but Naro Toneetsi never lived in it. He stayed in the teepee. That big house, ha! He put his best horses in it."

And now I live there with those horses, Daniel thought.

"He was truly of The People," Isa-tai said.

45

"But Quanah? I say he has forgotten the ways of The People."

Realizing he was holding his breath, Daniel slowly exhaled. Waiting. The only sound now came from yipping dogs and bawling babies.

Slowly Yellow Bear looked away from the corral. His eyes landed on a smoldering stick in the gray ash, and he deftly pushed it closer to the flames with the toe of his moccasin. Still staring at the fire, he said: "It is you who have forgotten the ways of The People. It is impolite to speak the name of those who have traveled to The Land Beyond The Sun, Isa-tai."

Men's heads bobbed around the fire, and Isa-tai stiffened at the rebuke.

"I meant no harm," he told Ben Buffalo Bone and Cuhtz Bávi.

The two Kotsotekas nodded their acceptance in return.

"It is hard to say what is right." The holy man, Nagwee, had spoken, although he still stared into the white smoke. "My teeth are gone. I barely taste the *taibo* meat. That is good. I like not the taste. But Quanah speaks with wisdom. Once The People were strong as the limb of an oak. Now we have grown weak. But if we are not careful" — he reached over and picked up a handful of ash, lifted it, and, opening his hand, let the wind carry the ashes away — "The People will become what this once strong oak limb has become."

Silence. Even the dogs had stopped barking.

"Soon," Quanah said, "I go to meet with Captain Hall, with the other *Tejano* ranchers. Nagwee will travel with me, for he speaks with much wisdom. Yellow Bear will come with me, for he wishes to see this city called Fort Worth, and his counsel is strong and wise." Quanah's eyes locked on Isa-tai's. "Anyone is welcome to come with me, and make sure that the decision I make is what is best for The People."

Isa-tai straightened. "I will go with you."

Quanah nodded. "It is done." He turned, and walked away.

"Bávi, why are you smiling?"

He turned, embarrassed, seeing Ben Buffalo Bone staring at him, laughter in Ben's bottomless eyes, found himself almost falling into the traps of the Pale Eyes with a lie — "Brother, I am not. . . ." — before stopping himself.

"I go to Fort Worth, too, bávi," Daniel told his friend.

"Fort Worth." Ben Buffalo Bone's head shook. "Very far. The agent has asked me to go to The Big Pasture. Longhorn cattle are there."

That stopped Daniel. Quanah had been holding that pasture for reserve, to strike up a better deal for The People when he negotiated a new lease agreement with the *taibo* ranchers.

"Would you like me to ride with you?"

Ben's head shook. "I go alone. My sister, Rain Shower, she saw the cattle. She saw no Pale Eyes. They probably . . . what Pale Eyes call them . . . strays?"

"Probably," Daniel agreed.

"I go alone," his friend repeated. "And you?"

Daniel smiled. "I will not be alone when School Father Pratt gives his talk." He wasn't looking at Ben Buffalo Bone any more. He watched Charles Flint, walking behind his father.

CHAPTER FOUR

Above the belching and hissing of the greasy black locomotive rose the crowd's roar. Daniel, who had just helped Yellow Bear out of the passenger car, turned and stared, amazed at all the spectators. The throng must have stretched half a block, with city constables in their black-visored navy caps forming a human fence to keep them from crushing the newcomers. The band struck up "Johnny Get Your Gun" as Quanah stepped onto the depot platform. It hurt Daniel's ears.

He felt a breath on his ear, turned, saw Yellow Bear but couldn't hear him. Daniel leaned closer.

"Ice cream," the ancient Kwahadi grunted.

Beside him, Charles Flint laughed.

"We must wait a while, *Tsu Kuh Puah,*" Daniel said with a smile, again using the term of respect for an older man.

Quanah was shaking hands with some red-headed *taibo,* his curly hair neatly combed and parted, a flowing handlebar mustache bending in the breeze, dressed in a brown suit with a red ribbon tie. He wore no gun, no badge, no epaulets, but over the din of music, applause, and modern mechanics, Daniel heard Quanah introduce the tall *Tejano* to Nagwee as a captain. He couldn't make out the man's last name.

"This is crazy!" Charles Flint had to shout in Daniel's ear.

"Haa," Daniel said, nodding, but did not take his eyes off Quanah and the tall man.

Quanah's mouth moved, and the *taibo* extended his hand toward Isa-tai. Frowning, Isa-tai folded his arms across his chest and glowered. The tall redhead, however, did not seem offended. He merely nodded at the holy man and moved with Quanah down the depot platform until both tall men stood in front of Daniel.

"His Arrows Fly Straight Into The Hearts Of His Enemies," Quanah said, speaking in the language of The People, and Daniel straightened. Rarely did people call him by that name any more. "Metal Shirt," Quanah said in English. "Ser-geant. Good Comanch'." As Quanah smiled, Daniel's pride soared.

"This Captain Hall."

Lee Hall extended his hand, and Daniel shook it. The *taibo*'s grip felt like a vise. His pale eyes, however, were soft, almost sad.

"Metal Shirt, eh?" Hall's voice sounded like hominy, not the harsh twang of most *Tejanos,* but something far more genteel, from deeper in the South. "Then we, sir, have much in common. Once I wore the cinco peso star of the Texas Rangers."

They slid down the rough pine planks of the depot, and Quanah introduced Captain Hall to Yellow Bear.

"It is an honor to make your acquaintance," Captain Hall said.

"Ice cream," Yellow Bear demanded.

"And this," Quanah said, "Tetecae. Charles . . . Flint. Work at post. He . . ." — Quanah took a moment to think of the right word — "cipher."

"That is a handsome suit, sir," the former Ranger said. "Better than anything one should find at Taylor and Barr's, I would dare say."

"Thank you." Charles Flint cast a nervous glance at his father, who still stood there, unmoving, his face a mask of copper granite, arms still folded.

The band paused, the applause died down, and mutely women in their bonnets and parasols and men with their cigars, pipes, and city hats stared, gawking at the Indians at the depot, some of them dressed in suits, others, Daniel included, in buckskins and leggings. The silence lasted only a moment before a tuba bellowed, a cymbal clashed, and some song Daniel had never heard wailed over the whistle of another Texas & Pacific locomotive.

"Hello, Daniel."

He turned, swallowed, stared into the eyes of School Father Pratt.

"It has been a while."

Those few years had aged him. Oh, although heavier, Pratt still stood erect, shoulders square, and wore the spotless uniform he had worn at the Carlisle Industrial School. His hair seemed thinner, however, more gray than brown, his eyes held a weariness, his nose had reddened like a whiskey drinker's (though, as far as Daniel could recall, Pratt did not imbibe), and his earlobes had grown.

"School Father." Out of the corner of his eye, Daniel saw Charles Flint snap to attention. Pratt saw it, too, and his smile seemed to reduce his age.

"Mister Flint," Pratt said, nodding. "I hear many great things about you." Looking back at Daniel: "And you, as well, Mister Kill-

52

straight. Do you enjoy being a peace-keeper?"

Did he? Daniel wasn't sure. "It is. . . ." He tripped over an answer.

It sets me apart from The People. Many do not trust me. Afraid that I will arrest them, take them to The Lodges That Are Always In Darkness, put them in chains. Whiskey runners fear me, and well they should. I can count my friends on one hand. But that has been the path the Creator must have laid out for me. Nothing has changed.

He was amazed those words ran through his mind. That he did not speak them did not surprise him.

School Father Pratt had turned to Charles Flint, shaking his hand, asking about book-keeping, admiring his clothes.

At the far end of the depot platform, Captain Hall spoke to a slight man with a neatly trimmed salt-and-pepper beard. The man pointed a walking cane, its gold curved top reflecting sunlight, toward three canopy-topped surreys. Captain Hall's head bobbed, and he called over the last notes of the band: "Captain Pratt, we should go!"

"Ice cream," Yellow Bear said.

The Wednesday Woman's Club engagement had proved uneventful. Ladies who smelled of lilac powder waving their handheld fans to fight off the oppressive heat, and afterward offering gloved white hands to shake with slight curtsies while serving punch and, to Yellow Bear's delight, ice cream — vanilla, however, and not, to Daniel's disappointment, peach or butter pecan — and lemon cookies.

An hour later, Daniel couldn't remember anything about School Father Pratt's speech to those women other than a few quotations from the Bible.

City Hall was different.

Men and women crowded the lawn as they had at the train station. Even more. They covered every blade of grass, no one could move up or down Weatherford Street, and people pushed for perhaps a full block down Houston Street and maybe halfway down Main. Far in the back, others stood in the stirrups of their horses or in the back of buckboards. Down Weatherford and Houston Streets, men and women leaned out of second-story windows. More than a few even sat on rooftops.

"Once," School Father Pratt began, "and not that long ago, you wonderful, gracious citizens of this magnificent city would be barring your doors and filling musket barrels with blue whistlers at the very thought

54

of Comanche Indians inside the city limits. And now . . . this!"

Laughter.

Daniel looked at his lap, saw his thumbs twiddling. Tried to stop. Started again.

"Ladies and gentlemen, when it comes to Indian civilization, I am a Baptist."

Fitting, Daniel thought. Just moments earlier, the minister from the First Baptist Church had given the invocation.

"I strongly believe in immersing the Indian in our civilization. Hold them under. . . ." Here, Pratt raised both fists, then pretended to be holding a head under the water.

Daniel straightened, a memory from ages ago coming to the forefront. He could picture old Isa Nanaka, now traveling to The Land Beyond The Sun, holding a buffalo hunter's head under the water of the river the *Tejanos* called the Pease, could see the man's boots thrashing in the mud until Isa Nanaka had drowned the fool.

". . . until they are soaked thoroughly." School Father Pratt's hands fell to his side. "This task would be impossible to do on the reservations of old. It could be done only at boarding schools. That is why I created the Industrial School in Carlisle, Pennsylvania. And rest assured, ladies and gentlemen, that we did not teach these Indians to be . . . *ahem* . . . Yankees!"

More laughter. To the left of the lectern, Captain Lee Hall slapped his thigh, leaned over, and said something to Fort Worth's mayor whose name Daniel had already forgotten.

"Good citizens of Texas, you know all too well the savagery of war, the butchery of barbarians. The rivers once flowed red through this country."

Now Daniel recalled Isa Nanaka dragging the man's lifeless body from the muddy water. Saw him unsheathing his knife. Remembered the warrior taking the *taibo*'s scalp.

"I served in the Army. I saw the carnage. I know what brave settlers went through. Indeed, I can understand the hatred you felt for Indians such as these that now share this stage with me. Wipe out the Indians, you once said. Nay, you demanded it. Send them the way of the buffalo."

He paused, letting the words take hold.

"But is this the way of a Christian?" His head shook. "My way is better, ladies and gentlemen. It is as I have long championed. Kill the Indian, not the man."

Applause built to a crescendo, echoed by a roar of approval. No one challenged Pratt.

56

No heckles. That, Daniel found hard to comprehend. Most *Tejanos* he had met likely still wanted to kill both Indian and man, with relish. Especially Comanches.

"My good friends, my fellow citizens of Our Lord Jesus Christ, I want to introduce you to two prime examples of how Carlisle works. These two young gentlemen came to Pennsylvania as heathens, as raw, wild savages, but through dedication . . . on their part, indeed, as well as on the part of my excellent tutors . . . they have proved themselves as champions for the Comanche race. They are no longer savages, but are men among the best of their fields."

Sand caked Daniel's throat.

"Texas, allow me to introduce you to Charles Flint, a clerk and accountant for George McEveety's trading post in Indian Territory." Applause. "And Daniel Killstraight, the head police officer for the tribal police on the federal reserve near Fort Sill."

Something grazed Daniel's moccasin. He looked down at a shiny black shoe, followed the trail up the dark pants and coat until he stared up into Charles Flint's coal eyes. He realized Flint was standing, no longer sitting, and although he couldn't hear Flint's words, he could read his lips, and that urgent expression on his face.

"Stand up!"

Daniel looked out into the crowd. He wondered if he could rise, and was surprised when he did not collapse and roll down the steps of the courthouse.

His prayer was answered. School Father Pratt did not ask either to make a speech. Still clapping his hands, his face beaming, Pratt nodded at the two, and Daniel dropped into his chair. Sweat poured down his face and neck. His heart pounded.

"Their education would not have been possible without the co-operation of tribal elders." Pratt gestured behind him. "This is Yellow Bear. His savage heart has been tamed by the love, thanks to the gracious ladies of the Wednesday Woman's Club . . ." — laughter — "for ice cream. And let me just say that ice cream tastes far better, and has better results, than bullets and powder."

Daniel mopped his brow.

"And here is Nagwee." He butchered the name, but no one seemed to notice. "Among the Comanches, he is a medicine man. He is wise beyond his years.

"On Nagwee's left is another medicine man. This, folks, is not Isa-tai's first trip to Texas. He led that fateful attack in the year of Our Lord Eighteen Seventy-Four at Adobe Walls. Only the keen eye and true

58

shots of those stalwart white buffalo hunters prevented the Comanches from setting civilization back thirty or forty years. Isa-tai's name means Coyote Droppings. Imagine, my friends, if your parent had named you Coyote Droppings."

Laughter swept across Fort Worth. Someone on the platform stopped his boots and howled like a coyote. "Coyote Droppings! Don't that beat all!"

Daniel shook his head at the pale-eyes translation. Isa-tai meant no such thing.

"Charles Flint over here came to Pennsylvania with a savage name, but he has followed the white man's road. Isa-tai is also the father of Charles Flint. Look at father and son, my friends. Cannot you see how much the Carlisle Industrial School has, can, and will accomplish!"

The roar sounded deafening. Charles Flint muttered a pale-eyes oath. Daniel fought the urge to look at Isa-tai.

When the noise at last subsided, Pratt stopped to mop his forehead with a handkerchief. "Lastly, this tall man sitting behind me is a warrior and leader, a man of war, a man of peace. He fought hard to keep his people free, but now works hard to hold peace. He is more respected, more honored, more cherished than Crazy Horse or Sitting

Bull or Cochise or Osceola. He is a judge. He is the chief of the Comanches. He is the Abraham Lincoln and George Washington and Robert E. Lee of the Comanche people. And, as many of you know, he is a native Texan."

Roars. Someone even fired a pistol shot into the air. A horse whinnied, and cymbals clashed. The band's trumpeter sounded the charge. More laughter.

Pratt even snickered. He wiped his face again, then slid the handkerchief into his vest pocket. "His mother was the dearly departed Cynthia Ann Parker, taken captive by the Comanches from Parker's Fort 'way back during the dark days of Texas in Eighteen Thirty-Six. Ladies and gentlemen, I give you . . . Quanah Parker."

Daniel found himself clapping, watching Quanah rise, bowing, moving uncomfortably as School Father Pratt beckoned him to the lectern. Everyone was clapping. Everyone, that is, except Isa-tai.

Gradually the crowd hushed.

A camera flashed, belching smoke and bad smells. Reporters scribbled on their note pads, which reminded Daniel that he probably should buy some Old Glory writing tablets, a Columbus lead sharpener, and two or three packs of Faber's No. 2 pencils.

60

Ever superstitious, Daniel practically refused to use anything but those brands for his police work, and they were hard to find on the reservation. Even McEveety didn't carry those. In fact, the trading post stocked few writing utensils.

"Ladies, gentlemen." Quanah's soft voice carried over the crowd. "Me once bad man. Now me citizen of United States. Me work for Comanche. Me work for you. Good friends here. Captain Pratt. Captain Hall. This used to be hunting ground for Comanche. Many rattlesnakes here."

"Still are!" someone shouted from Main Street.

"Hush up, Horace!" countered a feminine voice.

"I see many faces here. Good faces. White faces. I work for my people. Government say . . . 'Put Indians in school. Make Indians do like white man.' This I do. Me proud. Tet-*uh* Flint . . . Charles Flint. Daniel Killstraight. Make proud. Make you proud. They good. But some Indians no good."

Daniel found enough nerve to shoot a quick glance at Isa-tai, but the large Kwahadi seemed to be asleep in his chair.

"But me say some white man no good. Bring whiskey. Get Comanche drunk. Steal souls of men. Women, too. Others bring

61

cattle. But pay not. This wrong. This, Killstraight, he try stop. Good lawman. I come here to talk with friend Captain Hall. Come see friend Waggoner. Friend Burnett. Good to see many faces. See friends. I miss my mother. She good woman. Good mother. She white woman. I go now."

As he turned, Daniel saw Quanah wipe a tear before it rolled down his cheek. Daniel thought of his own mother.

CHAPTER FIVE

Like red ants, reporters swarmed. Most of them came from Fort Worth and Dallas publications, but Daniel heard a bald man mention Austin and a man with Dundreary whiskers say San Antonio. A tall gentleman in a silk hat and peculiar accent said he hailed from London, and Daniel also heard names like *Frank Leslie's Illustrated, Scribner's Monthly, Harper's Weekly,* and *National Police Gazette,* the last of which Daniel had not only heard of, he had even read a few issues. A woman, her hair neatly in a bun, stood sketching page after page. Photographers scurried about, setting up their huge boxes on tripods. One man with a sweaty hand pulled Charles Flint from his chair, urging him to pose for a photograph with his father. "Good Injun and bad," the photographer said through a nasal twang. "It'll sell like Bohemian suds."

Daniel stepped aside as the photographer

pulled a laughing Charles Flint toward Isa-tai.

"Come on, old-timer," another photographer called, trying to coax Yellow Bear from his chair. "It won't take but a moment for me to capture your likeness. Your grandchildren will love it, yes, sir, indeed they will."

Yellow Bear jerked his arm from the photographer's grasp, and barked in his native tongue.

The photographer straightened, turned, searching for help, and found Daniel.

"Hey, boy. Can you talk this old chief into posing for a photograph?"

"He says he will not let you steal his shadow," Daniel said, translating Yellow Bear's words.

"Huh?"

Then the photographer saw Quanah, surrounded by reporters, and quickly grabbed his camera and tripod.

Daniel filled his lungs with hot air, and slowly exhaled. A few newspapermen left Quanah, and hurried to join the throng that surrounded Isa-tai. Charles Flint sat in a chair, his photograph already taken, conversing with a reporter who furiously scribbled with his pencil, while the lady artist knelt, working her pens to capture

Charles Flint's likeness. A moment later, a reporter tugged on Flint's coat sleeve, urging him to translate what his father was saying. A woman brought Yellow Bear some ice cream, and the *puhakat* smiled a toothless grin, and took the cone greedily. Other artists and photographers knelt beside Nagwee.

Nobody would be leaving for a spell, so Daniel sat in the chair Flint had abandoned. He picked up one of the paper fans the ladies from the Wednesday Woman's Club had handed out to their guests. There was a quote from Proverbs stenciled on the yellow paper, but Daniel was too tired, too hot to read. He waved the fan in front of his face, closed his eyes.

"Hello, Daniel. We have not had much of an opportunity to talk. It's been rather a whirlwind since you arrived."

Eyes opened, fan lowered, Daniel started to rise, but School Father Pratt raised a hand to stop him, and settled into the nearest chair.

Daniel tried to think of words. "I thought . . . you would . . . newspapermen . . . why don't they talk to you?"

"They've talked to me for ages." Checking his pocket watch, he added: "Though I have an interview with Mister Etheridge at

65

the *Standard* in a little more than an hour." Pratt smiled, took the fan Daniel had dropped, and waved it so that it would send warm air toward him and Daniel both. "These are the celebrities. Quanah. Isa-tai. You should go up there, make yourself known."

Daniel's head shook strongly.

"I'm surprised they haven't circled around you like vultures. Maybe I should not have said all that about Isa-tai. No, there's no maybe. That was stupid of me. Those ink-spillers can't get enough of that old tyrant." He lowered the fan, let it fall, and pointed. "Look at him, Daniel."

Daniel glanced, shrugged, turned back to his former educator.

With a smile, Pratt turned in his chair, reached over, and tapped the shield pinned on Daniel's vest. "You've done well, Daniel. But, of course, I knew you would. You're a good peace officer from all that I hear."

No, Daniel thought. He remembered something Hugh Gunter had once said. They were camping in the Nations, one, no, two years ago, bringing the body of Jimmy Comes Last from Fort Smith to the reservation. Having breakfast, or maybe it had been supper. Daniel couldn't remember exactly, but he knew they had been sitting around a

66

fire, and the Cherokee had been sipping coffee. Daniel had asked if Gunter liked being a policeman. "Sometimes," Gunter had answered, before motioning toward the coffin in the wagon. "Not always." And moments later, Gunter had added: "I am good at it."

Daniel wasn't good at it. Oh, sure, he had been promoted to sergeant of the Tribal Police, but that was because he could speak English and Comanche, and understood a little bit of Kiowa. What he couldn't speak, he could usually sign with his hands. He was no detective, and not much of a peace officer. The law? What did he understand of white man's law? People — red and white — said he had solved crimes, had stopped whiskey-running operations, had sent murderers and thieves to prison, but Daniel knew better. He had bungled his way through any investigation. Good at it? Not hardly.

"I knew you were a leader when you first arrived at Carlisle." Laughing, Pratt shook his head. "You were quite the rebellious little red devil. Our School Mothers must have cracked three score rulers on your knuckles. Yet, eventually, you saw the light, realized that the Comanche . . . and all other Indian tribes . . . must learn to adapt

67

to the white man's ways. It is the only way for you people to survive. We must stop the butchery, the violence." He was sounding like the speechmaker again. Daniel bit his bottom lip. "You are the one to lead the Comanches to a better way of life, a better living. You and Quanah."

He could feel the School Father's eyes boring into him, knew Pratt wanted a verbal response. Daniel tilted his head toward Isa-tai. "He is a leader," he said. "Not me."

"Do you know what a chameleon is, Daniel?"

"No. That is a word I do not know." *One of many,* he thought but did not say.

"It's . . . never mind. Suffice to say that Isa-tai is not the right leader," Pratt answered immediately. "He proved that at Adobe Walls."

On that, Daniel had to agree.

Memories, clear as spring run-off in the Wichita Mountains, came flooding before his face: Isa-tai claiming his *puha,* telling The People he could heal the sick, he could even raise the dead. Saying that no bullets would hurt him. None of this was new. Though just a young boy, Daniel had heard other prophets. False prophets, the old *puhakats* would say. Yet many of The People claimed to have seen Isa-tai travel to The

Land Beyond The Sun, remaining there all night, then coming down from the sky on the following morning. Others had seen him belch out cases and cases of cartridges. Once, a comet had appeared in the night sky, and Isa-tai had told The People that the light would disappear in five days. Daniel had heard that prediction himself. Daniel himself had seen the comet. And five days later, as Isa-tai had concluded, the white light in the night sky had vanished, never to return.

The Kwahadis believed him. So did Daniel, for he was a child. The Cheyennes came to hear his words, as did the Kiowas and Arapahos. Isa-tai came to Quanah, asked him to help him destroy the *taibos* who were waging their war against the buffalo, which The People needed desperately. It would be a revenge raid. Quanah would avenge the death of his uncle, killed by the Pale Eyes. First, they would hold a Sun Dance, and The People had never held a Sun Dance.

They would attack the killers of the buffalo at their camp at the place called Adobe Walls. Bad medicine, Yellow Bear had warned. Years ago, The People had attacked a pale-eyes force led by the great white scout Kit Carson near those same grounds, and death songs were sung, and women, children, and men left mourning. Isa-tai had not listened. Nor had Quanah. Thus, they had attacked Adobe Walls.

Again, death songs were sung, and women, children, and men left mourning. The Pale Eyes had far-shooting guns. Guns that would shoot today and kill tomorrow. One bullet fired from the *taibo* camp had struck and killed a warrior more than a mile away. Infuriated, a Cheyenne had lashed at Isa-tai with his quirt, but Isa-tai had blamed the Cheyennes for the defeat. One had killed a skunk before the battle, Isa-tai had claimed. It had ruined his *puha.*

"I hear," School Father Pratt said, "that Isa-tai wasn't known as Isa-tai back then. The Comanches gave him that name only after the battle. It means Coyote Droppings. Right?"

Daniel smiled. "No. He has always been known as Isa-tai. At least, as long as I can remember. And it does not mean Coyote Droppings, or Rear End Of A Wolf, or anything like that."

"What does it mean?"

Daniel tightened his lips. He could not tell School Father that in the language of The People Isa-tai meant Coyote Vagina.

"Pa-cha-na-quar-hip did not mean Buffalo Hump."

Daniel looked up, wondering how long Charles Flint had been standing there. "But that's how you white men always translate it?"

"Is that so?" Pratt stood up and shook Flint's hand. "And what was Buffalo Hump's real name?"

Flint grinned, and when he answered — "Erection That Won't Go Down." — Pratt guffawed.

"Well, I can understand why that name got changed." Pratt's eyes beamed. "Lord have mercy, can you imagine how the Wednesday's Women's Club would have reacted?" He slapped his knee, leaving Daniel wondering how the School Mothers would have behaved if they could see School Father Pratt's amusement over such a profane joke.

Yet the name was no joke, and Daniel could not hide his frown, his disappointment in Charles Flint. Oh, it wasn't like the true name of Buffalo Hump, a legendary leader of the Penateka band who had been dead for years, among The People had been some secret. Still, Flint had disappointed Daniel. Like his father, the bookkeeper seemed to have forgotten the ways of *Nermernuh.* He did not remember, or maybe care, that for any of The People to speak the

71

name of someone who had journeyed to The Land Beyond The Sun showed much disrespect.

"And what of your father's name?" Pratt said.

"His name?" Flint's grin widened. "My father? He is called Isa-tai."

Names. Isa-tai refused to call his son by the name he had been given by the Pale Eyes. To Isa-tai, his son was only Tetecae.

They had moved from the Tarrant County Courthouse across Weatherford Street to the office of the Fort Worth *Standard,* where Pratt gave an interview to the newspaper editor, who then proceeded to discuss the grazing situation with Quanah, and finally turned his attention to Isa-tai, with Charles Flint again handling the translations. Daniel sat listening in silence, while Yellow Bear's stomach growled, and the old *puhakat* shifted his feet impatiently. By the time the *Standard* editor had filled his notebook, the cattlemen had arrived — Dan Waggoner, Captain Lee Hall, and a gangling man with a weather-beaten face named Burk Burnett who wore a silver-plated Colt revolver holstered over his stomach, the numbers *6666* engraved on the .45's ivory grip and tooled in the rich leather.

The air inside the stifling newspaper office began to fill with thick smoke from cigars these cattlemen fired up. It stank of *taibos,* of lies the *Tejanos* told with laughter.

"It's about time, Red," the one named Burnett told the former Texas Ranger.

The Mansion House Hotel was only four blocks down Rusk Street, but Captain Hall had summoned several hacks to drive the cattlemen and Comanche guests to the hotel for supper. School Father Pratt, however, did not attend. "I will see you gentlemen for breakfast," he announced, tipped his hat, and walked down Weatherford Street toward the courthouse, followed by the newspaper editor.

Elegant. That's the only word Daniel could think of to describe the Mansion House. He felt uncomfortable as soon as he entered the building, his moccasins gliding noiselessly across the rich velvet carpet.

A tall man with a gray silk tie and well-groomed mustache that looked as if it had been drawn on with a pencil nodded courteously at Captain Hall. "The dining room is all yours, sir," he said, and held open the door to let the men, red and white, pass.

This was not like the Pickwick Hotel. Oh, Daniel could feel the stares of the waiters, bartender, clerks, and hotel guests, even

73

from the *maitre d'* after leading them to the table — the same as he had felt at the Pick-wick. Yet soon he forgot those angry looks as cattlemen and Comanches found their seats around a long table, covered with white lace cloth, decorated by long, skinny candles in a spotless silver candelabra. He wondered why Quanah's group was not staying at this hotel, but imagined the rates probably had something to do with that.

When Daniel pulled out a chair next to Charles Flint, a firm hand gripped his arm, and Quanah said: "You sit by me." As Quanah led him around the table, he whispered: "Make sure I understand what these men say."

Soup came first. Well, first, actually was wine for the Texians, water, coffee, or tea for the Comanches. Daniel dipped his spoon into the creamy soup, tasted it, then found a napkin to wipe his tongue. Some sort of fish, and The People rarely ate fish. Naturally the *Tejanos* did not notice that they were the only ones slurping their bowls. The waiters came quickly, picked up the empty bowls and the full ones, disappeared, only to return with thick steaks, mounds of biscuits, ears of corn, boiled potatoes, and slices of watermelon. These, both Texians and The People enjoyed.

"Dessert, gentlemen?" the head waiter asked. "Brandy? Port? Coffee?"

Faces of the cattlemen turned toward Quanah, who wiped his fingers on his trousers, and said: "Full."

"Just brandy for us," Captain Hall said.

"I'll have a port, if you don't mind," Dan Waggoner interrupted.

The waiter snapped his fingers, and looked at Quanah. "Anything for you gentlemen? We have a wonderful strawberry rhubarb pie."

No answer.

"Very well," the man said, and turned.

"Ice cream."

Daniel looked across the table at Yellow Bear. "Ice cream," he repeated, and when the cattlemen began to laugh, the waiter joined them.

"Do you have ice cream, Stephen?" Captain Hall asked.

"I'm afraid not, sir."

"Run on over to the Queen City and fetch a gallon," Burk Burnett ordered, and the waiter nodded before scurrying back to the kitchen.

"Well, Quanah," Captain Hall said. "I guess we should get down to business."

"We need all of The Big Pasture," Captain

Hall was saying. "All of it. Every blade of grass."

Quanah spoke, and Daniel translated. "He asks if you know the size of The Big Pasture."

"Three hundred thousand acres," the redheaded *taibo* said immediately. "I know exactly how big it is. And how much we need. Burk here has ten thousand head of Durhams and Herefords alone. I have half that, longhorns, and Dan here a little less than half. We've had some dry years. Your pasture can support our beef, and we'll pay you handsomely for it."

Daniel translated. He felt uncomfortable, seeing the eyes of Isa-tai, Charles Flint, and Nagwee boring into him. Only Yellow Bear seemed to have no interest, working his spoon like a shovel in the gallon container of butter pecan ice cream.

Quanah leaned toward Daniel, whispering, although Daniel felt certain that none of the ranchers could speak a smidgen of Comanche.

"It is much land."

"Yes, *Tsu Kuh Puah,* it is."

"They have never requested so much land."

"They are Texians. It was only a matter of time."

76

Quanah smiled, started to straighten, then leaned back. "What is this Dur-ham and . . . ?" He could not form the word on his tongue.

"Some kind of *taibo* cattle," Daniel answered. "Not the ones with the long horns."

Quanah grunted. Now he sat straight, looked across the table at Captain Hall, and asked in English: "How much?"

"The board of directors has authorized me to pay you and your tribe three cents an acre."

Burk Burnett put in: "At three hundred thousand acres, that's. . . ."

Charles Flint cut him off: "Nine thousand dollars."

"Nine thou-sand dol-lars." Quanah's head bobbed. "Much money."

"Much money indeed," Captain Hall said, and pulled out several papers from the inside pocket of his coat. "Now, if you'll. . . ."

"But not enough," Quanah said.

Daniel grinned.

Captain Hall's face tightened. The papers were shoved back inside the pocket. "How much were you thinking?" Hall's voice no longer sounded smooth.

"Twelve cents."

"Christ!" Dan Waggoner's glass hit the

77

table so hard that the stem broke, and red wine stained the white lace cloth.

Quanah spoke again, and Daniel translated. "Twelve cents for only half The Big Pasture. The People have many horses that need grass, too."

"Unacceptable."

Silence — except for Yellow Bear's slurping of the now-melted ice cream.

"Give them four cents, Red," Burk Burnett said.

"Daniel," Charles Flint said, "that's twelve thousand dollars. That'll buy a lot of food and stores for our people."

Captain Hall's eyes locked on Daniel's, not Quanah's. "You heard the man."

So had Quanah. He held up both hands, extending all fingers.

Hall's head shook. "Ten cents! I'm not a fool, nor am I as rich as the Grand Duke of Prussia. I'm a cow-poor Texian. Four and a half."

"We go now." Quanah pushed out of his chair.

CHAPTER SIX

"Wait!" His face ashen, Burk Burnett gripped the table, as if he needed support. While Quanah remained standing, his face unreadable, Burnett turned to Captain Hall. "I need that grass, Red. Hell's fire, we all do."

Daniel hid his smile. These cattlemen weren't the first *taibos* who had underestimated Quanah Parker.

"Six cents. But we need all of The Big Pasture." A bead of sweat rolled down the captain's forehead. Hall and Burnett looked nervous. Still holding his broken wine glass, Dan Waggoner appeared angry.

"Seven." Quanah remained standing.

Burnett let out a heavy sigh. Waggoner released the wine glass, and clenched his fists. Captain Hall ran his fingers across his mustache, smoothing it, eyes studying Quanah.

"I can't go that high, Quanah." Desperation accented the Ranger's voice. "And that's the God's honest truth. It would bust Burk, bust me, bust the entire association."

"Then how you say . . . ?" Quanah looked again to Daniel for help.

"Six and a half?" Daniel asked.

The Texans glanced at each other. "No," Dan Waggoner said, but Daniel read something else in the eyes of Captain Hall and Burk Burnett.

Turning back to Quanah, Burnett asked hopefully: "For all of the pasture?"

Daniel didn't need to translate. "Big Pasture only."

Quanah's head bobbed. "Other pastures need for Comanche ponies."

The captain's facial muscles relaxed, and he found a handkerchief in his vest pocket, and wiped perspiration off his forehead. Once he had returned the white square of cotton, he lifted his brandy, took a sip, and started to say something, but what came out was: "Aw, hell."

His gaze went past Quanah and Daniel, and Dan Waggoner rose, mumbling: "What the hell is he doing here?"

Hearing the footsteps, Daniel turned in his chair.

A powerfully built *Tejano* strode toward the dining table, spurs chiming as his big feet clopped on the floor. Thick beard stubble and a giant, unkempt mustache hid much of his face, but Daniel could see the glare in the man's dark eyes, the crooked nose, the missing tip of his left ear. His jaw worked like a piston on the thick wad of tobacco in one of his cheeks, and, when he stopped, he spit out a river of tobacco juice that landed between Captain Hall's polished boots, ignoring the cuspidor next to the table.

The former Ranger's face flushed, but Burnett cautioned him: "Easy does it, Red."

Satisfaction replaced the anger in the newcomer's eyes.

"What are you doing here, Carmody?" Captain Hall asked, his voice unpleasant.

"I got me an invitation." The big man hooked his thumbs in the belt of his battered, dust-caked, cow-hide leggings, between grimy leather work gloves he had shoved behind the leather. He wore a wide-brimmed, beaten-all-to-hell hat, maybe gray, maybe white, maybe darker and just caked with dirt, dust, and sweat stains. A frayed, green calico bandanna hung around his neck, and huge muscles strained against the thin blue cotton of his shirt. His chest resembled a rain barrel, his neck, the back blistered red, might have been larger than

Daniel's own head.

"You are not a member of the Northern Texas Stock Growers' Association," Burk Burnett told him.

That, Daniel could believe. He didn't look much like a wealthy pale-eyes cattleman, but a working cowhand, though bigger than any thirty-a-month cowboy Daniel had ever seen.

"Get the hell out of here, Sol," Dan Waggoner said. "We've rented this dining room and are conducting business."

Sol Carmody shifted the tobacco into the other cheek. "Told y'all I got me an invite. And I got business here, too. Ain't that right, Chief?"

He was looking between Quanah, still standing, and Daniel. Daniel turned as Isa-tai rose from his chair, and began speaking in the language of The People. Out of the corner of his eye, Daniel saw Quanah's fingers ball into fists.

"This *taibo*," Isa-tai said, tilting his jaw at Sol Carmody, "already feeds his *pimoró* on the grass of The People, on what you call The Big Pasture."

"That he cannot do!" Quanah barked. "Tell him to remove his longhorns."

That's when the memory struck Daniel. Ben Buffalo Bone saying, around ration day,

82

that Agent Biggers was sending him to The Big Pasture, that someone had seen long-horn cattle eating grass there. Merely strays, they had figured, and Daniel, busy with the work of cleaning up the pens after rations had been issued and cattle butchered, and his mind preoccupied with thoughts of his trip to Fort Worth, had not thought to ask Ben Buffalo Bone about the matter. Following the ways of The People, Ben Buffalo Bone had not volunteered any information.

"No." Isa-tai grinned.

"He cannot feed his cattle on *Nermernuh* grass. Not without permission."

"He has my permission." Isa-tai leaned forward. "You said the grass belongs to The People, Quanah. You are just angry that you will not get rich."

"I do not do this for my own profit. I do this for the good of The People."

"Bah." Isa-tai waved his hand in dismissal. "Look at you and your shiny stickpin, your *taibo* clothes. You are the one who travels by the iron horse to Washington City. To Texas. You are the one these men . . ." — he spit on the table — "built that fancy *taibo* house for. I live in a teepee, not a pale-eyes contraption. You are the one the Pale Eyes have proclaimed the chief of The People, when you very well know that among *Nerm-*

83

ernuh, there is no one leader. You are greedy, Quanah. Greedy for power and the riches you think these *taibo* snakes will give you."

Quanah took a step, stopped himself, and Daniel knew why. He would not let any *Tejanos* see two leaders of The People fight each other.

"These *taibos* cannot lease till Car-mo-dy is gone." Isa-tai put his hands on his hips. "And he will not leave. This is my victory, Quanah Parker."

"Killstraight?"

Daniel faced Captain Hall.

"What's this all about? What are they saying?"

The big Texian answered before Daniel could think of the right words. "Ol' Isa-tai here's been tellin' Chief Parker the way things is." Sol Carmody spit again, this time into the brass cuspidor, then wiped his lips and mustache with the sleeve of his stained shirt. "I got three thousand head eatin' that fine green grass on the reservation, boys. All that grass, nigh a half-million acres, for my little ol' herd. And you boys say I ain't fit to belong to your cattle king's association."

"We need that grass, Carmody!" Dan Waggoner shouted.

"Well, so do I!" Sol Carmody's voice thundered across the practically empty dining room. "And I got it."

"We'll have the Army drive you off, you son-of-a- . . . ."

"Watch it, Waggoner. I'm bigger than you, and ain't one to abide no insults. You think you can drive me off, you try it. I'll have forty cowhands and gun hands up on the pasture by the week's end, and Isa-tai has agreed to send some of his Comanche boys out to help me protect my herd. It ain't Quanah's pasture, boys. It's all of the Comanches, and Isa-tai, he's Comanch'. I got me a deal with Isa-tai. Ain't that the way y'all work, Kill . . . what the hell did he call you, boy?"

"Killstraight," Daniel answered without meaning to.

Carmody sniggered at the name. "Well, I reckon my business here is complete." He tipped his hat, and walked out of the dining room, whistling.

Voices exploded from every direction. Daniel couldn't catch what Nagwee was telling Quanah, who pointed a finger across the table at Isa-tai and spit out words, most of them unintelligible. Captain Hall was saying something about a judge named Starr, Burnett had bellowed the name of the commanding officer at Fort Still, and Waggoner sang curses at both the now-

departed Sol Carmody and the grinning
Isa-tai. Yellow Bear told Quanah and Isa-tai
to settle down. Only Daniel and Charles
Flint remained silent.

"Killstraight!"

Again Daniel faced Captain Hall.

"We need that grass. All of it. You get Carmody's tick-infested cows off our range."

Not your range, Daniel thought, but held
his temper.

Suddenly Charles Flint spoke: "Isn't it
possible that you could share the pasture
with that man, Carmody? He has three
thousand head, but we have much grass."

Isa-tai glared at his son, although Daniel
was certain the *puhakat* did not understand
much English.

"We won't share one blade of grass with
the likes of Sol Carmody," Burnett said.

Which was the answer Daniel expected
from a Texian. They were all crazy, and all
greedy.

Waggoner roared: "My beefs'll starve if
we don't get that pasture, boy!"

"Shut up, Dan!" Hall was sweating again.
He started to say something, but Daniel
raised his hand.

"Let us talk among ourselves," he quietly
requested.

Once the ranchers had retired into the hotel's saloon next door to the dining room, Daniel found his place in a circle on the floor. No teepee, not even a council fire, but Nagwee had brought his pipe, tamped down the tobacco, and Yellow Bear lighted it with a candle. Behind him, Daniel heard the whispers, could feel the stares of the restaurant's wait staff and cooks.

When the pipe came to Daniel, he offered it to the directions, lifted it to his mouth, and drew in the acrid smoke. The pipe, he saw, was old, fashioned from a bone from an antelope shank, then wrapped with the ligament from the back of a buffalo bull's neck, its bowl made from soapstone. No feathers. No ornamentation. It smoked quite well. As Daniel passed the pipe to Charles Flint, he remembered the story his father had told him and his mother. On the way to Adobe Walls, Isa-tai had carried his sacred pipe with him, letting each society dance every night as the warriors made their way across the Staked Plains. That pipe had been a war axe, an engraved steel bowl on top, and an ugly, killing weapon on the bottom.

Another difference struck Daniel. The pipe he had just smoked was simple yet elegant. Nagwee had likely killed the antelope himself, punched out the marrow, smoothed and pared the end. He would have gathered the white soapstone, fashioned it, dying it red with pokeberry and grease. The pipe Daniel's father had told him about, the one that had belonged to Isa-tai, had not been traditional. Oh, Isa-tai had probably carved out the wood, but the pipe-axe end had undoubtedly been bought from a Comanchero, or stolen from a trader.

As the pipe passed from Comanche to Comanche, Nagwee prayed until the pipe returned to him.

After a respectful silence, Yellow Bear rose. "This is a hard thing," he said. "I do not like the taste of pale-eyes beef, but, with the buffalo all gone, it is better than the pig meat. Pigs are not clean. I would rather eat grasshopper. I do not understand the ways of the Pale Eyes. But they want to pay us money for grass. Grass that grows free. In the old days, which were not that long ago, we would not pay for grass. If there was grass, and it belonged to our enemy, we would take it." He pounded a fist into his open palm. "I do not need pale-eyes money. I have two wives, thirty-nine horses, but four are mares and will foal in two, three moons. I have many grandchildren. Quanah is a good husband to one of my daughters. He was a great warrior, a leader of the Kwahadi. My eyes are no good. His are strong. He sees far. He sees what we must do to work with, and live with, those who once were our enemies. I do not like the Pale Eyes. Except their ice cream. I like Quanah. He does what is best for The People. We should listen to him."

He sat. Daniel nodded in agreement, saw Isa-tai's black eyes boring into him, could feel the *puhakat*'s anger, then realized that Isa-tai was not looking at him, but at his son Charles Flint.

In the tradition of The People, the men remained silent, considering the words Yellow Bear had spoken. Nagwee looked at Daniel, who realized it was his turn to speak. He shook his head. Charles Flint also declined to speak.

It was Quanah's turn. He stood.

"Yellow Bear is a wise man," he said. "I have always listened to him, respected his opinion, even when we disagree. I am glad we do not disagree now. This paying for grass for pale-eyes beef is a subject as foreign to us as the god the Black Robes pray to, as trying to understand the ways of the Mexicans. I am *Nermernuh.* We are all *Nermernuh.* But we live with *taibos.* We must understand *taibos.* The Pale Eyes, these *Tejanos* with their many heads of cattle, they believe in money. Money is what buys our shirts. It buys our hats. Yes, these are clothes of the Pale Eyes, the *Tejanos,* but it also buys us coffee and sugar and blankets for when the north wind blows angrily. These ranchers have offered us six and a half cents an acre for three hundred thousand acres. I must ask the son of Isa-tai to tell us how much money that would mean."

Charles Flint cleared his throat. Avoiding the stare of his father, he withdrew a pencil and note pad from his coat pocket. "I have. . . ." He smiled shyly. "I can't do that ciphering in my head." He worked, scratched the eraser in his hair, pressed the lead point, nodded, said: "Nineteen thousand five hundred dollars."

A snort sounded, and Isa-tai turned his head to spit. His head shook, and he mumbled something that Daniel could not catch. Rude. Daniel could not believe a *puhakat* like Isa-tai would be so disrespectful. One did not interrupt any speaker during a council. Ever.

After thanking Daniel, Quanah continued. "Nineteen thousand five hundred. That is much." He removed his hat and held it toward the others. "This I bought at the store where Tetecae works for the *taibos.*" He used Flint's *Nermernuh* name. "It cost me one dollar and fifty cents, and it is a fine hat. Imagine how much nineteen thousand five hundred dollars could buy for all of The People. It could fill the bellies of our children, our grandchildren. It could keep our wives warm. That is how much the cattlemen I have spoken to will pay. I have not heard from Isa-tai how much his friend will give The People."

There was no time to consider Quanah's words. Isa-tai shot to his feet the moment Quanah sat and crossed his legs.

CHAPTER SEVEN

"What I have done, what I will do, what I do now, I do to protect The People," Isa-tai said. "My people. This Pale Eyes, Car-mo-dy, he will not pay as much as those friends of Quanah *Par-ker.*"

Charles Flint's father stressed the name Quanah had adopted, the *taibo* surname name that had been his mother's, a white girl taken captive during The People's raid in the pale-eyes year of 1836. Daniel looked into the faces of the older men, wondering how they would react, but trying to read any emotion in the face of a *puhakat,* or any Comanche, for that matter, always proved fruitless.

"That is true," Isa-tai continued. "I, however, do not believe that we should let any *taibo* feed any of his poor cows on grass that belongs to The People. It is not right. That is why I let Car-mo-dy bring his cows. To stop Quanah *Par-ker.*"

Daniel's head already hurt, and he decided against trying to figure out Isa-tai's logic. Instead, he just watched and listened as the *puhakat* paced around the circle as he spoke, waving his arms, his voice rising, his face animated. When he stopped in front of his son, Isa-tai extended his right arm and pointed directly at Quanah.

"See this man. He has become a *taibo.* Look at him. Look at his fancy clothes, his pale-eyes hat. He has even taken the name of a Pale Eyes. No longer do we know him as Fragrance. He has become Quanah *Parker.* He lives in a pale-eyes house built for him by Pale Eyes. He has learned to speak some of the tongue of the Pale Eyes. On this very afternoon, he goes into that big house and buys those Pale-Eyes clothes. That cloak, and what they call that dol-man. Bah!"

Now his left arm pointed at Charles Flint, then swept toward Daniel.

"They give my son and this son of a brave warrior the names of Pale Eyes, and this was done with the blessing of Quanah Parker. I do not call them by those names. My son is Tetecae, and this one will always be His Arrows Fly Straight Into The Hearts Of His Enemies. Good *Nermernuh* names." He touched the front of his buckskin shirt, and let his fingers stream through the blue-dyed fringe. "I do not wear the clothes of the Pale Eyes. I am *Nermernuh.* I will always be *Nermernuh.*"

Walking again, flailing his arms, his voice reverberating across the practically empty dining room.

"This Car-mo-dy will pay me two hundred and fifty dollars to let his cattle eat The People's grass. I do not know how much money that is. I do not care. I care not for pale-eyes paper. I judge my wealth by the number of my horses, by the scalps I have taken in battle, by the coup I have counted. This Car-mo-dy, he will also pay *Nermernuh* boys to help guard his cattle. This will put ten dollars a moon into the hands of those who wish to work for this Car-mo-dy."

Now he stopped. "But this is not the way of The People. Once, we stole horses from the Mexicans, and *Tejanos,* and the foolish travelers to the north of us. We stole horses from all of our enemies. This was the way of The People. It was a good way. We will steal this man's Car-mo-dy's cattle for ourselves. They are not fit to eat grass that belongs to The People. I am like Yellow Bear. I do not care for the taste of *pimoró. Cuhtz* is what a warrior, a *puhakat,* should eat, but the Pale

94

Eyes do not let us hunt the buffalo any more. They treat us like women. Like children. I will show these Pale Eyes that we are men. We are men who will not be tamed, that we will not become Pale Eyes."

He sat down, folded his arms, glared across the room at Quanah, who bowed his head, considering the words Isa-tai had spoken, but waiting for someone else to speak.

The words came from Nagwee: "If you steal or kill the *taibo* cattle, the Long Knives will arrest you."

"They will try," Isa-tai said, still looking at Quanah.

"I," Yellow Bear said, "would like to hear words from that one."

Daniel swallowed. The father-in-law of Quanah was pointing at him.

"I. . . ." Daniel could not summon any words.

"Rise and speak, His Arrows Fly Straight Into The Hearts Of His Enemies," Nagwee said. "Yellow Bear is right. We are old men. We do not understand the ways of the Pale Eyes. You have lived among them. You speak their tongue. Yet you also protect The People. You are a good Metal Shirt. This I know. You once arrested my son after he had drunk too much of the bad whiskey the

Creeks bring to our land. That was a good thing. My son could have hurt someone, could have hurt himself. Rise. Speak. We will not bite you, at least, not too hard. As for me, I cannot bite you at all." He pulled back his lips to reveal his missing teeth.

Laughter made its rounds across the circle. Only Isa-tai found no mirth in Nagwee's joke. Neither was Daniel exactly bemused.

That his legs supported him came as a surprise. Daniel did not attempt to walk around the circle. He cleared his throat, wet his lips, and tried to think.

"We are The People, yet we act like Pale Eyes."

Those words surprised him; indeed, they surprised everyone in the circle.

"Go on," Nagwee said.

Daniel took a deep breath, slowly exhaled, and found his courage.

"We argue over land. Land, that as we know, none of us owns. How does one own grass? It belongs to all. We fight over money. This is not something we would have done ten summers ago. I was sent, as was Tetecae, to follow the white man's road, and this was something I did not wish to do. But it is done. I am back. I try to find the right path. Sometimes I see that The People's path is the best. Yet there are times when I believe that we can learn from the road the Pale Eyes take. In this day, we must learn the white man's road, for the road of The People is becoming shorter, arduous, more difficult to travel."

He nodded respectfully at Isa-tai. "I have heard the words of Isa-tai, and know he believes in his heart" — Daniel tapped the center of his chest — "what he does is best for The People." Facing Quanah, he said softly: "Quanah has led The People in war and now in peace. His way would bring in more money for The People, not for himself. What Isa-tai proposes would lead to much trouble. I respect Isa-tai, but I do not think his plan is something The People should consider. He invites this rancher named Carmody to graze his cattle in The Big Pasture, yet at the same time he plans to steal those cattle? A lie? This is something I would expect from a *taibo.*"

Shit, he thought, and even silently mouthed the pale-eyes curse he had picked up working in the coal mines in Pittsburgh. It was, he had always thought, a good word. Yet he knew comparing Isa-tai to a *taibo* was wrong. There's no worse insult to a man like Isa-tai.

He couldn't look at Isa-tai, nor could he

apologize. So he stood there, trying to think of something else to say, but his tongue had swollen, and his brain refused to give him any words. Feeling the stares, he slowly sat down and crossed his knees.

"Good." Yellow Bear's head bobbed. "He speaks well."

"And we did not have to bite him," Nag-wee added, then looked at Charles Flint. "Would you like to speak?"

With a shrug, the young bookkeeper said: "I have nothing to say."

Grunting, Isa-tai stood, pointing at Daniel. "He Whose Arrows Fly Straight Into The Hearts Of His Enemies has become a *taibo,* too. He is no different than Quanah *Par-ker.* I no longer call him by the name his father gave him. I call him by the name he is known among the *taibo. Kill-straight.*" He spit, and sat down, but wasn't finished talking. "He disgraces The People with his words, and with his actions. Metal Shirt. *Bah!*"

Anger flushed Daniel's face. When he glanced at his hands, he realized his fists were clenched so tightly they shook. After sucking in air, he slowly exhaled, did it again, and again, waiting for the temper, that strong Comanche temper, to subside. Looking up, he saw Yellow Bear pushing himself to his feet.

"You speak of disgrace, Isa-tai," the old man said. "You say Quanah and this young one have disgraced us. You say they have betrayed The People." His voice was steady, but Daniel could feel the temper, the tension. "Should I bring up your disgrace, Isa-tai?"

The *puhakat* did not wait for Yellow Bear to finish. Shooting lithely to his feet, Isa-tai roared in defiance: "I have heard those insults since that day. I do not have to defend myself, old man. It was that fool warrior of the *Paganavo*." Meaning the Cheyenne, who The People knew as Striped Arrows. "When that idiot killed a skunk, he destroyed my *puha* for the entire raid. If that Cheyenne had listened, had followed my instructions, we would not have been defeated by those *Tejanos* with the far-killing rifles."

Yellow Bear simply stared, his black eyes like buckshot. "That is not the disgrace I refer to," he said bluntly, and sat down again.

"*Puha?*" Nagwee, still sitting, suddenly sniggered. "What *puha?*"

"You are old men," Isa-tai said. "I do not stand here to be insulted by old men, one whose belly is full not of buffalo, but a pale-

99

eyes sweet thing that is so cold it hurts one's teeth." Now, he sat down, and the floor was open.

It stayed that way, too, for five minutes, maybe longer, until Quanah rose one more time.

"We should not quarrel amongst ourselves. Not when the Pale Eyes can see us, hear us. On this matter, we will speak no more while in the land of the *Tejanos.* When we return to our country, then we will hold a council. Yet I have heard enough. Carmody will remove his cattle from The Big Pasture, and even if The People say that I am wrong, that Carmody's cattle should stay, we will not steal those cows." He glared at Isa-tai. "Not if you have invited him, Isa-tai. We do not lie. Not to ourselves. Not to *Tejanos.* We have not become that much like Pale Eyes."

No one else spoke, and, of that, Daniel was glad.

They gathered their belongings, and left the dining room, letting the waiters and cooks and the tall one with the thin mustache who Captain Hall had called a maître d' stare at their backs as they went through the door and stepped into the hotel's immaculate lobby.

More stares found them there, and all of

the Comanches stopped except for Isa-tai, who strode through the doors and stepped outside onto the boardwalk in front of Rusk Street.

Charles Flint started after his father, but Yellow Bear stopped him.

"Let him go."

Flint turned. "He is my father," he said, "and cannot find the Pickwick, I mean, the apartments near that hotel."

"Go, Tetecae," Quanah said. "Go with your father."

Charles Flint walked out the door.

"Well, Quanah?" The question came from Captain Hall, backed by the ranchers Waggoner and Burnett, and some other *Tejano* wearing a dusty, high-brimmed hat, wiry mustache, and goatee.

"We sign no papers," Quanah said in English. "We talk more on reservation. But I think your beef will eat our grass."

None of the cattlemen cared much for that answer.

"We can't wait long, Quanah," Burnett said.

Quanah's head bobbed, but he said nothing.

"Red," Burk Burnett said, suddenly grinning, "I'm a man of faith, and I believe in Quanah Parker. Everything'll work out.

We'll put Carmody in his place, our beefs'll get fat on Comanche grass, and the Comanches will have a lot of our coin to spend."

"I hope you're right, Burk," Waggoner said.

"I'm always right, Dan."

The smiles looked as forced as the silence, but when Yellow Bear said — "Ice cream." — the laughter that followed was real.

"All right, Chief," Captain Hall said, putting his right arm around Yellow Bear's shoulder. "Let's get you over to the Queen City. I don't think Missus Connor would have closed up yet, not as hot as tonight is."

So Captain Hall and Burk Burnett led the procession to the Queen City Ice Cream Parlor, where they were soon joined by Charles Flint, who said his father had retired to the room for the night at the Taylor & Barr building. Daniel, Flint, Yellow Bear, and the cowboy — who Dan Waggoner introduced as his *segundo,* George Briggs — were the only ones to partake in Mrs. Connor's butter pecan ice cream. The ranchers, Nagwee, and Quanah smoked cigars, with Burnett and Hall sipping coffee.

Yellow Bear lifted his bowl to his mouth, tilted it, and slurped, producing more grins on the faces of the *Tejanos.* Even Quanah, lowering his cigar, shook his head and laughed.

"Is it that good?" he asked in Comanche.

Yellow Bear nodded, and the bowl rattled on the table.

A loud ticking drew Daniel's attention, and he saw that Captain Hall had drawn a gold watch on a heavy chain from his vest pocket. "It's getting late. Been a long day."

Quanah nodded. "We go," he said in English.

Which suited Daniel, but not Yellow Bear.

"I want to see more of this *taibo* city," he said. "I am an old man. I want to see what else these Pale Eyes offer."

After Daniel translated, the cowhand, George Briggs, slapped his thigh. "Hell's bells, I'd be right proud to tree this town with a man like you." He glanced at his boss. "Be able to tell my grandkids that I once treed Cowtown with a renegade Co-manch'."

More laughter, and Quanah rose. "I go my way. To bed. You go yours. Don't wake me up."

"I'm going with you," Daniel said, and stood beside Quanah.

"We'll meet you tomorrow in the lobby of the Pickwick Hotel and go eat some break-fast," Captain Hall said. "Say, seven o'clock?"

Quanah grunted.

"My stomach hurts," Nagwee said. "I will go with you. Sleep. Feel better."

Daniel looked at Flint.

"I've got to get the post books in order. I promised Mister McEveety I'd get that done while I was here. So I guess. . . ."

Yellow Bear grunted. "My *Nermernuh* friends are women."

Daniel tried to fight down his smile, and Charles Flint shook his head. "All right, *Tsu Kuh Puah*," he said. "I will go with you. But just for a little while."

CHAPTER EIGHT

Church bells, chiming in the distance, woke him. Daniel swung out of bed, and rubbed his stiff, aching neck. He remembered waking up in the parlor chair, stumbling back to bed, still sweating. Even now, he felt damp and hot.

"This time of year, Fort Worth," he remembered overhearing someone say last night, "would make a good hell."

Again, he moved to the open window, sticking his head out, hoping to catch a cool breeze, only to feel no wind at all, just rank dampness and morning heat. With a sigh, he went back to the dresser, poured the last of the water from the pitcher into a bowl, and washed his face, his neck, under his armpits, and across his chest.

Already 7:00 A.M., the Progressor told him. He had overslept, if he could call how he had spent the night "sleeping." After drying his body, he opened the valise.

Who should I dress like today? he thought. *Nermernuh or Pale Eyes?* He grinned. *Or Mescalero?*

In the end, he went as he usually dressed, part The People (from the waist down), part *taibo* (waist up): moccasins and buckskin britches, red calico shirt, and the gray coat he had turned into a vest. He grabbed the wide-brimmed, open-crowned black hat and his room key, and hurried out the door.

What he saw across the hall stopped him. The door was cracked open, but the clerk at the Pickwick Hotel had said nobody was staying there. Curious, maybe even suspicious, Daniel stepped to the door and listened. The hinges creaked as he pushed it open. The covers were pushed back, the window open, and the room smelled of pipe smoke, but nobody was in. No grip. Nothing.

Feeling silly, he shook his head. Likely somebody checked in late in the night, and the clerk had sent him here. A drummer, already gone. Up early to make his sales.

Up early, Daniel thought, *and I'm late.*

He raced to the stairwell.

"I thought you Comanches got up with the sun," Burk Burnett said lightly, and extended his hand to Daniel.

"Only during a raidin' moon," the cowhand, George Briggs, said, chuckling, then spit tobacco juice into the street as Daniel shook hands with the rancher.

They had gathered in front of a coffee house on Houston Street — Burnett, Briggs, Waggoner, Charles Flint, and Nagwee. Isatai sat cross-legged near a hitching rail, away from the others. Moments later School Father Pratt and Captain Hall stepped through the doorway of the coffee house, holding steaming cups.

After Daniel shook hands with Pratt, he stepped off the boardwalk, and looked toward the Taylor & Barr building.

"Nobody gets up early in Hell's Half Acre," Pratt said.

He was right. Last night, or rather early this morning, the streets had been bustling with activity. Daniel remembered the drunken cowboy stumbling out of the alley toward the Tivoli Hall. He could still hear the cacophony of voices, the music, the laughter, the horses, the curses of the policeman. Now, as he looked across the street, the Tivoli looked worn-out, deserted. The hitching rails were all empty. So was Houston Street, except for a lone man with a broom, sweeping up broken glass in front of some beer hall far down the street.

"What's keeping Quanah?" Flint asked in English.

"Maybe ol' Yellow Bear," George Briggs said, shifting the quid from his left cheek to his right.

"Y'all tree the town, George?" Captain Hall blew over the rim of his coffee mug.

"Just wandered from the Club Room to the Bismarck to the El Paso and Occidental."

"You didn't get him roostered?" Waggoner asked facetiously.

"They don't serve Injuns, boss," Briggs said, and took off his hat. "And this morn', I wish they hadn't served me."

Every Pale Eyes chuckled.

"What time did you finish?" Daniel asked.

Briggs pushed his hat back. "Midnight. Early night for this ol' hoss."

Charles Flint laughed. "I was in bed long before that."

"I know," Briggs said. "You flew the coop about ten."

An hour and change after I left with Quanah, Daniel remembered. He thought again, remembering last night. He had heard a door shut down the hall, what sounded like the one to the room Quanah shared with his father-in-law, yet that had been 3:17 A.M. It had not been midnight. He studied

108

George Briggs and decided that, from the look of the *taibo*'s eyes, his memory, his concept of time, might not be trusted.

"Well, I had work to do," Flint was saying, and Daniel cut him off.

"Are you sure it was midnight?"

Briggs pushed his hat back. His bloodshot eyes locked hard on Daniel, and he reached into his vest, and withdrew a silver watch. "You see this here thing?" he said. He pressed on the stem, and the case opened. The hands were large enough that Daniel could read the time, 7:48, and the second hand was moving. "This here's an Illinois railroad watch. Ain't but ten years old, if that. It wasn't quite midnight when I taken Yellow Bear to that buildin' yonder and bid him a fine fare-thee-well. Then I wandered over to the Empress" — jutting his jaw down the street toward the man with the saloon — "for me nightcap."

"How many nightcaps, George?" Waggoner asked lightly.

"Daniel, Charles," School Father Pratt said, changing the subject, "would either of you care for coffee?"

That sounded good, but Nagwee spoke in the language of The People. "It is not like Quanah or Yellow Bear to sleep after the sun has risen."

109

"No, it isn't," Daniel said in English, and moved down the boardwalk, back toward the Taylor & Barr mercantile. Charles Flint caught up with him, and boot steps told Daniel they had pale-eyes company.

"You don't think anything's wrong?" Flint asked.

Daniel's head shook. He didn't. Oh, maybe Yellow Bear had eaten too much ice cream, or he was plumb tuckered out from wandering the saloons with George Briggs. Yesterday had been a tiring day. Maybe Quanah was exhausted, too. Daniel could have slept another three or four hours himself.

He looked back, found School Father Pratt and Burk Burnett walking behind them, concern disfiguring their faces. Back down the boardwalk, Dan Waggoner stood talking to George Briggs, while Nagwee was standing, arms folded across his chest, staring. Isa-tai remained sitting, face hard, not moving. He hadn't moved since Daniel had arrived, had barely even blinked.

Daniel and the others reached the outside staircase of the Taylor & Barr building. He took the steps two at a time until he reached the second landing, opened the outer door, and ran down the hallway. Once he had stopped, he could hear footsteps following him up. He knocked gently on the frame.

"*Ahó,*" he called softly, then louder. His knuckles struck the door, harder. "*Ahó! Tsu Kuh Puah!*" Now, he struck the door with his fist, and shouted the names of Quanah and Yellow Bear.

Charles Flint stood beside him, echoing his shouts. Gripping the handle, he turned the knob, pressed his weight against the door, pushed. "It is locked," he said.

He struck the door again.

"Quiet!" Pratt tried the door, but Flint was right. The door was locked. The School Father pressed his ear against the door, and spoke: "Quanah? Yellow Bear."

Sounds drew his attention. Daniel looked, saw that Briggs, Waggoner, and Nagwee had decided to come, too. Another figure came through the doorway, and Daniel straightened. Isa-tai.

"Could they have gone somewhere?" Pratt asked.

"Where would they go?" Flint replied. He hit the door with his fist.

George Briggs was rolling a cigarette — the chaw of tobacco gone from his cheek.

The men stopped when Pratt kicked the door, screaming Quanah's name.

"The clerk." Flint whirled. "The clerk. He will have another key. I will go."

"No time for that." Pratt stepped back.

"For the love of God, man," Burk Burnett said. "What are you doing?"

The School Father did not answer. Bending his leg, he slammed his boot just under the doorknob. Wood splintered and cracked.

"Jesus!" Dan Waggoner shouted down the hallway. "What the hell's up?"

The door swung into the room, banged against the wall.

Daniel stepped inside, tripped, landed on the rug. He rolled over, and gasped. Next to the bed, Quanah lay face down on the hardwood floor, his head turned toward the door. When School Father Pratt had kicked open the door, the door had just missed striking Quanah's face. Daniel had tripped over the great warrior's outstretched left arm.

Already Pratt was kneeling beside Quanah, lifting his wrist, feeling for a pulse. Charles Flint ran to the bed, yelling Yellow Bear's name. Gripping the footboard of the bed, Daniel pulled himself to his feet.

"Yellow Bear. . . ." Flint tugged at the sleeping *puhakat*'s sleeve. "It is I, Tetecae. Wake up, *Tsu Kuh Puah*." Flint turned his head to the side, coughed, turned back, started to say something, but coughed again.

Daniel coughed, too. Suddenly light-headed, he gripped the footboard for support, tried to lean over, tried to say something. He filled his lungs, and the cough doubled him over.

"Criminy." School Father Pratt went to his feet, whirled. "Burk," he cried, "tell that cowhand to put out that damned cigarette!"

"What?"

"Now!"

That's when Daniel understood. Pratt lurched for the lamp on one side of the bed. Putting an arm over his nose, Daniel moved to the other. He found the knob, turned it down, stopping the flow of gas. Across the bed, School Father Pratt nodded, then pointed across the apartment room.

"The window," Pratt said, then coughed, shook his head. "Open the window. Get some fresh air in here."

Daniel hurried, almost tripped again on the rug. He found the latch, pulled it, shoved the window open, leaned out, filled his lungs with fresh air. Below, on the streets, he saw Captain Hall chatting with a man in a plaid suit and gray hat. Unaware of what was happening upstairs.

He turned back, saw the other rancher, Waggoner, grabbing Quanah's bare feet. Burnett had long arms. They lifted, took Quanah. Nagwee barked something in the language of The People, but the two *Tejanos* could not understand.

"Take him to his room," Daniel translated. "Across the hall."

Pratt waved a pillow over the bed, circulating the air, forcing the poisonous gas out. He looked up, found Waggoner's *segundo*, George Briggs. Isa-tai was in the room now, too, standing beside the torn door, arms folded, staring, his face a mask of indifference.

"Briggs," Pratt said. "Fetch a doctor. Quick."

"What happened?" the cowhand asked.

"Must have. . . ." Pratt had to stop for a breath of air. "Must have blown out the lamps." He turned back to Yellow Bear.

"Holy Mother of God." The cowboy took off, running at an awkward gait, spurs singing a song as he raced down the hallway.

"We must get out of this room. Till that gas has cleared." Pratt sounded like a School Father again.

"Help me then," Flint said. "Help me with Yellow Bear."

"There's no need, son."

Fifteen minutes had passed, and they had returned to the room Quanah had shared with Yellow Bear. Nagwee remained across

114

the hall with Quanah, and the Pale Eyes waited for their own doctor.

"What's keeping that damned sawbones?" Pratt said angrily. Daniel could not ever remember hearing the School Father curse.

A song filled the room. Charles Flint looked over at his father, who had closed his eyes, raised his arms to the sky, and began singing.

Daniel looked at Yellow Bear. The old man's eyes were closed as if sleeping, and Daniel turned away. Again, he leaned out the window, closing his own eyes, trying to shake the image of Yellow Bear. As he ducked back inside, something on the window caught his eye. He peered closer at a reddish smudge on the glass below the latch. Like blood. Saw the lines. Like part of a man's finger. No, thumb.

Isa-tai sang.

Daniel turned, took a step, stopped, looked back at the window. Something was wrong. But what?

"Yellow Bear! Wake up!" Flint's voice cracked. Tears streamed down his face. The bookkeeper refused to believe the School Father's statement that Yellow Bear was dead.

Daniel started for the bed, only to stop again. He looked beyond Isa-tai and at the door, then to the small table next to a parlor chair. Quanah's coat draped the chair, and the table overflowed with Yellow Bear's clothes. Quanah's tie, even his diamond stickpin, lay on the dresser beside the water pitcher. He looked again at the table. There was the brass room key, on top of Yellow Bear's bone breastplate. Again, he looked at the door, then turned back toward the window.

Isa-tai sang, and soon his voice was answered by the song from across the hall. Nagwee's voice.

Both *puhakats* singing a song for the dead.

After shaking his head clear, Daniel walked to the bed, sitting on the edge, avoiding Charles Flint's face. He reached down until his fingers rested on Yellow Bear's forehead.

He looked strange, long silver braids matted from sweat, not dressed as *Nermernuh,* but in a long, bleached muslin nightshirt, the front unbuttoned, damp with sweat. Quanah wasn't the only one to have bought something downstairs in the mercantile the previous afternoon. Yellow Bear had traded an elk-horn knife for this nightshirt. A *taibo* shirt of coarse material, now stinking with sweat. It was not what a powerful *puhakat* of The People should be wearing when he died.

Daniel murmured his farewell.

"What's going on here?"

Daniel looked up to see a bald, sweating man holding a black hat. Behind him stood a panting George Briggs and a grim-faced Captain Hall.

"Yellow Bear's dead," Waggoner said. "Gas killed him."

"How's Quanah?" Captain Hall asked.

"I don't know," School Father Pratt said softly. "I couldn't even tell if his heart was beating. He is in the room across the hall with those two Comanche medicine men."

From the sound of Nagwee's song, Quanah was also preparing to begin his journey to The Land Beyond The Sun.

CHAPTER NINE

Asphyxiation.

A *taibo* word that held no meaning for Daniel, but that is what they said had killed Yellow Bear.

"So, the old medicine man . . . ," said a man in an ill-fitting, frayed, plaid suit, a reporter for Dallas *Herald*. "Let me get this straight. He comes to the room, in his cups, thinks the lamps are coal oil as they'd likely have up on the reservation. Not knowing they're gas, he blows them out. Goes to sleep, and the gas does its dirty work. Poor bastard just never woke up."

"That's what it looks like," Captain Hall said.

"Except," School Father Pratt added, "Yellow Bear definitely was not in his cups."

The man in the plaid suit winked. "He will be in our newspaper, Capt'n. Anything the Dallas press can do to make Fort Worth look bad, we'll do it, sir." He laughed, but, when nobody joined in, he grimaced, swallowed, and said meekly: " 'Course, Yellow Bear just made an honest mistake. Pity. I liked the ol' boy."

Their talk continued, but Daniel did not, would not listen. They had taken hacks to a restaurant on Bluff Street — Pratt and Hall, Daniel and Flint — to get away from the horde of newspaper reporters who had gathered at the Pickwick Hotel and Taylor & Barr mercantile.

"Gathered," Burk Burnett had said, "for the deathwatch."

Burnett had stayed behind. Isa-tai and Nagwee remained upstairs in the Taylor & Barr apartment, attending to Quanah with the Fort Worth doctor, an old man named Stallings whose breath, even at 8:00 A.M., reeked of rye whiskey. Daniel wished the pale-eyes sawbones was Major Becker — he trusted that bluecoat — but Becker was up at Fort Sill in Indian Territory. This reporter — Daniel glanced at the Old Glory writing tablet he had bought at the mercantile, saw where he had scribbled the ink-slinger's name, Kyne — had been enterprising enough to follow them to the café near the Trinity River.

The food smelled like the river, too.

"Best eat, Daniel." School Father Pratt's

119

voice was soothing, not scolding. "You too, Charles. You'll need your strength."

Glancing at the bowl of chili, Daniel lifted his spoon, and dug into the bowl of brown meat and grease, which reminded him of the mud on the streets at the edge of town. He left the spoon in the bowl, and stared out the window.

That was something he could never get used to, the way these Pale Eyes ate. The People were not used to having a noon meal. They would serve food on the flesh side of a dried hide, eating in the morning, in the evening. Rarely would they eat what the Pale Eyes called dinner. Oh, sure, if one got hungry, he could help himself to food in the day, pemmican maybe, or some dried beef. On the other hand, Daniel had not had breakfast that morning, not even coffee. Yet he couldn't eat. Not now. Not with Quanah back in that stifling room above the mercantile. Likely dying.

"Doc Stallings said Quanah Parker was in a coma?" the reporter, Kyne, asked.

No one answered, but that's what the frowning Dr. Stallings had said. When asked by reporters about Quanah's chances of recovery, the doctor had slowly, grimly said: "It is not good. Not good at all."

"What a shame." Kyne shook his head,

pulled a nickel flask from his coat pocket, and began to unscrew the top. "I liked that ol' boy, too."

Back in his room above the Taylor & Barr mercantile, Daniel leaned out the window, and drew in a lungful of fresh air. Well, as fresh as air could be in a dirty, cramped, and now noisy *taibo* city. The Progressor clock told him it was 4:37, and Hell's Half Acre had begun to come alive again. Above the sonance of Cowtown — clopping of hoofs, jingle of traces, plodding of feet down the boardwalk, the voices, laughter, and beginnings of music — the sound from across the hallway reached Daniel.

A song from Isa-tai. The shaking of a gourd rattle by Nagwee.

Stallings, the drunken doctor, had announced to the newspapermen in the lobby of the Pickwick Hotel that he had done all he could for Quanah Parker, that his recovery or demise lay in the hands of God, not medicine. The *taibos* had accepted that, but the two *puhakats* of The People would not give up so easily.

Daniel stepped back toward the pitcher and basin on the dresser, stopped, turned, looked back at the window.

Quickly he picked up his hat, strode

through the door, and walked down the hall to the room Quanah and Yellow Bear had shared. He pushed open the door, still broken from School Father Pratt's kick, and stepped inside.

Pratt and Burk Burnett had arranged for Yellow Bear's body to be taken to a funeral parlor to be prepared for burial. Daniel hadn't liked that at all, but he had kept his mouth shut. The Pale Eyes would put Yellow Bear in a wooden box, plant him in a cemetery. Burnett had promised it would be a fine funeral, with the best preacher Fort Worth had to offer. He had said a crowd of mourners would fill the church. They'd give Yellow Bear a great send-off.

Pale Eyes could not or would not understand the ways of The People. They would not sit Yellow Bear down so that he was facing east, to begin the journey to join his ancestors. Back home, along Cache Creek, Yellow Bear's belongings would be burned. Daniel regretted that they had traveled by train. Else, they could have killed one of Yellow Bear's best ponies to carry him to The Land Beyond The Sun.

Besides, what did these Pale Eyes know about mourning?

The thought stopped Daniel, and he glanced at his hands, his arms. He had forgotten, too. He should draw blood, cut a gash down his forearms. Maybe chop off his hair, or the tip of a finger. Anything to show how much he had loved Yellow Bear. That was how The People mourned. And they would never speak the name of Yellow Bear again.

Mourning would have to wait.

Refusing to look at the bed where Yellow Bear had died, or at the gas lamps that had killed him, and maybe would finally kill Quanah Parker, Daniel walked across the room. He stopped at the table. The belongings of both Yellow Bear and Quanah had been moved to the room shared by Isa-tai and Nagwee, but the brass key remained on the table. He picked it up, looked back at the door, and laid it on the table, then moved to the window.

It remained open, but Daniel pushed it shut. That's how he had found it. He knelt and studied the reddish print on the glass.

"What are you doing, kid?"

When Daniel turned, he saw Captain Lee Hall standing in the doorway, hat in one hand at his side, the other with a thumb hooked in his waistband.

Daniel closed the window all the way, and stood.

"It's a little hot, isn't it?" Captain Hall

said. "Don't you think you'd better leave that open?"

"Exactly," Daniel said, but walked away from the closed window. He stopped beside the table.

Lee Hall stepped through the doorway. His face had been curious, friendly, but the expression quickly changed. "I asked you a question. What are you doing in here?"

Daniel's fingers climbed up his vest, and he tapped the shield badge pinned on the lapel. "I am what they call a Metal Shirt. You, too, were once one."

"Meaning a Texas Ranger, that's right. I told you that already. But you best speak straight to me, Killstraight."

Daniel pointed to the lamps. "This was no accident."

Lee Hall's mouth dropped open. He started to say something, shook his head, and leaned against the wall next to the open door. He ran fingers through his red hair, swallowed, and inhaled deeply. After holding the breath, he let it out slowly, and once more shook his head.

"Son," he said, sounding much like a School Father who did not wish to scold an ignorant child, "I know this has been a terrible shock. But here's what happened . . . Quanah was asleep. Yellow Bear came back.

He dressed for bed, went to the lamps, and, tragically, thinking they were coal oil, blew them out. He went to sleep, and the gas killed him. The gas would have killed Quanah, but it looks like Yellow Bear, maybe in his death throes, kicked Quanah out of bed. Quanah must have tried for the door, but couldn't make it. The fact that his head was close to the crack between the door and floor likely saved him. Maybe. We'll see."

Daniel nodded. Yes, this Texas Ranger was a good detective. Perhaps as good as Hugh Gunter or Deputy U.S. Marshal Harvey P. Noble.

"So you see," Captain Hall said, "it was an accident."

Now Daniel shook his head. "No accident." He pointed to the window. "That's how the window was when we entered the room this morning. Only it was latched shut, too."

The former Ranger pulled on his hat. "So?"

"It was hot. Very hot. The newspaper this morning said the temperature reached one hundred and seven. Hot. It did not cool down much at night. Even the body of the one who is no more" — he wondered if Lee Hall would understand this need not to speak Yellow Bear's name — "was wet with sweat when we discovered him."

"So they got hot."

"Hotter upstairs here than even down-stairs. So hot I woke up in the middle of the night. After three o'clock. My window was open. Everybody's window was open. Everybody's but in this room."

Outside, a horse whinnied, followed by loud curses, and a whistle. Inside, Isa-tai sang, and Nagwee shook his gourd.

"I don't know, Killstraight. Maybe Yellow Bear had so much ice cream last night, he felt cold. He came in, closed the window, blew out the lamps. And died. An accident. Not murder."

Only now Lee Hall sounded as if he were trying to convince himself of it.

"Shortly after I woke," Daniel said, "I was leaning out the window, trying to cool off, and I heard a door open and close. This door." He pointed at the broken one the manager of the Pickwick had said he'd have to hire a carpenter to repair.

Captain Hall pointed out: "Yellow Bear coming back from his night on the town."

"According to the cowboy, Briggs," Daniel countered, "Yellow Bear was back here at midnight." He pointed at the dresser. "That clock put the time at between three-fifteen and three-thirty."

Glancing at the Progressor, Captain Hall pulled a gold watch from his vest pocket. "Then that clock's. . . ." He didn't finish. Instead, after looking at his timepiece, he slid the watch back into the pocket. "George Briggs could have been mistaken. Yellow Bear might not have been in his cups, but Briggs most definitely was."

That was one point Daniel could not dismiss.

"And another thing." Lee Hall had gathered up some steam. He pointed at the brass key. "The door was locked, wasn't it? That's why Richard had to kick open the door."

Daniel gave him a Comanche stare and let the *Tejano* Metal Shirt continue.

"Locked." Hall nodded. "That means Yellow Bear got here, locked the door, closed the window. Blew out the lamps. And died."

Daniel said nothing.

Captain Hall let out a mirthless chuckle. "I suppose you think the killer came in, locked the door behind him, blew out the lamps, crawled through the window, closed the window behind him, somehow managed to latch it shut, too. And drop, what, twenty, thirty feet, into the alley? Something like that?"

Shaking his head, Daniel picked up the key, tossed it, caught it, and held it between his fingers.

"The one who has joined his ancestors would not know what to do with this. Even I do not lock my door. Even Quanah, who lives in the Star House that you and other ranchers had built for him, he does not lock his doors. It is not the way of The People." He let the key fall back to the table.

"Then how did the door get locked?"

Daniel had been thinking about this. After they had found the door locked this morning, Flint had suggested that there would have been another key at the Pickwick Hotel, which managed the rental of the rooms above the Taylor & Barr mercantile. Daniel had stayed in enough hotels to understand that getting a key from behind the registration desk at night was not that difficult. The killer could have stolen the key, unlocked the door, blown out the gas lamps, locked the door behind him, and left the key back in its proper place.

Or there could have been another key.

Or. . . .

"One of us could have put the key on the table when we came into the room this morning? Is that right, Daniel?"

Charles Flint stepped inside, wiping his hands with a handkerchief. His tone had been far from friendly, but Daniel could not

128

deny that was his thinking.

"Everybody was in the room," Daniel said evenly. "Everybody but you, Captain Hall."

Hall straightened. "I was in here, too."

"Yes, but I had seen the key before. You had remained outside, did not come until the cowboy, Briggs, told you what was going on when he ran to get the doctor."

Hall blinked. "I could have stolen the key from the clerk at the Pickwick," he said. "Nobody really needed that key." He pointed at the one on the table.

Daniel smiled. Yes, this *taibo* was a good detective.

"Daniel," Charles Flint said as he slid the handkerchief into his trousers pocket, "who would have wanted to see Yellow Bear dead?"

Daniel grimaced. Flint had traveled the white man's road far too long, had forgotten that The People respected those who had joined their ancestors too much to speak their names among the living.

"Not him," Daniel said. He jutted his jaw toward the room across the hall where Nagwee and Isa-tai tried to bring Quanah back from death.

"Quanah?" Charles Flint stared out the door.

"Sure." Lee Hall's head bobbed in agree-

129

ment. "Yeah, we treat Quanah like royalty now, but I warrant there are plenty of folks in Fort Worth who'd like to see Quanah dead. Or any Comanch'. Your people made things rough on our settlers for a number of years. And what you did to our women. . . ."

Charles Flint bristled. "Your people made things rough on us Comanches, too."

"I won't argue that." Hall sighed. "All right. I still think this was a terrible accident. How do you prove it was murder and attempted murder?"

To that question, Daniel had no answer. He wasn't even sure where to begin.

"Who are your suspects?" Hall continued. "I think you're wrong about the killer leaving the key here this morning. None of us had reason to kill either Quanah or Yellow Bear."

Daniel tried to put this delicately. "There is the matter of The Big Pasture."

"Quanah was going to sign the lease agreement, Killstraight," Hall said. The *Tejano* did not like the accusation. "The association had no reason. . . ."

"The agreement was not signed," Daniel pointed out. "It might not have been signed. Might not be signed. And there is the other one."

"Sol Carmody? That rapscallion?" Hall

started to shake his head, but stopped. He whispered the name again: "Carmody."

"It is not Carmody that Daniel means," Charles Flint said. "Is it?"

Silence. Even the singing and rattling of the gourd across the hallway had stopped.

"He means my father," Flint said. "*Bávi,* you are wrong!"

Maybe. Daniel said nothing, but he intended to ask Nagwee not to leave Quanah alone with Isa-tai.

CHAPTER TEN

He had filled three pages of the Old Glory tablet, but as he reread his notes, Daniel decided what he had written added up to nothing.

The Progressor said it was 10:18. Yawning, Daniel pushed himself up, decided to check on Quanah. He opened the door, and stopped.

The door across the hall was shut. He stepped to it, put his ear against the wood, listening. Nothing from inside, though the sound from Hell's Half Acre echoed through the open windows.

"I am stupid," he said aloud, and returned to his room, grabbed his hat, two pencils, and the writing tablet, and hurried down the hall.

"If you do not leave, you will force me to call a constable and have you arrested."

The Pickwick Hotel manager's beady eyes

looked past Daniel toward the main door, as if hoping to summon a police officer.

"My request is not unreasonable," Daniel said again, not angrily, not pleadingly, but firmly.

"You will leave here." The manager wiped his waxed mustache, then ran a hand over his sweating pate. "I will call the police."

Daniel could feel the stares of patrons, but would not waver. "There are five rooms at the Taylor and Barr building," he said for the umpteenth time. Umpteenth. Another fine *taibo* word. One of the School Mothers at Carlisle had used it often: "Daniel, I've told you for the umpteenth time. . . ."

"Boy. . . ."

Daniel silenced him with a finger. "Five rooms. Four you let to us. Who was registered to the fifth room? That is all I need to know."

"For one thing, boy, it is not the policy of this hotel to give just anyone personal information about our guests." His tone had turned nasal and nasty. "Carlos, go fetch a copper."

Again, Daniel tapped his badge. "I am a peace officer."

"Peace officer my ass," the manager said. "Injun copper. What a joke." He shook his fist at Daniel's face. "You get out this moment. This is a respectable hotel."

Feeling his face flush, Daniel stepped back. Had School Father Pratt and those other teachers not taught him the white man's way, he would have struck the manager right then and there. Yet what honor could be found in counting coup on a worthless specimen like this sweating knave who did not even have enough hair to scalp?

"What's the problem here, Andy?"

Daniel sighed, resigned to the fact that he was about to be arrested. That would bring shame to School Father Pratt, to Agent Joshua Biggers, but he knew he had been in the right. All he wanted was an answer to an important question.

"This red devil's just being a nuisance, Billy. I've asked Carlos to bring in a policeman."

Turning just enough to see the newcomer, Daniel recognized him. He wasn't a peace officer at all, but the newspaper reporter from the Dallas *Herald.* Kyne. William J. Kyne, who extended his right hand toward Daniel.

"It's Killstraight, right?"

He stared at the hand, but did not accept it, expecting some ruse from this *taibo.*

The reporter didn't seem to be offended. Maybe newspaper reporters were used to such treatment. Instead, the right hand reached for a pencil tucked above his ear, and the left brought up a writing tablet. An Old Glory, with pages filled with indecipherable scratch marks.

"Billy," the Pickwick's manager began, "don't give this heathen. . . ."

"Quiet, Andy. Just give me a minute here. What's troubling you, Killstraight?"

Daniel remained mute.

The reporter returned the pencil to his ear, and set the Old Glory tablet on the registration desk. "All right. This ain't for the record. But I remember you at Norma's Café this afternoon when we were having dinner. I could tell something troubled you. Something about what happened to Quanah and that other ol' bird." He looked at the Pickwick manager. "Yes, sir, I could see why you wouldn't want to help out this detective, Andy. One guest dead. Another in a coma and likely not long for this world. It would be a shame if the Pickwick Hotel got sued by the Comanche nation. And it sure won't look good when all those Indian-loving Eastern papers like the Boston *Tribune* and *Harper's Weekly* start running articles about how the Pickwick killed Quanah Parker, chief of the Comanches."

"We are not responsible. . . ."

"You didn't tell the Comanches that those lamps were gas."

"Those rooms are owned by the Taylor and Barr. . . ."

"But they're managed by you boys." Kyne picked up the Old Glory, thumbed to a blank page. "Your mother was raped, killed, scalped, and mutilated by the Comanches, ain't that right, Andy?"

"My mother's alive and well in Mobile, Alabama."

"She won't be in the Dallas *Herald.* She'll be a motive that led to the death of Quanah Parker. That's the story that'll go out on the wires, that's the story all those Eastern papers'll pick up, and by the time you see a retraction, you'll be out of a job, my friend."

Daniel's head spun. He didn't know what to make of this conversation at all. The manager swore, and both hands dropped below the counter, returning with a leather-bound book, which he opened, then he flipped to a page, turned the book around, and shoved it toward the *Herald* reporter.

"There, you son-of-a-bitch. See for yourself. Nobody. *Nobody* stayed in Room Four last night. Or tonight. Or the night before."

Billy Kyne leaned forward. He wet his lips, and turned the book toward Daniel. "Can you read, Killstraight?"

The date marked under *Checked In* was yesterday. Rooms 1, 2, 3, and 5 were marked *N. Texas Stock Grw Assn,* and he could make out the handsome, almost feminine scroll of Lee Hall. No one had registered for Room 4. Daniel flipped back a page, then another. No one had stayed in Room 4 since July 2nd, and that was a man whose name, from what Daniel could make out, was Carmichael and who lived in Chicago.

"Satisfied?" The manager slammed the register shut, and drew it sharply off the desk, shoving it back onto a shelf underneath.

"The bed had been slept in," Daniel said. "The door was open."

"Get out of here!" the manager snapped. "Both of you. Especially you, Billy. You've worn out your welcome with me, you callous bastard."

Billy Kyne grinned. Putting his arm around Daniel's shoulder, he steered a path through the crowded lobby until they stepped outside onto the Third Street boardwalk.

"A copper's coming, lad," Kyne muttered. "Let's go back to your room before we both get hauled to the calaboose."

Daniel stopped in front of Room 4, and

gripped the knob. He turned it, pushed, and the door opened.

A match flared, and Billy Kyne stepped inside. He wasn't in the room long, before he shook it out, tossed the Lucifer into a cuspidor, and walked back into the lighted hallway.

"I tell you," Daniel said, reading the doubt in the reporter's face, "when I woke this morning, the door was open, the bed unmade."

"I don't disbelieve you a moment, Killstraight." He pointed across the hall. "That your room? Let's sit in there for a few minutes and figure out where you're headed."

A carpenter had repaired the door to Room 3, but to Daniel's surprise it was unlocked, too. Billy Kyne stepped through, and stared at the door.

"So you say Comanches don't lock their doors?"

Daniel nodded. "It is not our way."

"That's interesting," the reporter said, "but it doesn't mean much. A fellow, even an Indian, would be a fool to keep his door unlocked in this part of town. It's called Hell's Half Acre for a reason, you know."

Kyne moved to the wall lamp closest to

the door. He turned the knob, bathing the room in yellow light. Daniel moved to the window, and felt some measure of relief.

If he had imagined the open door and unmade bed, at least he had not dreamed this. He pointed to the smudge, and Billy Kyne joined him.

"What's this mean?" Kyne asked.

"I don't know," Daniel answered honestly. "But the window was shut."

Kneeling, Kyne squinted, pursed his lips, and looked at Daniel. "You reckon it's blood?"

Daniel shook his head. "Blood would have dried brown. That's still reddish."

"Uhn-huh. Ink, by my guess."

Ink. Daniel had not thought of that. Red ink.

"I use a pencil myself." Straightening, Kyne said: "But be that as it may, this thumb print . . . that's sure what it looks like . . . could have been here a day, a month, a year. Figure this. If they don't bother locking their doors at this place, then it isn't likely the chambermaids clean any window frequently, either."

"She made the bed," Daniel pointed out.

Smiling, Kyne reached into a pocket of his plaid sack suit, and withdrew a flask. "Sure you don't want a snort, Killstraight?"

Without waiting for a reply, he unscrewed the lid, and tossed his head back as he drank. "Was your bed made?"

Daniel had to think. "Yes, it was."

"Really. Even with all the commotion going on around here all day? That's impressive. All right, tomorrow, you wait on the maid. With luck, it'll be the same gal who cleaned your room today. You ask her if she made up the room across from yours."

He nodded. He had planned on doing that already.

"Why would they leave the door unlocked?" Daniel asked.

Billy Kyne shrugged. "Honest mistake, maybe."

Daniel threw Kyne's earlier argument back in his face. " 'But one would be foolish to keep his door unlocked in this part of town.' "

The reporter, however, wasn't listening. He was moving back to the globes of the lamps, looking at the one that was lit, then at the other. "Well, looky here." His grin revealed tobacco-stained teeth.

Daniel moved from the window to the bed. He didn't see it until Kyne tapped the smudge with his pencil.

Another red mark. Fainter, but clear enough.

"Don't expect no medal yet, Killstraight. Did you check ol' Yellow Bear's thumbs and fingers?"

His shoulders sagged, and he sighed. As a detective, he had much to learn. Billy Kyne read the answer on Daniel's face. "Too bad. Likely the undertaker's already cleaned up the ol' bird for his trip to the hereafter." He sipped again from his flask.

An idea struck Daniel, and his face brightened. "But the one who died here . . . he would not have used an ink pen."

Perplexed, Kyne lowered the flask. " 'The one who died here'?"

Daniel had to explain Comanche etiquette, and for the first time William J. Kyne scribbled something in his notebook. While he was writing, he said: "Well, you're forgetting the power of a celebrity, kid. And 'the one who died here' reminded me of ol' Sitting Bull, the Sioux."

"Lakota," Daniel corrected. At Carlisle, the Lakotas he had known hated being called Sioux.

Kyne didn't seem to hear.

"Before I landed in this dump of a town working at this dump of a newspaper, I was working in Saginaw, Michigan, when Buffalo Bill Cody brought his Wild West to town. Sitting Bull, the very red bastard who

141

killed Custer, was touring with Cody, and let me tell you he was the star of that spectacle. Signed autographs for scores of children, men, and women. Even soldiers, mind you. Dumb son-of-a-bitch that I was, I didn't get one. Mainly on account I didn't have a buck to spend on his John Hancock. That ol' boy made more money on autographs in one night than I'd make in a month, and that's on top of the fifty a month he was pulling from Cody."

Daniel frowned. "Then I must ask the cowboy, Briggs, if the one who is no more signed" — he tested the word — ". . . autographs . . . while he was wandering from saloon to saloon."

The pencil Kyne held waved in front of Daniel's face. "There's one other thing you need to consider."

Without speaking, Daniel waited.

"Quanah Parker, he who isn't dead yet, was signing scores of autographs yesterday. He could have blown out the lamp. And he could have closed the window."

That would be easy enough to check, but something else troubled Daniel. He kept thinking back to earlier that day, visualizing Charles Flint wiping his hands with a handkerchief. Charles Flint, the book-keeper. A bookkeeper wrote in ink, right?

He did not want to think that. He liked Flint. Flint's father, on the other hand. . . .

"I like your theory, kid." The reporter filed away pencil, notebook, and flask. "But even my idiotic editor, who plumb loves to give Fort Worth hell, wouldn't print what we have. That's because what we have, Killstraight, is a bunch of nothing. Now you get some evidence, and that'll be a whale of a story. 'Indian policeman suspects foul play in Cowtown.' That would be our headline. Or something a hell of a lot stronger. You said you told Capt'n Hall what you thought, and he didn't really believe it, right? You tell anybody else?"

Daniel shook his head.

"You trust me, don't you, kid?"

His lips just turned up a tad, not enough to be called a smile, but as close as Daniel could muster. Again he shook his head.

Kyne tilted his head back, and laughed. "That's good, boy. Don't trust the press. Especially the Dallas *Herald.* Especially Billy Kyne. You probably don't trust any white man, do you, Killstraight?"

No answer, although Daniel was thinking how much he wished Deputy U.S. Marshal Harvey P. Noble was in Fort Worth right now. Kyne opened the door, and stepped into the hall. After Daniel had joined him,

Kyne closed the door.

"Too bad we don't have a witness. Streets were full of people last night. Maybe somebody saw something."

Daniel was already ahead of Kyne on that front. He remembered the drunken cowboy in the alley, the police officer who had scolded him, almost arrested him. He didn't tell Kyne this, decided it would be better to keep that to himself. Although he had smiled when he had let Kyne know he didn't trust him, the truth was he didn't trust him.

"I'll have to do some checking," Kyne was saying. "Digging, rather. This won't be easy, not since I wore out my welcome with Andy at the hotel. And Tom Bode, that skinflint of an editor at the *Herald*, he sure won't cotton to the idea of me trotting back and forth from Dallas to this ol' burg every day. But I warrant I can talk him into it, for a couple days, anyhow. Anything to bring scandal to Fort Worth. First thing we need to do, though, is prove that Quanah didn't blow out those lamps, close that window."

He tilted his head to the door across the hall.

Daniel went to the room where Nagwee and Isa-tai tended to Quanah. Billy Kyne followed, but Daniel turned, raising his hand. "Not you," he said. "I will check."

"Now, kid. . . ." Daniel's stare ended Kyne's begging.

Turning, Daniel tried the knob — unlocked — and pushed open the door. He stopped, staring, not believing.

"Criminy." Billy Kyne quickly drew out both pencil and notebook. "Where the hell is everybody?"

CHAPTER ELEVEN

His heart sank, and he trembled, knowing that Quanah had died, that Isa-tai and Nag-wee had sneaked the body out of the Taylor & Barr building. Having learned what the Pale Eyes would do to Yellow Bear, they would not allow Quanah to be subjected to such sacrilege. Even Isa-tai, who despised Quanah, was too much *Nermernuh* to let Quanah receive a *taibo* burial.

Turning, bumping so hard into Kyne that he knocked the reporter against the wall, Daniel stepped into the hallway. *Where? How?* He started toward the stairs, stopped, turned.

"Damnation!" Kyne had hurried out of the room, slamming the door behind him. "I told Jason to let me know if that chief bought the farm." He shot Daniel a glance, saying — "I'll check the funeral parlor." — and ran toward the exit.

Daniel waited until he heard Kyne's feet

pounding the stairs out front, then he moved down the hall and entered Room 4. For the first time since arriving in Fort Worth, he felt a breeze. He walked to the open window, and leaned out.

Isa-tai and Nagwee would have known better than to take Quanah down the stairs, onto the crowded streets. It would have been difficult, but he could picture Nagwee nudging his way out of the window, stepping down onto the roof of the neighboring building that butted against the mercantile, grabbing Quanah's shoulders and carefully backing up until Isa-tai was outside, gripping Quanah's feet.

Daniel slipped through the window, and moved across the flat roof. Yes, he said to himself, nodding when he spotted the crates stacked against the alley wall. That's how they had done it. The wooden boxes would have been like stairs, and Daniel followed them until his moccasins touched dirt.

Although the alley was empty, noise echoed across the wooden and brick façades. A gunshot boomed. A whistle screeched. Hell's Half Acre was turning lively tonight.

"Where would they have taken him?" Daniel asked himself aloud, and looked north and west toward the Trinity River. Maybe. Not Main Street, not Houston. Too crowded this time of night. He hurried past Rusk Street, across Calhoun, all the way to Jones, and stopped.

Which way? Down toward Fort Worth's "Bloody Third Ward", toward the Texas and Pacific depot, the railroad? Or to the banks of the Trinity, heading north, trying to get Quanah closer to the land of The People? Perhaps East, toward the rising sun, out of town?

A nighthawk sounded, its cry carrying above the ruction from Houston Street, and Daniel walked toward it, moving down the dark, deserted street. After two blocks, doubt crept into his mind. He even wondered if he had actually heard a hawk, or was that just his imagination? He often thought of the marsh hawk as his *puha* — it had certainly been his father's — but now he wondered if he should just turn around, go back to the room, wait for Isa-tai and Nagwee to return. If they ever would.

The streets became more alive with glowing yellow light shining out of the windows of brothels and saloons. The breeze carried a mixture of smells: horse manure, stale beer, dust, vomit.

A drunken cowboy brushed Daniel's shoulder, muttered something he could not understand. A horse whinnied in front of a hitching rail. Daniel found more people on the streets as he moved southeast, and the tintamarre of laughter, words, and a strumming banjo echoed inside his head. When he reached the Waco Tap Saloon at Seventh Street, he stopped.

"Hey, sugar," a woman called from the corner, her words a slurred Texas drawl, "come on over here, hon'!"

Ignoring her, he bit his lip.

A horse raced from Calhoun Street, its rider pulling so hard on the reins the horse skidded to a stop in front of the saloon. The rider turned in the saddle, and yelled through the open doors: "Billy! Billy! Get your arse out of here, kid!"

That was pointless. Billy could not have heard the man's shouts unless he were standing outside the Waco Tap Saloon.

Swearing slightly, the cowboy leaped from the saddle, tripped on the boardwalk, and flew into the saloon.

"C'mon, sugar!" the woman called again. "Cleopatra will show you a good time."

Daniel sighed, crossed the street, and moved back toward Rusk.

"Two dollars!" the woman yelled with desperation. "And I got some mescal that won't cost you nothin'!"

A moment later, he stopped and turned.

The cowboy and his companion had burst through the saloon's doorway, and Daniel thought he had heard the one called Billy say something about a teepee.

The cowboy swung into the saddle, while Billy moved down the hitching post until he came to a small bay.

"I tell you, Billy," the first one said, "there's a damned teepee in the middle of the wagon yard."

"You're drunk." Billy backed the bay onto the street, tipped his hat at the woman on the corner, and spurred his horse.

They galloped past Daniel, wheeling their horses at the next intersection, disappearing as they rode north on Rusk. Billy was likely right. His friend must be drunk, yet what were the odds? Daniel took off running, crossing the street, leaping over a cowhand sleeping off a drunk in the middle of the boardwalk. The cowboys had vanished, and there were two wagon yards just up the block, the Texas and the City, but Daniel knew the one he wanted.

A crowd was already gathered, fighting for a better look inside the Texas Wagon Yard on the corner of Rusk and Sixth.

"Excuse me," he said, and slipped between a man in a bell crown hat and a snuff-dipping woman leaning on a cane before being stopped by a *taibo* wall. He tapped a shoulder, asked for a path, but nobody listened until the snuff-dipping woman spit into a coffee can she clutched with the hand not holding the cane yelled: "Hey, let this Injun through. Maybe he knows what's goin' on here!"

Shoulders parted, eyes stared, voices whispered.

Something resembling a path appeared, and Daniel meandered through, trying to ignore the stares. One person even ran his fingers through his long hair, then told a companion: "I touched me a red savage."

"Should have taken his scalp, Lou," another voice said, answered by a chorus of sniggers.

The last two people, a blacksmith in his work apron rubbing rough hands through an even rougher beard, and a one-eyed Negro with thumbs hooked in his waistband, stepped aside, and Daniel stepped clear, halting beside a wheel-less phaeton, its axles propped up on thick blocks of wood.

By The People's standards, it would not be much of a lodge. Lacking the needed ten to twenty buffalo hides, Isa-tai and Nagwee had fashioned canvas they must have borrowed from the wagons parked along the

Sixth Street side of the sprawling yard, and fetched cedar poles out of two black birch farm wagons parked in the middle of the yard.

A *Nermernuh* teepee could be raised in fifteen minutes, but The People considered that women's work. He could not imagine Nagwee and Isa-tai getting this set up, especially since they had to improvise, yet there stood a teepee, the entrance facing east, smoke wafting through the hole, and a loud roaring coming from inside.

"What's that noise?" someone asked.

"I ain't goin' in to find out."

In front of the teepee, a two-foot deep ditch had been dug running north and south for roughly six feet. Floating in the breeze was an eagle feather attached to the top of an iron lantern rod at the edge of the corner closest to the teepee's doorway.

Taking a deep breath and slowly exhaling, Daniel walked to the split in the canvas. He removed his badge and coins, leaving them at the edge of the pit, for metal was not allowed inside a curing lodge, leaped into the ditch, jumped out, and entered the teepee.

Anyone could enter a curing lodge, though usually only other sick ones would come in except for the *puhakat*'s singers and helpers. Daniel moved clockwise around the fire, and sat cross-legged on the north side.

Quanah lay on a blanket along the west-facing side of the teepee. *At least he's still alive,* Daniel thought.

Above Quanah stood Nagwee, draped in a heavy buffalo robe, sweating profusely, whipping his *yuane,* the bull-roarer known among The People as "warm wind", over his head. When Nagwee whirled the thin piece of wood attached by a long string, the roar of wind made Daniel's head throb. Isa-tai had stopped singing and sat beside a drum. He gave four beats, then stopped, arched back his head, and yelled.

Outside, the crowd's voices grew louder.

This was *pianahuwait,* the Big Doctoring of the Beaver Ceremony. The People were never much for group dances. They had performed the Sun Dance only once, at Isa-tai's urging, and that was right before the disastrous raid at Adobe Walls. Daniel had performed the Eagle Dance, but never had he actually seen a Beaver Ceremony. Usually a loved one would request a great *puhakat* to perform the ritual for someone suffering from the lung sickness or maybe after a witch's hex.

He held his breath, observing. From what he understood, there should be a cotton-wood trunk in the center and rising all the way to the top of the teepee, but, undoubtedly, that would have been too hard for Isatai and Nagwee to find in the middle of Fort Worth. Yet they had managed to secure a thick wagon tongue where the tree trunk should have been. The *puhakats* had taken time to dig ponds on the north and south, edging the rims with willows that they had likely found along the riverbank. They had filled each pond with water, undoubtedly from the troughs outside. Mud had been used to form effigies shaped in the form of beavers just outside each pond, facing west.

The roaring fire told Daniel that the ceremony was just beginning.

Isa-tai unwrapped deerskin, revealing a pipe. As he tamped tobacco into the bowl, Daniel remembered enough to move to the fire, pull out a stick, and offer the glowing red end to Isa-tai. With a nod, Isa-tai accepted the gesture, and lit the pipe.

Daniel stared. Isa-tai had to grunt angry guttural words before Daniel realized that Charles Flint's father was offering him the pipe.

He accepted it, shamed, took three puffs, and handed it back to Isa-tai, but the *puhakat* sternly shook his head.

"Ayarocueté," Isa-tai said in a hoarse whisper, and held up four fingers.

Of course. Now Daniel remembered. Four puffs. Four was the mystical number. Four beats of the drums. Four songs. Four puffs. He took another drag, and Isa-tai nodded and accepted the pipe this time.

Daniel stared as Isa-tai smoked. He had donned a buffalo skull headdress and ceremonial clothes, but what struck Daniel was Isa-tai's face. Two lines had been painted across his cheek under his eyes, and four smaller vertical lines ran from his bottom lip to his chin. All of the lines were the color of vermillion.

Red ink . . . red paint . . . like what he had seen on the windowpane and lamp's globe in Quanah's room.

Isa-tai drew four times, and handed the pipe to Nagwee. After the healer's puffs, the pipe returned to Daniel, who suddenly remembered that it was a woman's job to clean the pipe. He wished Rain Shower were here.

After Nagwee prayed, he grabbed feathers and strode to the north beaver pond, dipping them into the muddy water, before heading, still singing his prayers, to the south pond to repeat the process. He moved clockwise, always clockwise and, hovering over Quanah, began fanning the Kwahadi leader with the feathers, water dripping off

155

them onto Quanah's face, his chest, his arms.

Isa-tai spoke, and Daniel turned away from Nagwee. Isa-tai pointed at the pipe, made the sign to refill its bowl, and Daniel did as instructed. After Nagwee had finished his prayers, the three men smoked again.

As Daniel cleaned the pipe, Nagwee moved back to Quanah. Now he knelt, and began rubbing herbs — Daniel did not know what kind — on the comatose man's chest, over his forehead, his eyelids, his throat.

At last, Nagwee straightened, and let the heavy buffalo robe slide off his body, which glistened with sweat. Suddenly he darted to the upright wagon tongue, and began shimmying up the pole. Daniel held his breath. The wooden tongue leaned slightly, and, for a moment, Daniel thought it might break or at least collapse under Nagwee's weight.

Isa-tail barked something, and hurried to the pole, motioning for Daniel to help him. They pressed both hands against the wagon tongue, putting their weight into it, grunting, straining, sweating. Daniel wanted to look up, but couldn't, wouldn't.

Outside, a woman screamed, echoed by the shocked voices of men and women.

"Look at that!"

"My God!"

"It's a head!"

"What the hell's that buck doin'?"

Nagwee had reached the top, had stuck his head through the opening. Now he announced that he was coming down, and Daniel and Isa-tai backed away. The holy man's feet hit the sand, the wagon tongue quivered and tilted to one side, but did not fall.

Daniel backed away, watching Nagwee as he ran around the fire before stepping, from the east, into the bed of coals. Daniel bit his lip. Tears welled in his eyes. He smelled the burning of moccasins, of flesh. He could feel the pain, yet Nagwee's face showed nothing while he moved his arms like a burrowing owl flitting its wings. At last, Nagwee backed out of the fire, moccasins smoldering, and walked to the south, stopping at the western edge of the curing lodge.

Nagwee moved to the south pond, where he chewed bark from the willow sticks. Tilting his head back, the *puhakat* let out a gush of air. The smell, Daniel remembered, reminded him of beaver.

He looked at Quanah, who still breathed, still slept, but did not look any better.

The crowd parted as Isa-tai and Nagwee

157

walked out of the Texas Wagon Yard. Daniel stopped outside the ditch as School Father Pratt, Captain Hall, and other men in fancy duds and worried expressions approached him. Kyne, the newspaper reporter, came with them.

"What's going on, Daniel?" Pratt asked.

"It is what we call *pianahuwait*," he said, and explained the Beaver Ceremony as best he could.

"The singing?" Hall asked.

Daniel had joined Isa-tai and Nagwee in the final song, as was custom for The People, then Nagwee had extinguished the fire inside the lodge, and, after each had left the teepee, they had jumped into the ditch and climbed out on the east side.

"It is how we close the ceremony."

Church bells chimed. It was midnight. Nagwee had timed this perfectly.

"Let me get this straight," Kyne said. "Those two medicine men fetched Quanah out of the hotel, rigged all this up?"

Daniel nodded.

"Damn!" The reporter slapped his notebook against his thigh. "Wait till my editor hears about this. Comanche Indians are so discouraged with Fort Worth's doctors, they decide to heal their chief themselves. That'll make that ol' miser Bode happy! Damn!"

He tilted his head back and howled.

Others were not amused.

"How's Quanah?" Captain Hall asked.

"Better?" Kyne added hopefully.

"It is just the first night," Daniel explained with a shrug of his shoulders.

"You mean," said a man wearing a fancy badge, "this Beaver thing isn't over?"

CHAPTER TWELVE

"It lasts three days," Daniel said, hoping he remembered correctly.

"Three days!" The badge-wearer shook his head. "There's no way this circus can stay here for two more nights."

"Hold on, Charley," said a man in duck trousers and a sweat-soaked muslin shirt. "This here's my property, and, if they want to work on their chief in my wagon yard, I sure ain't complainin'."

The city lawman and wagon yard owner stared at each other.

"Daniel," School Father Pratt said suggestively, "Quanah needs a doctor's care. He needs to be in his bed in the apartment." He gestured behind him. "Look around. This is no place for a sick man."

"I will stay with him," Daniel announced. He hated the look on Pratt's face, felt the School Father's disappointment.

"This is going to be a nightmare, Zeke,"

the city policeman said.

"You tell Mayor Broiles that I'll pay for a permit if that's what it takes, but this is gonna be good for my business, Charley, and I say this is my property, and that teepee stays put."

"Good for you. Not me." The marshal spit. "I'll have to put two officers here all day, all night. You know what my force consists of? Two mounted officers, two patrolmen, a jailer, and two sanitary officers. Now how in hell can the city afford this? We've already blown our year's budget just because of these red niggers!" He hooked a thumb angrily, just missing Daniel's nose.

"Marshal," School Father Pratt said, "watch your tongue, sir."

There was no breeze, and tension hung in the air like humidity.

Captain Hall stared at the teepee. "I'll have some of my men help you police the wagon yard, too, Marshal. You can make them special deputies if you like, and the association will foot the bill."

When most, but certainly nowhere near all, of the crowd had scattered across Hell's Half Acre, Daniel returned to the teepee, stopping to pick up the metal he had left near the ditch. He found the badge. Some son-of-a-bitch had taken the coins he'd left. Sighing, he pinned the shield on the lapel of his vest, knowing he should feel some relief. Most thieves would have taken the tin badge, too, if for nothing more than a souvenir.

"You held out on me, Killstraight. I thought we were pals."

He turned to find William J. Kyne standing on the other side of the ditch, dribbling his fingers on the Old Glory writing tablet.

Daniel felt no need to explain, to tell this reporter that he had not known what had become of Quanah.

Kyne tilted his jaw toward the lodge. "Be all right if I took a look-see in there?"

Daniel answered with surprising venom, but Kyne appeared to take the rejection. To Daniel's surprise, the *Herald* journalist smiled.

"What would it take to show you that I'm not the typical white man? I don't hate Indians, not even you Comanches. Hell, I don't even hate Fort Worth. I'm just practicing what my paper preaches, and that's that Dallas is a hell of a finer city than this cow town."

Daniel had been to Dallas. In fact, some roughnecks had beaten the hell out of him there. He didn't care much for either Texas town.

"What do you need? For Quanah? For your witch doctors? You tell me, and ol' Billy Kyne'll produce. Won't cost you a thing."

Except my soul.

Ignoring Kyne, he ducked inside the lodge. He could still smell the scent of beaver, over the last wisps of smoke from the fire. He scanned the teepee, then quickly pulled himself back outside.

Kyne was walking away.

"Are you serious?" Daniel called out.

The reporter turned. Several long seconds passed. "You name it, kid. The *Herald* will get it."

Daniel pursed his lips, thinking, finally deciding to chance it. "I need the trunk of a cottonwood tree."

Kyne blinked. He found his flask, drained it, shoved it back into his coat pocket. "A cottonwood tree?"

"Just the trunk," Daniel said. "But . . ." — he glanced at the teepee — "it should be fifteen feet high or thereabouts."

"How big?"

Big enough to hold up Nagwee, Daniel thought, and could not hide his smile. He held out his arms in a circle. "About like that?" he requested. "And I need it by early morning."

With a chuckle, Kyne turned toward Rusk Street. "I'll see what I can do, Killstraight."

He jerked awake to the bells of St. Stanislaus Catholic Church. Groggily he stumbled out of the healing lodge, and headed for the water trough. Whispers reached him before he even realized he had an audience, and, after splashing water on his face and wetting back his hair, he saw the crowd. A few school-age boys, black men and women, white women and men, a family of Chinese, nowhere near the size of the throng last night, but plenty considering if the church bells were right, it was just 6:00 A.M.

After filling the gourd, he returned to the teepee, squatted beside Quanah, lifting his head into his arms, pouring water down his throat.

The canvas flap flew open. Charles Flint stepped inside. "How is he?" Flint asked.

Daniel shrugged, and lowered Quanah's head onto the blankets.

Flint looked around, his face masked with a curiosity. "What . . . ?" He shook his head. "What is this?"

Of course, Daniel realized. Having come of age on the reservation and at Carlisle, Charles Flint would not know about the

Beaver Ceremony. Daniel barely compre-
hended it himself. Before he could explain,
wagon traces sang out, accompanied by a
squeaky wheel, braying mules, and a string
of cuss words that left the God-fearing
women in the Texas Wagon Yard gasping.

Daniel followed Flint outside to see a
gray-bearded Mexican in a battered straw
hat snapping a blacksnake whip over the
left mule's ear. The crowd quickly moved to
the Sixth Street side, and let the wagon ease
past the wheelless phaeton and come to a
halt near the ditch. A figure leaped off the
back of the market wagon, and Daniel
recognized Billy Kyne's voice.

"You fellas, lend a hand. *Pronto,* boys.
Pronto."

Daniel moved around the ditch, and
stared, unbelieving, as black and white men,
under the supervision of Billy Kyne, pulled
a huge cottonwood trunk out of the wagon.

"Where you want this piece of fine furniture, Killstraight?" Kyne asked.

Nagwee grunted as he walked around the
cottonwood, putting his hand against it,
nodding, eying Flint and Daniel with suspicion, and finally looking at Isa-tai and asking something too low for Daniel to understand.

Isa-tai snorted and spat.

"It is better than that skinny thing that felt as slippery as a fish," Nagwee said, and nodded his final approval at Daniel. "We will begin the *pianahuwait* soon," Nagwee said. "When the bells ring again."

Flint struggled for words. "I do not know what to do."

"Then go do books," Isa-tai said harshly in English, and his son's head dropped.

"I will tell him what he needs to do," Daniel said, eyes angry, staring at the *puhakat*. Isa-tai wore the same red paint on his face.

The Kwahadi spit. "How? You do not know the way yourself?"

Daniel couldn't deny that.

A train's whistle cut across the morning air.

"They will do fine," Nagwee said. "We must prepare for the Big Doctoring."

"You're a real bastard, Daniel."

Daniel dumped water from an oaken bucket into the pond, and stared at Flint.

"You think my father did this." Flint switched to the language of The People.

"I do not think anything." Daniel rose. "Yet," he added, and he exited the lodge and walked back to the water trough. Flint caught up with him.

"My father would not harm one of The People." And in English: "No Indian would harm a member of his tribe."

Daniel shook his head, and dropped the bucket into the trough. "You have not been back from the East very long, my friend. Everything has changed on the reservation. And I remember the story of a powerful *dohate* of our friends the Kiowas. When the one that was chosen to speak for all the Kiowas told the Pale Eyes to send this *dohate* to the prison at Fort Marion, the *dohate* placed a spell on the peace chief. The peace chief died."

"I know that story," Flint said. "Kicking Bird died, then Maman-ti went to Fort Marion, where he died. Of malaria. Or dysentery. But not because he had killed another Kiowa."

Angrily Flint sent his bucket splashing into the trough, jerking it up, letting water slosh over the sides as they returned to the healing lodge.

"This was an accident," Flint said after dumping water into the pond. He jutted his jaw toward Quanah. "Yellow Bear paid for his mistake, but that's all it was, Daniel, a mistake."

Daniel glared at the bookkeeper. "It was no mistake," he said flatly. "It was murder.

Attempted murder."

An angry wail exploded from Flint's lungs. "Do you hate my father that much?"

"I do not know that it was your father," Daniel said again, silently adding to himself: *But he is certainly . . . what was it he had heard the* taibo *judge named Parker say in Fort Smith? A man of interest.*

Remembering seeing the bookkeeper wiping his hands, Daniel's eyes dropped to Flint's hands. *And I would like to see your fingers, too.*

"I will prove to you that my father committed no crime," Flint said.

"Tzat." Daniel nodded. Good. "I can use much help."

"Bávi, then it is a good thing we are here."

Daniel stepped back, his jaw dropping as Ben Buffalo Bone stepped inside the lodge. His best friend's uncle, Cuhtz Bávi, followed, stopping and staring grimly at the unconscious Quanah. The flap moved yet again.

"The former bluecoat called Pratt and the *taibo* Metal Shirt named Hall," Ben Buffalo Bone explained. "They used the talking wires to tell the agent, Biggers, what has happened here."

Ben's uncle looked around. "What has become of the one who journeys to The

168

Land Beyond The Sun?"

Daniel's head dropped. How could he tell a man like Cuhtz Bávi that Yellow Bear had been given a white man's burial? The undertaker had planted the corpse in some potter's field the same day, had not even let The People attend the funeral.

"Biggers gave us all passes to come to Texas," Ben Buffalo Bone said. "Frank Striker came with us as he speaks English good."

Striker was the agency interpreter, a big Texian who was married to a Kiowa. Daniel was glad Ben had changed the subject from Yellow Bear.

"Striker is outside. He talks to a *Tejano* Metal Shirt." Suddenly Ben announced excitedly: "We took the iron horse."

"It stinks," said Cuhtz Bávi. "Smells nothing like a good pony, and I do not like the places where they make us sit. It is not as comfortable, or as cool, as my brush arbor."

Daniel barely heard Ben Buffalo Bone's uncle's complaints. He stared at the woman who had followed Cuhtz Bávi into the healing lodge.

Her hair, shining with grease, looked blacker than midnight, parted in the middle in the fashion of The People. Her face was round, and she wore copper bracelets adorned with bright stones, a bone necklace strung with sinew that held three German silver crosses. Her dress was made of doeskin. She looked away from Quanah, tears welling, and stared at Daniel.

"You should not be here!" Daniel shouted.

Immediately he regretted his sharpness, saw the hurt in her face, replaced almost immediately by anger.

"I am here!" she barked back at him.

Which she always was. Here. For Daniel.

Rain Shower, perhaps with assistance from her mother and sister Oajuicauojué, who had just reached puberty, had made his britches. She had sewn the stripes — chevrons, they were called — on his jacket's sleeve to show that he was a sergeant. After he had cut off the sleeves, she had stitched the stripes onto the front of what was now his vest. She had helped him find his way, his path, his medicine, since he had returned from Pennsylvania.

If the government had paid him more than $8 a month, he would have bought many horses and brought them to her uncle. He would marry her. He. . . .

His lips tightened. And he remembered the nightmare. The hand grabbing Rain Shower, jerking her out of Daniel's sight.

Before he could speak, Nagwee returned

to the lodge. "We will begin," the *puhakat* announced. "It is time."

By noon, the second day of the curing ceremony was complete. It had pretty much been a repeat of last night, but this time Rain Shower had cleaned Nagwee's pipe, while Daniel, Ben Buffalo Bone, and Flint had sung while Ben's uncle and Isa-tai had beaten drums.

"So what happens next?" a reporter from some newspaper in Austin asked.

Daniel felt uncomfortable talking to so many reporters, yet Nagwee had told Daniel that they must pacify the Pale Eyes, else they might take Quanah out of the healing lodge before it was time. Daniel would speak for The People. He would make the Pale Eyes happy, let them understand the ways of *Nermernuh*.

But there are so many!

A cacophony of questions assaulted Daniel's ears. There must be more ink-slingers in this wagon yard than breast collars and buggy harnesses combined.

"We will start again tonight," Daniel said. "The ceremony will be over by tomorrow at noon."

Pencils scratched. Every reporter but Billy Kyne scribbled furiously.

"Is it helpful to have more Comanches here?" a reporter asked.

Daniel nodded.

"So what happens at noon tomorrow?"

A shrug. He would not tell them.

"Will Quanah die?" a Fort Worth reporter asked.

"I do not know."

"You must be thankful," said a woman reporter from some Eastern paper, "to have so many of your own kind here to assist you."

"I am thankful," Daniel said, "that a white man brought a cottonwood trunk this morning."

Leaning against the Sixth Street stone wall, Billy Kyne gave Daniel a mock salute.

By six o'clock that evening, the crowd at the Texas Wagon Yard had tripled. An hour later, that number had doubled. Now Daniel could see why the city marshal had been so worried, and he did not see any cowboys helping the police officers as Captain Hall had promised.

Holding their Chicago nightsticks, two policemen forced some of the onlookers back. One of the peace officers cursed as Daniel entered the healing lodge. He watched the policeman for two or three

172

seconds, no longer, and stepped through the flap.

"Tsu Kuh Puah," he whispered to Nagwee. "There is a man outside that I must talk to."

Nagwee's face hardened.

"If you say I must stay, I will," Daniel said. "But I need to speak to this man."

"A *taibo?*"

Daniel nodded.

Nagwee shot a glance toward Quanah, then shook his head, and waved his hand in Daniel's face. "Go. Do what you must."

He wanted to apologize, thought better of it, and stepped through the flap. Billy Kyne was not in the crowd, which Daniel considered lucky. The *Herald* reporter, likely in one of the saloons, would have been almost impossible to sneak past. The newspaper horde, however, had divided into groups with a handful of reporters agreeing to alert the others of any new news. Billy Kyne would right now be in one of the saloons, drinking. Maybe with Frank Striker. Daniel didn't see the interpreter, either.

He looked through the opening, saw Rain Shower's questioning glare, then faced the newspaper men.

"It is about to begin?" one bespectacled reporter asked.

"Soon," Daniel said. "It will be over by noon tomorrow." He moved toward Sixth Street.

"Well, where the Sam Hill are you going?" the reporter said.

Daniel forced a smile. "The Comanche have bodily functions same as white men."

That got several chuckles, and the newspaper reporters turned away, rolling cigarettes or pulling bottles of beer from an ice-filled bucket resting on the ground.

Daniel moved past some of the younger employees of the wagon yard and railroads, and walked away from the lodge, the ditch, the smoke, and the smell of beaver. He made a beeline for the policeman with the Irish brogue.

CHAPTER THIRTEEN

He had not seen anyone resembling the cowboy he had glimpsed in the alley, but he knew this Pale Eyes was the same one Daniel had spotted on the streets. Maybe the Metal Shirt had seen somebody enter the Taylor & Barr's upstairs apartments.

Once he reached Rusk Street, Daniel stopped, caught a glimpse of the policeman as he turned east onto Eighth Street. Daniel broke into a sprint, weaving past men and women, careful not to knock anyone over. He took the corner, and spotted the officer passing a two-story structure on the corner of Calhoun. Twirling a nightstick in his right hand, the man moved at a lively clip, and Daniel, already out of breath, wished he had that copper's gait. The cop turned south onto Calhoun, heading toward the Third Ward.

Sucking in air, Daniel chased after him.

He didn't catch up with him until the officer had heard his footsteps, and stopped, turning, raising his nightstick while reaching for a holstered pistol. Sensing the policeman's alarm, Daniel stopped, held out his empty hands, and tried to catch his breath.

"My name . . . is Daniel . . . Killstraight," he said. "I would like . . . to talk to . . . you."

The police officer didn't move, didn't speak. He was almost to Eleventh Street.

Laughter echoed across the Third Ward, someone sawed a fiddle, terribly, and Daniel could hear the clinking of glasses, the curses and catcalls.

"Step into the bloody light." The policeman had finally spoken.

Daniel moved until he stood under a gas lamp next to the City Gas Works building.

"That's good. Just keep your bloody hands where they are."

The officer moved closer to him, hands nervously, but determinedly, clutching the club and the butt of a Smith & Wesson revolver.

"You're one of those Comanches," the man spoke.

Daniel nodded, and tapped his badge. "I, too, am a peace officer."

The policeman let out a mirthless chuckle and spit onto the street. A tall, angular man in the navy blue uniform of the Fort Worth Police Department, he had deep-seated blue eyes that never seemed to blink, a crooked nose, dark walrus mustache flecked with gray, thin lips, and a cleft in his chin. A scar ran from the corner of his right eye, then up to his temple like a check mark. Two items hung from his neck: a whistle, part of the police force's equipment, and a golden medallion that Daniel had seen worn by many of the miners in Pennsylvania who followed the Pale Eyes religion of the Black Robes.

"Peace officer. There's no peace in the bloody Third Ward, boy. Best get your arse back to the wagon yard."

Often, Daniel felt that way about the Comanche, Kiowa and Apache reserve near Fort Sill.

"On Wednesday night," Daniel said, "early Thursday morning, actually, you were patrolling on Houston Street."

The police officer released his grip on the revolver, and lowered the billy club just a little. "Aye. And what of it?"

"That was the night Quanah Parker, our chief, was poisoned by the gas and another was killed."

"So?"

A grunt, curse, and thud sounded behind

him, and the officer turned, gripping the Smith & Wesson again, flattening himself against the wall. He saw a cowboy pushing himself up from the boardwalk, slipping again, trying to pick up a bottle he had dropped, but unable to make his right hand co-operate.

"Jesus, Mother Mary, and Joseph," the policeman said, shaking his head, glancing at Daniel before moving down Calhoun Street toward the buffoon.

Upon reaching the drunkard, the officer reached down, grabbed the cowhand by the collar and waistband, jerked him to his feet, and slammed him against the picket wall of a ramshackle building. "You've had a wee too many tonight, you dumb bloke," the officer said.

The cowboy slurred words Daniel could not understand.

"Aye, and your breath reeks of a brewery."

Daniel eased down the boardwalk. "There was another drunk on that night," he said. "He had relieved himself in the alley, was trying to make his way back to the Tivoli." Hoping he pronounced that right. "Do you remember this?"

The officer had fished metal bracelets from his belt, had slapped one on the drunk's right wrist, was trying to get the other hand secured.

"What are you talking about? Can't you see I'm busy here."

"I just wish to know if you saw anyone entering the Taylor and Barr building around this time. Or coming out of it."

No answer. Having managed to get the handcuffs on, the copper jerked the drunk around. The cowboy tilted toward the officer, but the billy club caught him in the sternum and forced him back against the wall.

"It is important," Daniel said. "Do you remember?"

The policeman whirled, his blue eyes fierce. "Here's what I remember, you bloody red heathen. I remember that tonight is me daughter's birthday, but I'm patrolling this hell-hole instead of celebrating with my family on account of you Comanch'. I remem—"

Like water from an artesian well, vomit hurled from the cowboy's mouth.

"Damnation!" The officer tried to turn to his side, but the stinking wretchedness caught the right side of his uniform, his arm, his nightstick. His boot heel fell into a hole in the warped pine planks, and he turned, twisting, cursing as he crashed into the fine dirt and horse droppings. The

179

cowboy slid down the wall.

Daniel moved for the officer, who rolled over, and sat up, lifting his billy club, snapping: "Get the bloody hell back to the wagon yard, you stupid son-of-a-bitch."

"But. . . ."

"Bugger off! Or I'll run you into the jail with this cad!"

Well, he thought while walking dejectedly back up Calhoun Street, *that's probably what I should have expected. He hadn't even gotten the officer's name, but Daniel refused to give up. My fault. Policing the Third Ward has to be more stressful than policing the reservation. I caught this Metal Shirt in a foul mood. But he has not seen the last of me.*

He remembered the conversation he had overhead with the city marshal. How many officers? Two on horseback, two patrolmen, a jailer, and two sanitary officers. Something like that. All Daniel had to do was go to the jail, wait for the patrolman to return. Offer to buy him a cup of coffee — providing Charles Flint would loan him money. Meet this Irishman on friendlier surroundings. But not tonight. Better to let the man cool off, and clean his uniform.

Turning left onto Eighth Street, he saw her.

At the same time Rain Shower spotted him, and halted in front of the two-story building.

Two men walking west angled around her, ignoring her, but another man, leaning against the building between a window and batwing doors, smoking a cigarette, pushed himself off the wall, flicking the cigarette into the street, and approached her from behind.

Like in Daniel's nightmare.

Rain Shower smiled, started again toward him. Daniel wanted to shout a warning, but he couldn't quite comprehend what was happening. She stopped, sensing the presence behind her. Daniel found his voice, roared out a warning in the language of The People, knowing he was too late.

As she started to turn, the cowboy wrapped a massive hand around Rain Shower's mouth, while his left arm wrapped around her waist. Her eyes showed fright. The man was a giant. Laughing, he dragged her through the doors, and they disappeared inside the two-story building.

The two men who had passed Rain Shower on the boardwalk stopped, turned, but did nothing else, other than to grin. The one on the left elbowed the other.

Daniel ran, watching the two men turn

back around to continue their journey as if they had not seen the abduction.

A laughing man staggered into Daniel as he made his way toward the batwing doors. "Watch where the hell. . . ."

The man never finished. Daniel slammed a left fist into the man's temple, and he crashed into the trash can, pulling it over as he slammed onto the boardwalk.

Daniel pushed his way through the batwing doors. Light from the chandeliers and wall sconces made him squint, yet his vision soon adjusted. He wasn't aware that the musician had stopped playing, lowering his fiddle. Wasn't aware that the rough-looking men lining the bar had stopped, turning, staring. Wasn't aware of the meaty woman in the corner, tossing a cigar into a spittoon and hefting a bung starter.

He moved to his right, toward the table. Two giggling men stood in front of it, one of them with his arm around a red-headed woman wearing nothing but calf-length drawers and a camisole.

The redhead saw him first. She started to utter a warning, then pulled herself away from the snickering man's grip, and leaped away.

"What's wrong, Cynthy?" He saw Daniel. His partner didn't.

Daniel grabbed the man's shoulder, jerked, sending him sprawling to the floor. He ignored the one who had been holding Cynthy.

The big man had thrown Rain Shower on a table, his left knee between her legs, hat on the floor, his face pressing against her neck, moving up to her face, her lips. He jerked back suddenly, spitting out blood from where Rain Shower had bit his bottom lip.

"You little . . . !"

Daniel grabbed him by the collar and waistband — just as he had seen the Irish policeman handle the drunk earlier. He threw the man, off-balance, to the floor. Rain Shower rolled off the table, black eyes malevolent — but not as angry as Daniel's.

The one who had taken Rain Shower off the street had to be taller than six-foot-two, and likely weighed better than two hundred pounds, with muscles tearing at the sleeves of his calico shirt, and a face covered with scars. Like most Comanches, Daniel was short, stocky — no match for this man who began pushing himself off the floor. No match under London prize ring rules, that is.

"Well, well, well," the man said. "Reckon I get you first, her second. Suits me to a T."

Daniel kicked him in the face.

The man crashed back to the floor, and Daniel was on top of him, slamming a knee into the man's groin, left hand wrapping around the man's throat, right hand smashing into his nose, his mouth, feeling the teeth break, carve into his knuckles. Blood splattered his face. He stopped hitting, grabbed a fistful of hair, jerked the man's head off the floor, slammed it onto the hardwood. Again. Again.

Behind him, the giggling man suddenly wailed. Daniel turned, saw the man writhing on the ground, his left leg drenched in blood. Rain Shower held a broken beer bottle.

The redhead screamed.

Cowboys, muleskinners, and railroad men left the bar, moving toward Daniel.

He didn't care. He turned back to the man, kneed him again in the groin, slammed a right, then a left into the man's face. The nose gave way. The jaw bone broke. Daniel locked both hands on the man's throat, pressed harder, harder.

Suddenly his head rocked with fire.

He shook off the pain, turned away from the unconscious giant's unrecognizable face, spotted the fat woman, her face plastered with rouge like mud on a Mexican's *jacal.* The woman raised the bung starter over her head again, started to bring it down a second time.

Daniel swung his right arm, catching the woman just below her knees. She yipped as her feet flew out from under her, and fell hard onto the floor.

"Get that sum-bitch!" one of the men cried out.

"Aiiiyeeeeee!" Rain Shower leaped in front of him, and the men suddenly stopped, watching her warily as she waved the bloody end of the broken bottle. She taunted them as women, as worthless as Pawnees, afraid of one warrior and one woman. She said they had no honor, that they were dogs. They could not savvy her words, but they certainly understood her meaning.

Daniel pushed himself to his feet, took one step toward Rain Shower, then fell.

The first cowboy he had thrown to the ground had jerked Daniel's ankle. Daniel rolled over, felt the cowboy jumping on top of him. He saw Rain Shower turn, and tried to warn her. . . .

Too late. A wiry man in buckskins took advantage, whipping out his right hand, locking on Rain Shower's wrist, wrenching the beer bottle from her hand. Daniel swung his fist upward, a glancing blow, but the

185

man holding him did not budge.

Rain Shower screamed.

A boot crashed into Daniel's shoulder. Another struck his ribs. Something smashed his face. He tasted blood.

Something roared, but Daniel couldn't see. Vaguely he was aware that the pressure was off his chest, and that nobody was hitting or kicking him.

Words reached him.

"Stop him!"

"He'll kill him!"

"Mickey, for the love of God!"

He heard Rain Shower. Opened his eyes. Saw her face. He shook his head, trying to shake off the fog, pulled himself up.

The policeman came into view. He had struck the man in the buckskin britches with the barrel of his pistol. He struck him again. The man lay on the floor.

"Mickey!" the fat woman cried. "Stop!" She turned. "Find another marshal!"

The Irish officer muttered something about his daughter, brought the pistol down on the man again, missing his head, but clipping his ear and smashing the collarbone. He spoke again, raising the pistol, using words Daniel did not understand. Not English. Something else.

"Stop!" the woman named Cynthy yelled.

"Stop him, in God's name! He'll kill Petey!"

None of the men moved, either intimidated by the Irishman's badge, his Smith & Wesson, or his savagery.

The copper was about to strike the man again, when Daniel — who didn't even remember climbing to his feet — grabbed his arm, pulled him back, spun him away.

Blood pooled on the floor underneath the buckskin-clad man's face, but his lungs still worked. Cynthy ran to him, turning his battered head upward, looking up at the crowd, uttering a plea: "Get a doctor. Somebody get a doctor!"

There were plenty of volunteers, for the room quickly emptied.

A metallic click brought Daniel's attention back to the Irish patrolman.

The Smith & Wesson's hammer was cocked, and the barrel trained on Daniel's heaving stomach.

Daniel wiped the blood off his face. His eyes locked on the policeman's. "It is over," he said.

CHAPTER FOURTEEN

"I don't know what came over me." A sigh escaped the police officer, and he shook his head, and lifted his coffee cup. "That wasn't you I saw in that disorderly house, but me daughter." He sipped, set the cup back on the table, and leaned back, clenching his fists. "I hate this bloody town. It ought to be in England, not Texas."

The waitress brought another ice-filled rag, swapping it out for the one Daniel had been pressing to the side of his face.

"You need anything else, Mickey?" she asked.

The patrolman's head shook, and the woman left.

They sat in the Queen City Ice Cream Parlor, leaving the blood, carnage, and confusion behind at the sporting house on Eighth Street. Daniel did not know what had become of the man the policeman had buffaloed, the one Daniel had almost beaten to death, or the one Rain Shower had stabbed with a broken beer bottle. He didn't even know what had happened to the drunk the patrolman had been carting off to jail. They had left the bawdy house together, backing out of the saloon, the officer warning the big woman he called Loretta that, if he heard a peep from her house or a complaint, this place would go up like Chicago in '72.

"Will the woman make things difficult for you?" Daniel asked.

Sergeant Mickey O'Doherty shook his head. "Loretta? She knows to keep her bloody mouth shut. That was no idle threat I gave her. Me name in the old language is Dochartaigh. It means hurtful, and that I can be, laddie, lassie. That I can be. Now, what do your names mean?"

Rain Shower answered for both, then Daniel said: "But I am called Daniel Killstraight." His fingers lifted the bottom of his vest, and he pointed to the chevrons. "I, too, am a sergeant."

"Sergeant Killstraight." O'Doherty let out a chuckle. "That's an apt name, laddie, seeing how you almost killed that one fellow." He looked across the table. "But I don't know if Rain Shower fits you, lassie. Not after that ruction. You fight mighty well. I warrant you could give John Sullivan, the Boston Strong Boy himself, a run for his money."

Rain Shower's eyes dropped to the bowl of butter pecan in front of her, but Daniel could tell she was smiling.

"I should not have been curt with you earlier, Sergeant." The patrolman's tone turned professional. "This is not a pleasant town, however, and it can be quite stressful. What is it you wish to know?"

After Daniel explained, the patrolman sadly shook his head, and Daniel's heart sank.

"Even by Fort Worth standards, that was a wild night for a Wednesday eve," O'Doherty said. "I remember the lad. Drunk he was. I was about to run him in, but some b'hoys started a row over at the Occidental. I had to run over there and keep that bucket of blood from being dismantled."

He drained his coffee, and shook his head again. "But, sorry to say, I can't say I saw anything that drew me attention to the Taylor and Barr, or the Pickwick Hotel. Usually I'm watching the rowdier places, the saloons, the . . . *ahem, ladies boarding houses.* No, I just don't remember seeing anyone around those stairs that lead to those apartments. How's your chief doing, by the way?"

"He lives." That was all Daniel could think to say.

"Well, I should be on me way." Once he pushed himself to his feet, he brought out some coins, gestured to the waitress, and set them on the table. "My treat. Can you make it back to the wagon yard safely? Or, better yet, the Taylor and Barr?"

"We can," Rain Shower answered.

O'Doherty tipped his cap, and turned to leave, stopping at the door to call back: "If I remember anything, I'll let you know."

The bell rang as the officer opened the door.

"That *taibo*," Rain Shower blurted out, and the patrolman stopped.

"Excuse me?"

Daniel stared at Rain Shower blankly.

"The one who had lost his reason to whiskey. The cowboy. On that night. Did you recognize him?"

"Just a drunken saddle tramp," O'Doherty said flatly. "I've seem him around, but I can't put a name on him." Another tip of his hat, and the police officer was gone.

Daniel adjusted his bundle of ice, looking at Rain Shower. The ice cream shop was empty again, except for them and the waitress.

"You should find this *Tejano*," Rain Shower instructed.

"The drunken cowboy?" Daniel shook his head. "Even had he seen something, the whiskey would rob him of his memory."

Silence. Rain Shower focused on the ice cream. Mad. At him. Daniel shook his head, and lowered the ice.

"I would not know where to begin to look for this cowboy." The alley had been so dark, Daniel had never gotten a good look at the man's face.

"The place you mentioned," she said, not bothering to look up.

Herman Kussatz's Tivoli Hall. He considered this, and shook his head.

"They would not let me in that place. I am *Nermernuh*."

Another spoonful of ice cream. Still not looking at Daniel, she said: "They let in the one who has gone to The Land Beyond The Sun."

"But he was with a *taibo*."

Now Rain Shower raised her spoon, pointing the handle toward the door. "The Metal Shirt, he is a *taibo*. He would assist you. Striker, who has traveled from our country with us, he, too, is a Pale Eyes. He likes you.

He would help."

This he had to consider.

Rain Shower spoke again. "There is another thing you should investigate, Daniel." He flinched. Whenever she called him by the name the Carlisle teachers had given him, it meant she was angry with him.

"This cowboy. He was drunk on whiskey. Could he have entered the building? Could he have gone into the room where Quanah and the other one slept? Could he have accidentally, or purposefully, blown out the lamps?"

For a long moment, Daniel thought about this, but finally shook his head.

"No." The door to Quanah's room. He had heard it being closed after he had seen the drunken cowhand's encounter with Sergeant O'Doherty. He explained this to Rain Shower.

"And after this, did you hear footsteps down the hall?"

This took him longer to remember. "No," he said at last.

"So maybe all the others are right. The other one comes in. He blows out the lamps. It is an accident. He dies, and Quanah fights to stay with the living. But that is all it is. An accident."

His head throbbed. He sat there, feeling

the ice melt in the rag he held, looking at Rain Shower but not really seeing her.

She dipped her spoon in the ice cream again, began eating. "You do not want to believe," she said. "Your head is hard."

Harder than a bung starter. Harder than the boot that had kicked him.

"The door was locked," he explained. "The People have no use for keys."

Focused on the food, she answered: "You do not want to believe." She swallowed, and looked up at him, her black eyes firm. "You want to think Isa-tai is responsible. You hate him, and it clouds your reason."

"That is not true."

"Bah." The ice cream was all but gone, but she scooped up the soupy melt.

He found another argument. "The *Tejano* who accompanied the other one. The one named Briggs, who works for the rancher, Waggoner. I asked him. He said he sent Quanah's companion upstairs at midnight. When I saw the cowboy and the Metal Shirt, it was three seventeen."

"That *Tejano* had been drinking whiskey, too. You cannot believe him."

"I do believe him." Flatly.

"I do not believe it is Isa-tai," she said. "He uses his *puha* now to save Quanah."

"What *puha*?" Daniel said, remembering

194

Nagwee's insult.

The spoon clattered in her bowl, and she stared defiantly across the table at Daniel. "Tell me this . . . was not Isa-tai sharing a room with Nagwee?"

Daniel nodded.

"Nagwee does not sleep well. Would he not have heard Isa-tai had he sneaked out of the room to commit murder?"

He had not thought of that. He hadn't even asked Nagwee.

"Isa-tai would not kill another *Nermernuh*," Rain Shower said. "Nor would Nagwee. Or Tetecae. It is not done among The People."

"You should not be here." Daniel had heard enough of this. He thought back to his nightmare that had almost come true tonight. Rain Shower had almost been killed, and Daniel would have had no one else to blame but himself.

"I am here," she said. "Agent Biggers thought that I should go."

"You were almost killed." He felt tears welling in his eyes.

"*Bah.* I would have killed that Pale Eyes. He was nothing. He was no warrior."

His head fell. A small hand reached out and touched his, and Daniel looked up.

Rain Shower smiled. "A *taibo* cannot harm

195

me, my precious one. But I have forgotten my place. I should have thanked you. You counted many coup tonight. We will sing songs of your bravery upon our return to Cache Creek."

He liked her touch, and felt more pain when she returned her hand to grip the spoon.

"So if you still think this was . . . what is it the Pale Eyes say . . . a crime? Yes, crime. If that is what your heart tells you, then you must seek out that *Tejano*."

He repeated his excuse. "I cannot go into the Tivoli by myself."

She shook her head, and Daniel wondered if she thought that he was revealing cowardice. "Then ask the Metal Shirt. Ask Striker, who speaks true." The bell above the door rang. Rain Shower looked up and pointed the spoon. "Or ask that *taibo*. He is your friend. He would help you."

As Daniel turned around toward the door, he heard Rain Shower's voice drop. "He would do anything to drink the Pale-Eyes whiskey."

Hat in hand, smile creeping across his face, Billy Kyne walked toward their table, and sat down in the seat that the patrolman had recently abandoned.

■ ■ ■ ■

"You been holding out on your old pard, Billy Kyne," the reporter said after ordering a cup of coffee from the waitress. "I'm cutting the dust with some of the boys at the watering hole at the Commercial Hotel, and come back to the Texas Wagon Yard only to find that Daniel Killstraight has up and flown the coop. And this pretty Comanche squaw has taken off after him. Sounds peculiar to me, so, with my nose smelling a story, I roam across Hell's Half Acre. And what do I find? Besides a waddie sleeping off a drunk with his hands manacled behind his back down on Calhoun Street? I discover a hell of a lot of commotion at a sporting house."

He paused as the waitress placed a steaming cup of coffee on the table, then scooped up the coins Sergeant O'Doherty had left behind, and handed them to the waitress. "Will this cover everything, darling?"

She rolled her eyes, muttered a sarcastic thanks, and left for the cash box.

Kyne brought the flask from his pocket, sweetened the black coffee, and held out the flask. "Care for a snort?"

Comanche eyes glared back at him.

197

"I admit, it's an acquired taste, but, once you get used to it, there's few things better than Manhattan rye."

"I could get used to eating dirt," Rain Shower said, "but why should I want to?"

His eyebrows arched as Billy Kyne shook his head, screwed the lid on tight, and dropped the flask back into his coat pocket.

"Well, I do have to say my editor will be pleased as punch at the story I'll file when I get back to Dallas. Comanches on warpath in Cowtown. According to my findings, a Comanche buck and his squaw. . . ."

"I do not care for that word . . . *squaw.*"

Kyne stopped, studied Daniel, and took another sip. "All right, this Comanche princess and her warrior left one gent with his jaw broken, nose flattened, and he won't be able to go back to work at the Texas Express Company for nigh a month. Two other blokes didn't make out good, either. One got his brains almost beaten out of him." He drank more rye-spiced coffee. "Not quite sure I've got all the particulars on that. There might have been another red savage in the mix." The cup sank below the table onto Kyne's lap. "And the third victim, his end is a heartbreaker. Got a bottle shoved into him. Doc says he'll likely loose that limb for sure. Poor Leo Barton. Never again will he dance with a pretty gal unless he can learn to do the Virginia reel on a peg leg."

Rain Shower leaned forward, eyes wide. "It is true? The one will lose his leg?"

Kyne winked. "He will in the Dallas *Herald,* pretty warrior. Till Leo Barton demands a retraction."

The cup returned to his lips, and Kyne drank heartily, ignoring the black brew's heat. He put the cup on the table, and brought out his Old Glory tablet and a pencil. "So set the record straight, folks. What happened tonight?"

Daniel and Rain Shower exchanged glances, but did not answer.

Kyne sighed, and emptied his coffee cup. "And after I've done your work for you," he said. "I found that maid, Killstraight, and talked to her about Room Four. Good thing I've learned some Spanish living in Texas. Not that she knew anything, but, yes, she made the bed that morning. Says they never lock the doors. Got tired of drunks busting them down to break into empty rooms, but that they warn lodgers to lock their doors, it being Hell's Half Acre. So anybody could have slept there. Anybody."

The bell rang above the door, and Daniel turned, surprised to find O'Doherty making his way back inside the ice cream parlor. He stopped at the table, studying Kyne with a mixture of suspicion and contempt, then looked at Daniel.

"A word in private, Sergeant Killstraight?" O'Doherty said stiffly.

When Daniel started to rise, Kyne said good-naturedly: "Oh, whatever you can say to Daniel, you can certainly share with me, Sergeant. We're pards, me and Daniel. Share and share alike. Ain't that right, Daniel?"

Daniel planned on ignoring Kyne, until the newspaper reporter added something in a less friendly tone. "Or have you forgotten that cottonwood trunk ol' Billy Kyne fetched for you Comanch' to help with poor, sickly Quanah Parker?"

He sank back into his chair, suddenly ashamed. When he found his voice, he nodded toward Kyne and told the Fort Worth policeman: "You can speak in front of this man."

O'Doherty didn't like it, but he cleared his throat. "Something came to mind," he said. "The drunk from Kussatz's dram shop. I remember him. Not his name, but I know the brand he rides for. He's *segundo* for Sol Carmody's outfit on the Elm Fork, and that's fitting, that he'd ride for Carmody. They're two of the hardest rocks in Texas."

CHAPTER FIFTEEN

After the police sergeant left the Queen City Ice Cream Parlor, Billy Kyne pushed back his hat with the end of his pencil, whistled, and began writing furiously in his notebook. Finished, he tucked the pencil over his ear and looked at Rain Shower, then at Daniel, his face beaming.

"That theory you have about foul play is perking up something considerable, Danny, my boy. Sol Carmody. That copper was right, kids, when he said Carmody's hard. Hard and mean. And if my memory hasn't been clouded by Manhattan rye, I'd say he's got as good a motive as anyone hereabouts to see Quanah . . . or any Comanch' . . . done in." He let out a chuckle, and shook his head. "You two Indians are going to get Billy Kyne back on staff in New York City for the *Tribune,* and that'll sure have Horace Greeley spinning in his grave."

He leaned forward, elbows on the table,

head held by his hands, and whispered: "Carmody's wife and two sons were massacred by Comanches in 'Seventy-Two. The newspapers hereabouts wouldn't even print what you-all had done to Missus Carmody."

Daniel pushed himself up. "Come," he said. "We must go to the saloon."

"That's an offer Billy Kyne would never turn down." He stood, too, but Rain Shower stopped them.

"No."

They looked down at her. Her face was rigid.

"Have you forgotten *pianahuwait?*" she asked. "We must return to the Beaver Ceremony. Nagwee needs us. As does Quanah."

The sun rose, the church bells pealed, yet they continued to dance, drum, and sing. Fighting exhaustion, they went on until shortly before noon, when, as they sang the closing song four times, Nagwee loosened the ropes securing the teepee to the stakes. Still singing, they rose, and ran out of the curing lodge in all directions.

The Big Doctoring was over. The People would have to wait and see how strong Nagwee's *puha* would prove to be.

From the size of the crowd, Daniel figured

Fort Worth's curiosity had dwindled. He could count the spectators — including five hymn-singing women led by a Bible-clutching man with a long black beard and flat-brimmed black hat shouting that the city should not condone such sacrilege, that Fort Worth was a Sodom for allowing this heathen practice. The only newspaper reporters there were Billy Kyne, a Negro from a Dallas newspaper, and four Fort Worth reporters. *Harper's Weekly, Scribner's,* and the *Police Gazette* were gone. So were the journalists from Kansas City, Jacksboro, Austin, London, and San Antonio.

"I must help take Quanah back to his room," Daniel whispered to Charles Flint. "Can you answer their questions?" He hoped Flint's anger at him had subsided.

It must have, because Flint stammered before finally nodding. "I will try. But what if I'm wrong?"

Smiling, Daniel put his arm on the book-keeper's shoulder, and squeezed. Lowering his voice, he whispered: "They won't ever know."

Following the two *puhakats,* Ben Buffalo Bone and Daniel carried Quanah on a litter provided by the city fire department back upstairs above the Taylor & Barr mercantile.

Rain Shower, Cuhtz Bávi, and Frank Striker trailed them, as Flint went to the reporters, already firing questions at him. Nagwee opened the door to the room he shared with Isa-tai, and they laid Quanah on a buffalo robe on the floor near the window.

Frank Striker said he would retire to his room, and headed downstairs for the Pickwick Hotel.

The window was open, and a surprisingly cool breeze filled the room. Daniel hadn't noticed until now that the skies had darkened. Thunder rumbled. Rain Shower prepared a pipe, and Nagwee accepted it and sat, the other men joining him in a circle.

As always, the first puff of smoke was offered to the Great Spirit, and the next to the sun. They smoked, and, when the pipe returned to Nagwee, he nodded.

"It was a good ceremony," he said. "Considering."

"Not so good," Isa-tai said with bitterness. "Polluted by *taibo* hands. *Taibo* cloth instead of buffalo hides for the lodge. Not even a cottonwood trunk on that first night of prayer." He looked at Quanah with contempt, then stared directly at Daniel. "He will die."

Rage boiled inside Daniel, but Nagwee spoke calmly. "Not if my *puha* is strong."

Isa-tai started to comment, but stopped.

After a moment of silence, Ben Buffalo Bone said: "I thought the Pale Eyes were helpful. Not all of them. But many."

"This is true." Nagwee's head bobbed.

"They helped kill him," Isa-tai said.

Cuhtz Bávi looked from face to face, but said nothing.

Lightning flashed. Several seconds later, thunder rolled. No one spoke, and Daniel sensed a presence. They had left the door open, and, when he turned, he saw Billy Kyne leaning against the frame, nodding his head politely, then tilted it in a gesture that it was time to go.

Daniel looked back at Nagwee, who frowned and said: "I suppose you must go again, He Whose Arrows Fly Straight Into The Hearts Of His Enemies."

Daniel dropped his head.

"Go. This is not a pleasant smoke." He glared at Isa-tai, then painted on a smile, and lifted his hands toward Rain Shower. "Help an old holy man to his feet, dearest one."

Rain Shower was staying in Room 4, while Ben Buffalo Bone had thrown his gear in Daniel's apartment, and Cuhtz Bávi was rooming with Charles Flint. Since Frank Striker had a room in the Pickwick Hotel, obviously the management did not realize he had married a Kiowa. The room where Yellow Bear had died remained unoccupied.

"Give me one minute," Daniel told Kyne, and gestured at Ben Buffalo Bone. They walked down the hall to Daniel's room, went inside, where Daniel grabbed two pencils and his Old Glory tablet. *"Bávi,"* he said, "I ask you to do a huge favor for me."

"It will be done, *bávi.*"

Daniel ran his tongue across his lips. "Watch Quanah. Make sure he is not left alone with Isa-tai."

Ben Buffalo Bone frowned. "Isa-tai . . . do you think . . . ?"

He silenced his friend by holding up his hand. "I am not sure of anything. That is why I go with this *taibo.* Just keep your eyes and ears open."

"Bávi, it will be done." Ben Buffalo Bone nodded.

He left Ben Buffalo Bone, saying — *"Pbah vee."* Take care. — and followed Billy Kyne down the hall. They met Charles Flint on the stairs outside, and Daniel stopped.

"How did it go?"

Flint's eyes were glassy, but he nodded. "Well . . . I guess."

Daniel gave him a thankful nod, took a few steps down, and stopped. "Will you do me one other favor?"

"Yes."

"Watch over Rain Shower. This place can be unpleasant."

"It will be done," Flint said, and Daniel joined Billy Kyne, who was waiting at the bottom of the stairs.

The beer-jerker at Tivoli Hall wiped down the edge of the bar with a damp towel, started to answer Kyne's question, but a shout from the other end commanded his attention, and he moved down the bar, drawing a foamy beer from a tap, and slid a pewter stein down to a waiting customer. Seconds later, he stood in front of Daniel and Kyne.

It was not much after 1:00 P.M., and Herman Kussatz's saloon was crowded with men in suits, farmers in denim, cowhands wearing big hats. Various languages rang out, most of which Daniel recognized from his mining days as German. He could understand the saloon's popularity. Kussatz offered a free lunch all day long, and it was dinnertime. Even Kyne had ordered a draft beer and was spreading something yellow on the thick slice of bread he was about to use to cover a chunk of ham.

"Vednesday night?" The barkeep snorted.

"Ja, I vork dat night. You expect me to remember Vednesday? *Nein.*"

Daniel had known this would be a long shot.

The bartender pointed down the bar at a big box labeled Gurley's Patented Refrigerator. "Kussatz buy that. Keeps beer colder than ice, vill hold one hundred fifty kegs. Place is very busy. *Nein, nein,* I don't know the cowboy."

Kyne bit into the sandwich, chewed, chased it down with a long pull from his stein, while the bartender went back to draw three more beers and pour a shot of bourbon.

"The Hun's right," Kyne said with a mouthful of beer and sandwich. "I wouldn't let that miser I work for in Dallas know my true feelings, but this beer hall is finer than anything in Dallas, that's for certain. Ranchers, mayors, newspapermen, cowboys, cattle buyers. Everybody drinks here. Probably the best dram shop in all of Texas."

When the German returned, the bartender asked: "Vot does the cowboy look like?"

"He wore spurs," Daniel answered.

The beer-jerker laughed, and Kyne joined him. "Most do in this city," Kyne said. "You need more of a description than that."

Daniel tried to remember. He could not

remember anything about the man's face, wasn't even sure he had seen the face. The hat the cowboy had worn was indistinguishable. Even the spurs sounded as did most he had heard in Fort Worth, Dallas, Wichita Falls, Fort Smith, and on the reservation pastures.

Kyne drained his beer, and addressed the German: "He's *segundo* for Sol Carmody. You know Carmody, don't you?"

The bartender tossed the rag into a tin pail behind the bar. "Ja. Most do."

Kyne pushed the empty stein toward the German, who scooped it into a huge hand, and moved back to the line of taps. When he returned, and set the beer in front of the newspaperman, Kyne said: "All we want is the *segundo*'s name?"

"*Nein.* I don't know the cowboy." He took the empty plate, and moved back down the bar.

After sipping his second beer, Kyne looked at Daniel and shrugged. "Well, it was a long shot, Killstraight. But if that copper was right, and it was Carmody's ramrod, I should be able to find his name directly. Or you and I could ride out north to the Elm Fork, pay a visit to Sol. I take it you want to question this fellow yourself?"

Daniel stared at his full glass of water and

the bowl of beans he had not touched. Deep in thought, he did not answer Kyne, who finished his beer, and fished out three coins, which he slapped on the bar. "Come on, Killstraight. I need to get to the depot and hop a train back to Dallas."

The bartender was back, staring at Daniel's bowl, swiping the coins into the deep pocket of his apron. When he turned to leave, Daniel spoke. "*Herr* Bartender." He remembered the miners calling the beer-jerkers that back in Pennsylvania. When the big German looked at him, Daniel asked: "Was Sol Carmody here on Wednesday night?"

"*Ja.*" He nodded, and hooked a thumb toward a table facing the Houston Street window. "Sit there. Vit your Injun."

Kyne's shoe slipped on the brass rail. He bumped into the well-dressed man standing next to him, excused himself, and pulled the pencil from his ear. "Carmody was drinking with Yellow Bear?"

"*Ja.*" The bartender nodded. "*Ja.* Now I remember. The cowboy. He sit vit them, too. Vear spurs, ja. Dark hair. Mustache. But his name?" He shrugged apologetically. "*Nein.*"

Daniel and Kyne exchanged a quick glance, then Daniel asked: "How many were sitting at that table?"

"Injun chief vit feathers. Carmody." He held up two fingers. "Zwei cowboys." Another shrug. "Others come, go, sit, talk."

The bartender went back, this time carrying Daniel's untouched bowl of beans.

Daniel thumbed back three or four pages of his Old Glory tablet. He found the name. "George Briggs," he said.

"Right." Kyne scratched something on a blank page. "Foreman for Dan Waggoner."

"I thought Waggoner and Carmody did not like each other," Daniel said.

Kyne wrote something else. "That's an understatement, Killstraight. Nobody in the Northern Texas Stock Growers' Association cares for Sol Carmody, and he hates everybody."

Daniel chewed on the end of his Faber's pencil for a moment, then removed the pencil. "But could Briggs and Carmody . . . could they be friends?"

" 'Misery acquaints a man with strange bedfellows,' Shakespeare wrote in *The Tempest*. Or as Charles Dudley Warner, who gave me my first newspaper job at the Hartford *Courant,* put it . . . 'politics makes strange bedfellows.' And to quote William J. Kyne . . . 'Cold draft beer and a free lunch can absolutely make the bitterest of enemies temporary pals.' "

The beer-jerker was back, bringing a plate of smelly beef and a tumbler of whiskey to the gent standing beside Kyne, and placing a stein of beer into the hand of a tall, blond man.

"On the other hand," Kyne continued, "Briggs might hoist some beers with Sol Carmody's ramrod, but share a table with Carmody himself? Not a chance in hell, Killstraight. Not if he wanted to keep his job riding for Dan Waggoner."

"*Ja, ja.* Vagner," the German said. "He come, too. Sit for a few minutes." He looked at Daniel and Kyne. "You finished?"

Kyne stared at Daniel, who leaned on the bar and asked: "Dan Waggoner sat down with Sol Carmody?"

"*Ja.* Not long. Five minutes maybe. Then he left."

"What time did everybody leave?"

He shook his head. "*Nein.* I can't say."

"Horse apples, you damned Hun!" Kyne straightened, tried to look bigger, but no matter how much he sucked in his stomach, he would not be a noon shadow to the bruising German. "You might not remember when those two cowhands left, or even Sol Carmody or Dan Waggoner, but a Comanche all decked out like Yellow Bear. You wouldn't forget him. You'd be watching

212

him on account you're curious as everybody else, and you'd never seen a Comanche back on the Rhine or the Danube or wherever you come from. You know. Put that little brain to moil and give us an answer."

It was not the approach Daniel would have chosen, but it worked. The beer-jerker frowned, but answered. "The chief left vit von cowboy at midnight." Shrugging. "Near midnight. Before, after, I can't say."

So George Briggs had been telling the truth.

"Just Yellow Bear and Waggoner's cowhand, George Briggs?" Kyne spoke with urgency. "Not them other two? Or Waggoner. Yellow Bear walked out with just one man?"

"Don't know the name of the cowboy, but *ja,* von left vit the chief. Vagner, he vas gone long time before."

"And Carmody," Daniel asked, "and the other?"

"Nein." Another shake of his head. "I don't remember." Glaring at Kyne. "Dat is so."

Again, a customer called, and the barkeep moved down the bar.

"That's something," Kyne said, gathering his tablet and pencils. "I don't have a farthing what it means, but it must mean something." They headed for the batwing doors. "I'll find out that gent's name. You want to ride out to Carmody's ranch? I can rent a buggy. Take us all day to get there."

Daniel shook his head. There was no guarantee Carmody or his foreman would be at the ranch, and, besides, Kyne was right. Maybe they had something, but what?

"And when I see Dan Waggoner, I'll nail his hide to the barn. What's he doing, meeting with Sol Carmody?"

They pushed through the batwing doors, and Daniel ran straight into Ben Buffalo Bone.

His Kotsoteka friend's face looked troubled.

"It is Quanah," Ben said. "Come quick."

CHAPTER SIXTEEN

Large, hard drops of rain pelted them as they ran across the street and up the stairs. Daniel was soaked and cold by the time he reached Nagwee's room. The door was open, the window now closed to keep out the dampness, and Rain Shower and Charles Flint knelt over Quanah.

His heart sank as he entered the room, squeezing past Nagwee and Isa-tai. Cuhtz Bávi sat on the floor, tamping tobacco into a pipe bowl.

Rain Shower looked up, smiling, and Quanah turned his head. His eyes focused, and he worked his lips before calling out in a weak voice: *"Maruaweeka."*

A grin exploded, and Daniel sank onto the blanket, reaching down, grabbing Quanah's extended hand — "Hello yourself." — he said in English.

Behind him, Billy Kyne's voice thundered: "Damnation. No other reporters here?

215

Excellent. Just excellent. Is he going to live?"

Turning around, Nagwee spoke in his native tongue. "My *puha* is strong." He was speaking, not to the *Herald* reporter, but Isa-tai, and he was smiling with satisfaction when he said it. Isa-tai's face grew harder, his frown deeper, and he folded his arms across his chest, and turned away from Nagwee, staring at the wall.

"What's that mean?" Kyne wiped his notebook on his coat, which was dripping wet. "What did he say?"

"He said his power is strong," Daniel said.

Quanah added, summoning strength from somewhere deep within, in English: *"I will live."*

Kyne wrote, tried harder, gave up, flipped his notebook to another page, and tried again, before cursing and sending the pencil flying across the room, where it bounced off the wall and landed in Nagwee's bed.

"Wet pencil. Wet pages. Damn, I gotta get this in now." Thunder drowned out Kyne's farewell. Lightning flashed, more thunder rolled, and Billy Kyne was gone.

"It is good to see you," Quanah told Daniel.

Tears rolled down his cheeks. "My friend, it is great to see you."

Flint lifted Quanah's head, and Rain

Shower gave him water from a tumbler. Some dribbled down Quanah's chin, but, when the glass was empty, he said: "More."

Flint rose, and, as he poured from a pitcher, Quanah's eyes wandered around the room.

"Where is Yellow Bear?" he asked.

Charles Flint held up Quanah's arm, letting Daniel wrap clean linen strips around the cuts the Kwahadi leader had carved down his forearm with Cuhtz Bávi's knife. Personally Daniel had not thought this had been a good idea, weak as Quanah was, but Quanah had insisted, and Nagwee had grunted that it was good, that the one who had gone to The Land Beyond The Sun should be mourned by his daughter's husband.

"There." Gently Flint lowered Quanah's arm.

Releasing a heavy sigh, Quanah sadly shook his head. Tears streamed down his face, shaming Daniel as he remembered he had not properly mourned Yellow Bear.

"It is hard to believe he is gone," Quanah said. "I have lost too many wise men whose counsel I often needed."

Daniel bit his bottom lip. Isa Nanaka and now Yellow Bear had died. Teepee That Stands Alone was broken, shattered, living

217

alone, hardly seeing anyone, south of Saddle Mountain. Others had fallen victim to the pale-eyes whiskey, no longer caring for The People, for their families, living for nothing except another drink. Other than Nagwee and Cuhtz Bávi, who was left? Isa-tai? The thought made Daniel shudder.

"You are cold," Quanah said. "Tetecae, close the window."

"I am all right," Daniel said.

"But something troubles you. Speak, He Whose Arrows Fly Straight Into The Hearts Of His Enemies."

Daniel glanced at Charles Flint, but, when his eyes met the bookkeeper's, he quickly looked away.

"Go ahead," Flint said. "Ask him."

"Ask me what?"

"You are weak," Daniel said. "You should rest."

Quanah reached over, grabbed Daniel's forearm, and squeezed tightly. *"Ask me what?"*

Daniel swallowed. Lightning flashed, followed by a deafening roar of thunder. The rain, which had been falling off and on all afternoon, had turned into a downpour. He wondered about Isa-tai, Nagwee, Rain Shower, and the others. School Father Pratt and Captain Hall had come upstairs, paid

Quanah their respects, then taken the others to a steakhouse to eat supper. How long had they been gone? Thirty minutes? An hour?

"Speak, my friend. What is on your mind? What troubles you?"

He looked into Quanah's eyes. His lips moved as he tried to find the words.

"What do you remember about the night?" It was Charles Flint who had spoken.

"The night?" Quanah blinked.

"The night you were almost called to The Land Beyond The Sun?" Flint explained.

Quanah's eyes closed, and his brow furrowed. "I went to sleep," he said. "I was very tired for it had been a long day." He motioned for a drink, and Daniel filled the tumbler and handed it to him as Flint helped raise his head.

"I have a vague memory of falling onto the floor. My head was spinning. My lungs did not wish to work. I pulled myself toward the light."

"The light?" Daniel asked.

"*Haa*, the light. It marked the door."

Light . . . shining through the crack between the door and the floor. Which meant the lamps were off in their room. Well, Daniel had known that already.

"Yellow Bear had kicked you out of bed,"

Flint said, and Daniel saw Quanah cringe. Flint had done it again, dishonoring the dead by speaking their names. "He saved your life, undoubtedly."

"He who is traveling to The Land Beyond The Sun saved my life more than once."

No one spoke for a long while. Rain pounded the windowpanes. The breeze felt almost cold.

"That is not all you wish to know," Quanah said.

Daniel ran his fingers through his hair, nodding. "The *kupl-ta*." He pointed to the lamp, turned off, on the wall over Nagwee's bed, then decided to explain. "Did you turn it off?"

"Haa." His head bobbed. "After I came in and prepared myself to sleep."

Flint cleared his throat. "Blow it out, or turn it down?"

Quanah's answer made Daniel's heartbeat increase. "Turn it down. The kupl-ta was gas. This, Captain Hall explained to me."

"This was explained to you," Flint said, "and what of . . ." — this time he remembered — "the one who is no more?"

"I told him." His eyes narrowed, and he looked first at Flint, then at Daniel. "What are you trying to say?"

Daniel pointed to the window, where rain

dribbled on the sill and splattered against the glass. "Did you open the window when you came back from our supper?"

Quanah's head shook. "No."

Daniel frowned, and Flint shook his head.

"I had no need to open it, for it was already open. You two young Kwahadis have short memories. It was not always so cool. It was stifling when we first arrived in this place. We always left the window open."

"The father of your favorite wife?" Flint asked. "Do you remember when he came back? Did he wake you?"

Shaking his head, Quanah said: "I remember nothing, except falling to the floor and crawling toward the light, and I am not certain I even remember that. It seemed more like a dream."

"Could he who is gone," Flint asked, "could he have blown out the lamp by mistake?"

Quanah stared.

"Could he have closed the window?" Daniel asked.

First, Quanah wet his lips, then he clenched his fists. Lightning flashed, and the rain seemed to slacken as the thunder pealed somewhere to the east. "Why would he have done either of those things? You two are foolish boys. He who has traveled to The

Land Beyond The Sun was no fool, which you two seem to think he was."

Daniel started to protest, but Quanah would not let him.

"He was a *puhakat,* and a very wise man. I always listened to what he had to say, for he was a man who spoke with great wisdom. He never touched the *taibo* spirits that rob our young and old of their tact, their reason, their souls. If I told him that these lamps were not coal oil but gas . . . and this I did tell him . . . and that he should not blow them out, he would have remembered. He was very wise." Angrily he rose one arm to lean on his elbow and hooked a thumb toward the window. "Nor would he have closed the window. As I once heard a Pale Eyes say . . . 'One does not make hell any hotter.'"

Daniel hung his head, and tried to explain. "We did not mean to insult a great *puhakat.* He was a man Tetecae and I always respected and admired. We just had to know these things."

"Why?"

Again, Daniel pointed to the gas lamps on the wall. "When we found you the next morning, the lamps were on, but the fire had been put out." He pointed to the window. "And the window was shut and even latched shut."

Flint cleared his throat, then added: "The door was locked. We found a key on the table."

"School Father Pratt kicked the door open," Daniel added. "We barely got you out before you began the great journey."

His eyes closed tightly, Quanah lay there, not moving except for the slight shaking of his head, as he tried to comprehend everything.

"Could . . . ?" Flint hesitated, tried again. "Could that *puhakat* . . . could he have made a mistake?"

Eyes still closed, head still moving, Quanah said tightly: "No."

"He was tired," Flint said. "As you were. He had been up till midnight with the *Tejanos*. Is it possible . . . ?"

"He would not have blown out those lamps," Quanah said, his eyes open, blazing. "And what kind of fool would have closed the window. The windows in my Star House are always open during the summer. Otherwise my wives and I would not be able to live in such a place."

"Then it is settled," Daniel said. He did not want to upset the great Kwahadi any more.

"I meant you no disrespect," Flint added.

"We just need to know for certain," Daniel said.

"The key?" Flint said cautiously. "What of the key? Did you lock the door?"

This time Quanah thought for a minute or two, recalling details from a memory clouded by a coma.

"We had one key. The man gave it to us in the hotel." His Adam's apple bobbed. He pressed his lips together. "I do not believe in locking doors. If anyone wants to visit me, my door is open. At my home. At the many hotels I have stayed in pale-eyes cities." Another pause to remember. "When we got to our room, I put the key on the table by the bed. It was always there."

Daniel straightened. "The night table?"

"*Haa.* I put the key by the Jesus book."

Flint looked at Daniel, then back at Quanah. "Not on the dresser? The wooden tower with boxes where Pale Eyes keep their clothes."

"The table by the bed. It was there when I went to bed. I know this because I thought to pick up the Jesus book, but I do not understand all of those marks."

Again, Daniel and Flint stared at each other.

"Why do you ask me these questions?" Quanah said. "What does this mean?"

Daniel looked at the sick chief of The People. "*Tsu Kuh Puah,* I do not believe this was an accident," he said. "The window was found shut, locked. The key was found on the dresser, not on the table by the bed. The lamps were on, the flames blown out, filling the room with poisoned air. We found red markings, prints from someone's thumb, on the lamp's globe, and on the glass of the window. I believe that someone was trying to kill you."

"And the father of my favorite wife?"

"His death was an accident," Flint said. "You were the one he meant to kill."

Far off in the distance, thunder rolled across the night sky. The rain had stopped, and the streets of Hell's Half Acre became alive again.

Quanah's tears resumed their flow. "Who would want to kill me?" he asked, and choked back a sob for Yellow Bear.

"That is the question we must answer," Flint said.

The sobs ceased, and Daniel saw that Quanah was asleep. Good. He needed more strength, and Daniel felt guilty for draining Quanah so. He should have waited, asked Quanah these questions later. On the other hand, he had read in the *National Police Gazette* that it is best to interview witnesses immediately, and not wait until their memories are clouded by ideas of what they thought they had seen, thought they remembered. A detective should, he recalled, have all his questions written out before him. A good detective must know what to ask. His Old Glory tablet was in his room down the hall. He hadn't even thought to bring it to the Tivoli Hall.

Some detective I am.

"I have told you," Charles Flint said, "that you think my father did this, but I say he did not. I will prove to you that he did not."

"We must work together," Daniel said.

Flint stared, eyes as black and as untrusting as Isa-tai's.

"Do you know what an alibi is?"

"It is. . . ." Flint finally flashed a rare smile. "It is something one needs not know to keep books for a trading post."

Daniel grinned back. "It is something that proves one did not, could not commit a crime."

"My father could not have committed this crime."

"So he must have an alibi. He has motive, and this you cannot deny. He had opportunity."

"Then his alibi is that he was asleep in the same room with Nagwee."

"We will ask Nagwee about that night. My friend Hugh Gunter, a Cherokee police-man, says that one must investigate a crime with an open mind." Actually Hugh Gunter hadn't said that at all. Hugh Gunter's philosophy was often: *If I think the sum-bitch did it, he did it, and I'll prove he did it, and see the bastard gets what's coming to him.* "I have an open mind. I do not wish ill upon Isa-tai. I hope he did not have any hand in this. And he is not the only person who is what Deputy Marshal Harvey P. Noble calls a suspect."

He let Flint digest this. Maybe he could make Charles Flint a Metal Shirt. As ser-geant, he could always use someone willing to risk his life and hair for $8 a month, someone who didn't mind the taunts from The People. Someone who could be spit on in the afternoon by a grandmother for ar-resting her son or grandson.

"We eliminate the suspects," Daniel ex-plained. "We find who has an alibi that says they did not commit the crime. But first we must find out why the crime was commit-ted." He posed the question to Flint. "So who would want to see Quanah dead?"

While Flint chewed on that, Daniel was already thinking: *Who was in the room when I saw the key on the dresser? Nagwee and*

Isa-tai. Flint and School Father Pratt. George Briggs. Burk Burnett. Dan Waggoner.

He frowned.

Or there could have been another key. That gave him more suspects. Sol Carmody. The thousands of Pale Eyes who hate The People and were in Fort Worth. And what do I really know of this Pale Eyes newspaperman, Kyne? Why is he so curious about what happened?

Still, another thought struck him.

Or Quanah could be wrong, and Flint right. Yellow Bear might have moved the key. No matter how intelligent he was . . . and in my heart I know he was a great, wise man . . . this is not the land of The People. He could have locked the door, closed the window, blown out the lamps.

Daniel sighed. Tonight, he would fill up his Old Glory tablet. He'd have to buy another at the Taylor & Barr mercantile tomorrow morning.

CHAPTER SEVENTEEN

He studied the list:

Isa-tai
~~Nagwee~~
~~Pratt~~
G. Briggs
Burnett
Waggoner
Carmody
Kyne
~~Capt. Hall~~
Cowboy in alley?
~~Tetecae~~ Tetecae

Nagwee would not have tried to kill Quanah. Never. Nor could Daniel suspect School Father, even though both the holy man and Pratt had been in the room, and could easily have placed the key on the dresser. Captain Hall was the only one who hadn't been upstairs in the room. So Daniel had scratched their names off his list of suspects. He thought about the cowboy he had seen in the alley, and while Daniel knew the drunken man who worked for Sol Carmody was in the alley when he heard the door close, he had put a question mark beside that entry.

Kyne had been right. Daniel needed to find this cowboy who worked for the Comanche-hating Sol Carmody. Needed to ask him some questions.

He looked at Flint's name. At first, he had scratched through it, but then he had to reconsider. He liked Tetecae well enough, wanted to like him even more if only for no other reason than he needed someone to trust.

"I do not understand those bird-track marks," Ben Buffalo Bone said from over Daniel's shoulder.

Which made Daniel smile. He was glad that his Kotsoteka friend had joined him in Fort Worth. He could trust Ben Buffalo Bone.

"Do you remember how we used to steal the chickens from the coop at the missionary school after I first arrived on the reservation?" Daniel asked.

Ben Buffalo Bone had a hearty, rich laugh.

"My father would say that The People

have fallen on hard times," Ben said, "when their young braves must go on raids for stupid birds that cannot even fly, and not horses or Mexicans to turn into slaves."

Tears welled in Daniel's eyes. "My mother would just shake her head, when I showed her our plunder. But she would glare at the Black Robes when they came to tell her that we must be punished, that stealing was wrong in the eyes of their Lord."

"What does a *taibo* god know about The People?"

School Father Pratt's words echoed in Daniel's mind: *Kill the Indian, not the man.*

Ben's broad hand slapped his shoulder. "Those were fine days, *bávi.* Not as fine as when the Kotsotekas, and you, the Kwahadis, roamed free to hunt, free to do as we pleased, but we made the best of those days, did we not?"

"Surely, we did."

A fat finger pointed to one of the words. Tetecae's name.

Daniel frowned. He just could not get around the fact that Charles Flint had been in the room. He could have slipped the key onto the dresser.

"But I do not understand why the Pale Eyes have to put down stories on paper. Some of them speak well, and there is nothing better than sitting around a circle, smoking, telling stories. The People do not tell stories this way."

Daniel wrote another line — *Accident?* — and flipped to a new page in his new Old Glory writing tablet.

"But we do," he told Ben Buffalo Bone. "We draw pictures on our hides to tell the stories of what happened during a year. We tell stories in pictures on our war shields."

"*Haa,* but when we paint a *chimal,* this paper is only good for stuffing the insides so that a *chimal* might turn away the arrow of an enemy. And pictures make more sense than these marks."

Ben Buffalo Bone walked around the writing table, and sat in the chair across from Daniel.

"Nagwee and Isa-tai say that Quanah is no longer in danger, and the Pale Eyes doctor agrees. Soon, we will return home. So what is it that troubles you, my brother?"

What troubled him was Rain Shower, and the nightmare. Maybe that had been not a dream, but a vision, foretelling of the ruction at the sporting house when Daniel had almost killed a *taibo* with his bare hands. He raised a finger, and gently touched the bruise between his eye and hair, just above the temple.

He left out his concerns about Ben's sister, and told him instead about what he suspected had been an attempt to kill Quanah Parker.

Typical of The People, Ben Buffalo Bone's face betrayed no emotion, and he never interrupted Daniel to ask questions. When Daniel had finished, his friend just sat there, staring, thinking.

"One *Nermernuh* would not kill another *Nermernuh*," he said at last. "I will not believe that."

"Even Isa-tai?" Daniel said.

"Especially Isa-tai. It is true that Isa-tai and Quanah do not often agree on what is best for The People, but Isa-tai is a powerful *puhakat*. It was not his fault for what happened all those years ago. The stupid Striped Arrows brave killed a skunk and destroyed Isa-tai's *puha* during the raid. Isa-tai vomited up thousands of cartridges for our fast-shooting rifles. My own father saw this with his very eyes."

Daniel glanced at his list. "Then one of the Pale Eyes cattlemen. This Sol Carmody, he despises The People for what they did to his family."

Daniel's mind flashed to another cattleman, a *Tejano* named J.C.C. McBride who had hated The People. Immediately Daniel tried to block out that memory. He had killed the rancher, and had done it in a way that The People of old — especially his father, and old Isa Nanaka, Quanah, too — would have appreciated, except that he had not taken the *taibo*'s scalp.

"I do not know this Pale Eyes that you call Sol Car-mo-dy." Ben Buffalo Bone shook his head.

Daniel stood and walked toward his bed, found the original Old Glory tablet in his valise, and returned with it to the desk. He flipped through some pages, read a few notes, and looked up at Ben Buffalo Bone.

"His cattle graze at The Big Pasture. Weeks ago, you rode there when we learned that there were longhorns eating The People's grass. Do you recall this?"

Ben Buffalo Bone's head bobbed. "*Haa,* I rode there. There were cattle. Twice Bent Nose came with me. Many cattle. Three *Tejanos.*"

"But they had no right to be in The Big Pasture."

"No, *bávi,* they did. One of the Pale Eyes shows me a piece of paper with the scratch marks. He says it gives him the right. I do not know about this. Nor does Twice Bent Nose. But the *Tejano* says that I can take it to show Biggers. This I do."

"And what did Agent Biggers say?"

"He reads the markings and says that the paper seems to be . . . I do not remember the *taibo* word. . . . But that the cattle should stay in The Big Pasture for now."

"What did Quanah say?"

"I did not tell Quanah."

Daniel pressed his lips tight. "Why did you not speak of this with Quanah?"

Ben Buffalo Bone could only shrug, but now his face showed emotion.

Smiling, Daniel reached across the table and put his hand on Ben Buffalo Bone's shoulder. "It is all right, my friend. You did nothing wrong. Did Agent Biggers keep the paper?"

The young Kotsoteka nodded.

Daniel found his new writing tablet, flipped back a page, and studied the list. George Briggs . . . Burk Burnett . . . Dan Waggoner.

He made a mark through Burnett's name. Like Captain Lee Hall, Burk Burnett needed Quanah. So did the Northern Texas Stock Growers' Association. Quanah supported these cattlemen, and they, in turn, supported Quanah. Quanah's death would have complicated any future lease on The Big Pasture or the other grazing areas controlled by The People.

That brought him to the names of Briggs and Waggoner.

Waggoner needed grass, or his ranch might be ruined. He had said so himself, but, then, if he could trust his memory, so had Burk Burnett. Yet Waggoner's words had been the sharpest, and Waggoner had been seen with his foreman in the Tivoli Hall, sharing drinks with Sol Carmody and his *segundo.* On the other hand, Dan Waggoner hated Sol Carmody. Or had that been an act? Or maybe . . . if Waggoner were desperate enough, would he have aligned himself with Carmody?

The ways of the Pale Eyes Daniel had learned. Quanah had signed one agreement, or was about to, that would lease The Big Pasture to Captain Lee Hall and his organization. Isa-tai had signed an agreement with Sol Carmody. They would fight this out for months, maybe even years, in courts. He thought of Greer County, a section of land north of the Red River that bordered the federal reservation of The People, the Apaches, and the Kiowas. Texians claimed that land belonged to the state of Texas. The government in Washington City said it was part of Indian Territory. Nothing had been decided, and this argument had been going on since before Daniel had been born.

So if two men said they had rights to The Big Pasture, what would happen? Lawyers would get rich. Eventually somebody would win, but by then many cattle might be dead from starvation. The Northern Texas Stock Growers' Association had no cattle on the land of The People. Sol Carmody did, and removing those cattle might take forever under the pale-eyes law. When you considered that, Daniel thought, it would make practical business sense for Dan Waggoner to agree to a truce with Sol Carmody.

"Would a truce be enough to commit murder?"

He hadn't realized he had said those words aloud, until Ben Buffalo Bone asked what did he mean.

"*Bávi. . . .*" Daniel gave him a weary smile. "I don't know what I mean."

It was a whole lot easier trying to solve disputes in the Nations, even if The People looked down on Metal Shirts. Judging a horse race would not cause Daniel's head to ache as it did now. Putting his elbows on the table, he reached up and massaged both temples.

If Quanah were dead, who would become leader of The People? Nagwee? Maybe, but he was no leader, just a holy man. Isa-tai? The Pale Eyes did not like him much, but they could not ignore his influence with The People. They might think that by naming him chief — which The People always considered silly for no one man led all the bands — it would make him easier to control.

Of course, they had thought that about Quanah, too.

He dropped his arms, staring at the names, thinking something else. Nagwee would not replace Quanah. Nor would Isatai. The Pale Eyes would first look to Yellow Bear. He was not only Quanah's father-in-law, but perhaps the most powerful *puhakat* on the reservation, even more powerful than Nagwee. Yellow Bear was a man much respected by both The People and the government of the Pale Eyes. Agent Biggers had once told Yellow Bear how much he enjoyed the old man's company, despite the fact that Yellow Bear spoke hardly any English and Biggers understood only a few *Nermernuh* words, despite their different opinions on religion.

Yellow Bear would have replaced Quanah.

Charles Flint had said that Yellow Bear's death had been an accident — probably not the correct *taibo* word — and that Quanah had been the intended victim. Maybe the man who had blown out the lamps, closed

238

the window, and locked the door had wanted both men to die. The more he thought about that, the more it seemed so reasonable.

Why haven't I considered this before?

"Tell me what you are thinking, my brother," Ben Buffalo Bone said. "I am no holy man, so I cannot read what is in your mind."

After Daniel had explained, Ben Buffalo Bone shook his head. "I will never understand the ways of the *Tejanos.* Or the Long Knives. You think this *taibo,* or *taibos,* they wanted to kill both Quanah and the father of his favorite wife? That sounds crazy to me, bávi."

Daniel shrugged. "I have known many *po-sa taibos.*"

Ben Buffalo Bone finally managed a smile. "That is true. And I have known many crazy *Nermernuh.* Maybe you should show this paper to Tetecae. He is smart, and understands both the *taibo* and The People."

Daniel shook his head. "I can talk to Tetecae, but I don't think I should show him this." Not with Flint's name on the list. Not with his father at the very top. He thought of something else. "Do you think Tetecae would make a good Metal Shirt?"

Doubt creased Ben Buffalo Bone's round

face. "When he works at the big store, which is full of the hard candy and coffee that I like so, and dresses better than many *Tejanos,* why would he want to be spit on, to have rocks thrown at him? To be shot at?"

Why do we? Daniel thought, but did not say.

"You should ask Rain Shower."

Daniel looked amused. "To be a Metal Shirt?"

"No, *bávi.* But she knows much. You have often talked to her about matters that trouble you. This I know. And you should take her for your wife, have many *Nermernuh* babies. You should do this soon, my brother."

The smile had faded instantly. Daniel shook his head.

"You do not like my sister?"

He shook his head violently. "No, I like her very much. I have no ponies to give your uncle."

"Cuhtz Bávi would not want many. Rain Shower is not as pretty as Oajuicauojué. Some brave will pay many ponies for my younger sister, but Rain Shower?" He snorted.

Daniel stared at the writing tablet.

"*Bávi,* I am not as smart as you. Nor as brave. But I do know one thing, for my eyes

240

see very well. You should speak to Cuhtz
Bávi about Rain Shower. Before Tetecae
steals her away from you."

CHAPTER EIGHTEEN

It did not surprise Daniel.

When the Pale Eyes doctor insisted that Quanah sit in the wheelchair and be rolled down the hall, carried down the steps, wheeled to the hack, driven to the depot, and pushed to the train, Quanah said: "No."

"But. . . ."

"Damn no."

The doctor started to protest again, but School Father Pratt cut him off. "Leave your contraption here, Doctor. Quanah will walk."

"He is too weak. He cannot make it down those steps. I dare say he will collapse before he even reaches the door."

"My money's on Quanah." Captain Hall smiled.

As for Quanah? He was already standing, ramrod straight, face pale, lips chapped, and arms still bandaged, but his eyes a firm, unblinking black. The doctor began shaking his head, and Quanah started walking.

He led the procession, followed by Nag-wee and Cuhtz Bávi, then the doctor, Captain Hall, School Father Pratt. Isa-tai gave them a good lead before he stepped through the door with Frank Striker, carrying both his and Quanah's grips, trailing. Ledger in one hand and valise in the other, Charles Flint let Rain Shower go ahead of him. Daniel brought up the rear, a few feet behind Ben Buffalo Bone. Most of the luggage had been taken to the depot already by two Negroes. Daniel carried only his grip, and one of his Old Glory tablets.

He kept his eyes on Rain Shower as they made their way down the stairs and into the waiting cabs on Houston Street. School Father Pratt helped Rain Shower into the last hack, and Flint climbed in beside her, with Ben Buffalo Bone sitting next to the bookkeeper. Daniel had to sit in the driver's box, and School Father Pratt ran to climb into his vehicle. While waiting for the cabs to begin their journey, Daniel glanced at Tivoli Hall, but, from all appearances, it was closed. It was, after all, 8:00 A.M.

They rode down Houston Street, past the sporting houses, gambling halls, the saloons, hotels, into the Third Ward, and finally arrived at the depot for the Texas & Pacific. A big, greasy, black 2-8-0 locomotive belched thick smoke, as eager to get out of Cowtown as Daniel was.

Captain Hall stood on the platform, talking to Quanah. Daniel only made out a few of the rancher's words, but knew the former Ranger's concern was more on leasing The Big Pasture than on Quanah's recovery. They shook hands, and Quanah headed to the car, stopping to sign an autograph for a freckle-faced red-headed boy whose father hid nervously in the shadows.

"Daniel."

He turned, finding School Father Pratt extending his right hand, using his left to tip the old military hat he wore at Rain Shower. "Charles."

The former bluecoat shook hands with his two students, who had to lay ledger and writing tablet on the platform to free their hands. "I wish to express my sympathy over the loss of Yellow Bear. It was a terrible accident." His eyes looked questioningly at Daniel, as if he wanted a confirmation that it was an accident. Looking away quickly, Daniel saw Captain Hall taking to Frank Striker. Hall must have relayed Daniel's suspicions to Pratt.

Daniel looked back at Pratt, but said nothing.

"You two Comanches are excellent representations of what the Industrial Boarding School is all about," Pratt said, giving up on prying any information out of Daniel. "You are traveling the white man's road and leading your people into a new era." He tilted his head toward the train. "Like Quanah Parker."

"Thank you," Flint said.

Daniel could only nod.

"Kill the Indian, not the man. That's what I preach and teach. When you get back to the reservation, do what is right. Help Quanah lead your people. We have accomplished much, but there is much left to accomplish. It will be a long journey."

Another handshake, another tip of his hat and a polite farewell to Rain Shower, and Pratt walked back to one of the waiting hacks.

"Come, let us board the train." Flint's voice. When Daniel turned, he saw the bookkeeper had already picked up his ledger and was escorting Rain Shower up the platform, following Nagwee and Cuhtz Bávi aboard.

"I warned you," Ben Buffalo Bone muttered, and headed to the train.

Always too much going on, Daniel thought. *Metal Shirt work, much of it nothing more than drudgery, but now more. Yellow Bear dead. Quanah had barely survived. A fight among Tejanos over The Big Pasture. A fight among The People over that same grazing land. One and a half Old Glory tablets filled with mostly nonsensical notes. Theories and superstitions, but nothing solid. And now Rain Shower is laughing at something Charles Flint had said.*

Spitting onto the dirty planks, he picked up his tablet, and headed for the train.

"Killstraight!"

Turning, he straightened, tensing, as William J. Kyne ran down the boardwalk. Kyne's Congress gaiters slid to a stop, and he caught his breath, looking around. "Damn. I just made it. Take it everybody else's on that train?"

Daniel's head bobbed.

"No chance I can get a fare-the-well quote from Chief Quanah, eh?"

A conductor yelled the answer: "All aboard!"

Kyne sniggered, and shook his head, and, when Daniel resumed his walk to the train, Kyne walked alongside him.

"We're still partners, aren't we, Killstraight? We're still working on this story together, right?"

No answer.

"Listen, I'll work on the Sol Carmody end

down here, but I'm going to need your help when you get back to the reservation."

Daniel slowed his pace, and shot the *Herald* reporter a glance.

"I got the name of the cowboy, Carmody's *segundo,* the one you likely saw drunker than Hooter's goat in the alley on the night ol' Yellow Bear up and went to the happy hunting ground. Vince Christensen. Word is . . . and this isn't from the Dallas *Herald,* so it's likely accurate . . . that Vince spent three years in Huntsville for manslaughter. The way I see it, it's not hard to get someone who has already killed one person to murder another. Especially if all you're asking him to do is to kill one or two Indians."

Daniel walked on, but knew he would write the name of the cowboy in the tablet as soon as he settled into his seat.

"You need to talk to Vince. Wire me what you find out. The *Herald* will pick up the charges."

Sticking the Old Glory underneath his arm, Daniel grabbed the handle, and pulled himself onto the step. The train lunged, started to pull away. He looked down and back at Kyne.

"Me talk to Vince?" he called out.

Kyne nodded. "Carmody sent him up to the reservation. To make sure his herd of longhorns stays on The Big Pasture." He blinked. Smiling, Kyne waved his hat over his head, yelling: "Don't be surprised, Killstraight, to find old Billy Kyne paying you a visit in Indian Territory in a couple of weeks. But find Vince Christensen! Talk to him!"

He longed to sit close to Rain Shower, but Quanah motioned for him to sit across from him and Nagwee, so Daniel obliged. The car rocked without rhythm, and the smell of smoke and cinders lay heavy in the late morning air. Fort Worth became a distant memory, and the rolling hills stunted with trees replaced the landscape, gradually losing the trees, soon flattening.

The train increased speed.

"This Iron Horse breathes much fire," Nagwee said, staring out the window. "Not good."

Daniel knew what the holy man meant. Even despite the recent rains, the land here was brown, the coarse, dry grass nowhere near as high as Daniel had seen it in previous years.

Quanah agreed. "The grass is not as green as it is in our land."

"That is why the Pale Eyes want it so."

Quanah grunted. "Of this we will speak

among the elders when we return to the land of The People."

"It will be good to be home again."

"*Haa.*" Quanah nodded.

Turning, Nagwee revealed a mischievous grin. "You will be happy to be no longer where you can hear my snores."

"Snores? I thought those were pale-eyes cannon roaring in my ears."

Daniel smiled, then fetched a pencil and hurriedly opened his tablet. He had almost forgotten to write down Vince Christensen's name. He looked back at some of his notes, put the end of the pencil in his mouth, and chewed. The train whistle blew. Ahead of him, Rain Shower laughed at something Charles Flint had said. At the rear of the car, Ben Buffalo Bone began playing a song on his flute.

He barely heard the words, wasn't quite sure he understood, and, removing the pencil from his mouth, he looked at Nagwee.

"I am sorry," Daniel said, "*Tsu Kuh Puah,* what did you say of Isa-tai?"

Nagwee and Quanah stared. With a frown, Nagwee answered: "I said that Isa-tai liked not my snores, either." Flashing another grin at Quanah, he added: "My wife minds not, though."

"Your wife is deaf," Quanah said.

"No. She just cut off her ears because I snore."

This was something Pale Eyes did not understand about The People, that they had a wicked sense of humor, that they were devoted to their family. *Taibos* found Comanches to be solemn, heartless, cruel. Yet Daniel knew The People laughed often, loved with all their heart, only he was not in a mood to hear Nagwee and Quanah's jovial banter.

"But did you say Isa-tai left because of your snoring?"

Nagwee grunted. Quanah frowned. Nagwee crossed his arms over his chest and glared at Daniel. "I said that. You were not listening. Isa-tai got up in the middle of the night. He opens the door. I wake up. 'Where do you go?' I ask him, and he says . . . 'To get away from this racket where I can sleep.' "

"So he went down the hall?"

"I did not ask him the next morning. He did not say."

"Was that the . . . ?" No, he would not bring up that night, especially not spoil the fine spirits Nagwee and Quanah were in. Daniel thanked Nagwee, and filled the page of the Old Glory tablet.

Isa-tai left room. No alibi from Nagwee.
Took Room 4. Had to be. Where else?
But what time? Nagwee would not know.
He could not read a clock, and the roof
hides the stars.
Could that have been the door I heard
shut? No. I would have heard footsteps
pass my door. Or would I, had he been
quiet?
Red paint on Isa-tai's face. Red marks on
window, globe.
Theory: Isa-tai leaves. Nagwee wakens.
Isa-tai lies. Shuts door. Waits for Nagwee
to fall to sleep.
Enters Quanah's room. Shuts window.
Blows out lamps. Grabs key off table.
Locks door. Sneaks to Room 4. Sleeps
there. Next morning returns key when no
one is looking after Quanah discovered.
?????????
Shit!

Quickly he looked up and flipped the page
as Charles Flint passed by on the way to
the water bucket at the end of the car. The
notes from Ben Buffalo Bone's flute wailed
sadly, and Daniel looked down the aisle and
found Rain Shower. Her face seemed happy,
but he noticed that she was watching
Charles Flint. She must have felt his stare,

251

because she turned, but by then Daniel had avoided her eyes, and looked out the window, watching the burned, ugly land pass by.

The train took them to Wichita Falls. From there, they boarded wagons, filled with corn bound for Fort Sill, and traveled on. After crossing the Red River at Hill's Ferry, they wove along the trail through gullies and over tree-lined hills, and toward the Wichita Mountains.

Past Crater Creek . . . to Blue Beaver Creek. Sage shined across the land.

"This is holy place," Cuhtz Bávi said.

"Once it was," Nagwee said, "but no more. It is owned by the Long Knives."

Daniel knew what the *puhakat* meant. Among The People, wherever one found natural sage, the land was holy. Once, this had been The People's domain; now the bluecoats controlled it. In the year the Pale Eyes called 1875, Quanah had camped at Crater Creek before riding on to Blue Beaver Creek to meet Bad Hand Mackenzie to surrender the Kwahadis.

"Is that not right, Isa-tai?" Nagwee said. "Was this not once the land of The People? Our most holy land?"

Isa-tai did not move. Legs buried by corn,

252

he sat with his back against the hard side of the wagon, arms folded, black eyes unblinking.

Frank Striker changed the subject. "You want to get off at your home, Quanah?" The trail led just past Quanah's Star House. Isatai lived near there, too. In fact, Daniel could have gotten off here along with Cuhtz Bávi, Ben Buffalo Bone, and Rain Shower. Despite wanting to meet with the Indian agent, he now realized that's what he should do. He would have been alone with Rain Shower. Most likely Charles Flint would have to journey on to the trading post with his ledger books.

"No. I must meet with Biggers. With the bluecoat chief."

Besides, the bearded Pale Eyes driver yelled back: "Striker, my orders is to get all of these bucks to Fort Sill!"

So it was settled.

A kernel hit him on the nose, and Rain Shower exploded with giddiness. Daniel found her, saw he picking another kernel, tossing it, but laughter spoiled her aim. This one bounced off the crown of his hat.

Ben Buffalo Bone played his flute. Rain Shower threw a handful of corn. Daniel loved the way she looked, how she laughed.

253

He shielded the cannonade of corn, plucked a kernel from between his legs, and fired a salvo that sailed over Rain Shower's head.

The corn fight was on.

Cuhtz Bávi hit Frank Striker. Quanah buried the toe of Nagwee's moccasins. Nagwee dumped a handful on Quanah's bowler. Corn and laughter flew with the musical notes. Only Ben Buffalo Bone, who played a merry tune, and Isa-tai and Charles Flint did not participate. Ben would have, Daniel felt, had he not been enjoying the flute. But Isa-tai and his son? They just did not seem to know how to laugh.

"Cut out that damned foolishness!" the driver of the wagon called out, and sprayed tobacco juice onto the road. "Cut it out, I say! We're almost to the fort!"

They did not listen. The war went on until Ben Buffalo Bone lowered the flute. He raised his head, and then they all heard.

Strains of music from the bluecoat band reached them, and they pulled themselves to their feet, corn spilling off their bodies into the wagon or down their clothes. Daniel reached up, grabbed the top of the side, and pulled himself up.

They drove into the parade ground at Fort Sill. It looked as if the entire Army was out there, standing at attention in the hot, humid afternoon, in dress uniforms, brass buttons reflecting the sunlight, brass horns of the regimental band wailing, drums rolling like thunder.

Metal Shirts were there, too. Daniel recognized Agent Joshua Biggers, Bible in hand, and Twice Bent Nose. Other Indians — not just The People, but Kiowas and Apaches — stood. They were singing songs, welcoming Quanah back.

Daniel dropped back down. Tears streamed down Quanah's face. Ben Buffalo Bone tried to match the band's melody with his flute.

It was a happy time, and, when Rain Shower reached up and took Daniel's hand, he knew he had not felt this way in months. Everyone in the wagon sang.

Except for Isa-tai and Charles Flint. Isa-tai's sharp eyes locked on Nagwee. Flint stared acidly at Daniel. But holding Rain Shower's hand, seeing the laughter in her face, hearing the music in her voice, Daniel scarcely noticed.

CHAPTER NINETEEN

"I prayed for Quanah. I will continue to pray for him. He looks weak."

Agent Joshua Biggers, the Baptist minister from North Carolina, ducked behind his desk, and opened a drawer filled with papers.

"Don't you think so, Daniel?"

Weak? That's what Isa-tai had been telling several *Nermernuh* men outside by the corrals. Quanah felt so weary from his near-death that his wives had returned him to that pale-eyes-built Star House so they could care for him. He lacked the strength, Isa-tai railed, to guide The People. The blue-coats and the agent should appoint a new leader. Isa-tai should be that leader.

Said Daniel: "Quanah is strong."

"Yes, that he is." The young preacher returned his attention to the papers. "We also held a memorial service for Yellow Bear. A great number of Indians and whites attended. A fine turnout. I'm sure Yellow Bear would have been glad." Biggers's head shook. "What a tragic accident."

Daniel did not respond. *Tragic? Yes. Accident? Hardly.*

Not far from Cache Creek, headquarters for the Comanche, Kiowa, and Apache reservation was a small cabin, hotter than Hades except during the bitterest winter. A drawing of the Easter resurrection, done by a Kiowa girl on ledger paper, had been tacked to the wall, book-ended by portraits of Grover Cleveland and Jesus. Unlike his predecessors, Joshua Biggers kept his desk relatively free of filth, unless you considered the dust that spread across everything. The only thing not coated with the fine powder was the Bible in the center of the desk.

"Ah, here it is." Biggers rose, turned, and slid the yellow envelope across the desk. "This came for you the day before yesterday."

The last thing Daniel expected was a telegram. Especially one from William J. Kyne less than a week since they had left Fort Worth.

THINGS ABOUT TO BOIL OVER HERE STOP CARMODY HAS NO NEED FOR COMANCHE GRASS STOP LEASES

WITH CHEROKEE FOR HIS HERDS STOP TELLS ASSN HE WILL SELL HIS COMANCHE LEASE STOP NOW WE KNOW REASON STOP BLACKMAIL STOP HAVE YOU TALKED TO CHRISTENSEN YET STOP

"I trust this is not bad news, Sergeant."

Daniel shook his head. Not bad news, but what did it mean? If what Kyne said were true, blackmail was an obvious deduction. Sol Carmody had bought rights for a full year to lease The Big Pasture for $250. The Northern Texas Stock Growers' Association had offered . . . what? Daniel wished he had his Old Glory tablet with him to check. His memory said it had been $17,000, $18,000 . . . no, $19,000 or thereabouts.

"Christ Almighty!" Immediately he felt shamed. He looked up, saw the ashen look on Joshua Biggers's face, and apologized for taking the Lord's name in vain. For breaking one of the Ten Commandments back in Carlisle, the School Mothers would have pounded his knuckles with their rulers until he bled.

He studied the wire.

The People would get $250 under the agreement Isa-tai had signed with Carmody. That *Tejano* would net $19,000. Men,

258

women, and children — red, white, all colors — had been murdered for a much smaller sum than that. Carmody would have a big reason to silence any protest from Quanah, or Yellow Bear.

He shoved the telegram into his vest pocket, and looked back at the agent. "Before we left for Fort Worth, you were brought a paper. An agreement to lease The Big Pasture. Signed by Isa-tai."

"Yes, that's true."

"Do you still have it? May I see it?"

Biggers returned to the drawer. A minute later, Daniel had stepped into the doorway for better light.

To who this konserns

this leter is a agrement Btwen Sol Carmody, Elm Fork of trenety Rver, Tex, and Kiyota Dropins, reeprezentin the Comanch nation

in xchang for $250 per anum, the Comanch nation aagres 2 let "The biG pastir" to the S-C⅚, Ω5, ††† and .45-70 brands — all regestred Dallas, Tex, Sol Carmody OwNer.

no Othr Brands wil be allwed 2 Share grazin leese withot Carmodys apruval

This leter is Legaly bindin 2 all parteys.

Signed on this 12th day off jewLie in year of our Lourd 18 and 88

Solomon R. Carmody

X [Kiyota Dropins]
Witnesd by
V. Christensen
X [Tony johnsoN]
George McEveety

Daniel reread the letter. Carmody's *segundo,* Vince Christensen, had been one of the witnesses. He didn't know any Tony Johnson, but suspected that he could be found riding for one of Carmody's brands. George McEveety's signature, however, surprised him. Maybe that would give the document more of a legal standing in the pale-eyes courts. Daniel just didn't know.

"I didn't do anything wrong, did I, Sergeant?"

Shaking his head, Daniel returned the letter to Joshua Biggers. That was something new. Previous agents would have told Daniel to shut up, warning him that this was none of his affair, and that the letter was legal, valid, and nonnegotiable.

"The handwriting is atrocious, the spelling a comedy of errors," Biggers said. "Immediately I took it to the trading post, and Mister McEveety confirmed that he had signed it. I found Charles, and asked him to take me to see his father, just to make sure. I knew Quanah had something in mind for

260

The Big Pasture, but Isa-tai himself said he signed it. I decided that if anything were wrong, Quanah would let me know, take it directly to the colonel at Fort Sill, or, knowing Quanah's connections, all the way to Washington City. I guess I should have asked you about it, Sergeant."

Daniel shook his head, thinking: *No, I should have asked Ben Buffalo Bone.*

"I will speak to Mister McEveety about this," Daniel said. "Thank you, Reverend Biggers."

Once the trading post had been a brilliant red building that stood out on the prairie for miles, but an unrelenting sun and constant wind had faded the paint to more pink than red, and dust and dirt made it look more brown than pink. Still, by reservation standards, it remained impressive — a two-story building of wood planks with a fancy façade and plenty of windows on the top floor. The awning over the front porch sagged a little, as did the porch, and one of the steps was missing, and chickens squawked and pecked in the coyote-fenced coop to the side. Two Kiowa women sat cross-legged in the shade by the door, and a burly black man stood on the other side of the porch, broom in one hand, cigarette in the other. Dogs yipped as Daniel rode up, but it was too hot to be barking, so the ugly, bone-thin mongrels quickly retired under the porch, growling steadily to inform the newcomer that they weren't too tuckered out to take a chunk out of his leg if provoked.

Daniel expected to find George McEveety upstairs, where he lived in a small room in the back — the rest of the floor a warehouse, stockroom, something like that. Rumors around Fort Sill said the upstairs were also used for something more stimulating than the chicory he sold, but less sanitary. Instead of sweating in his quarters, the gray-bearded merchant sat on an overturned barrel, fanning himself with a newspaper, and slaking his thirst with a bottle of root beer.

"Well, if it ain't Gen'ral Metal Shirt hisself," McEveety said. "Step off your high horse, Killstraight." He held out the bottle. "Want some firewater, chief?"

The Negro exhaled smoke as he laughed at his boss' joke.

After swinging from his horse, Daniel wrapped the hackamore around the hitching rail, carefully climbed the steps, and greeted the two stone-faced Kiowa women who ignored him.

He stopped and leaned against a sun-rotted column, as much as he dared, and looked through the open door to see Charles Flint showing off a bolt of yellow calico to one of Twice Bent Nose's daughters. When he returned his attention to George McEveety, the trader was gulping down the rest of his root beer, and had stuffed the newspaper into a knothole. His face was pasty, hair matted with sweat, and the armpits of his shirt dark and stained. From where Daniel stood, he could smell McEveety's stink.

"I wish to ask you some questions, Mister McEveety," he said.

With a burp, McEveety leaned forward on his makeshift chair and pitched the empty bottle over the porch railing. "If it's them Old Glory writin' books you want, I still don't carry none. Ream paper and envelopes. That's all I got, and not much of them. Not much of a market, or a profit, for writin' when most of the customers is ignorant savages. Ain't that right, Buck?"

The black man laughed again.

"This is about an agreement you witnessed for the Texas rancher named Carmody."

McEveety's smile vanished instantly, and he shot from his chair. "Don't you. . . ." He stopped, turning, half smiling as Twice Bent

Nose's daughter — Daniel couldn't recollect her name — passed through the door, holding three yards of the calico in her hand. She sang out a hello to Daniel, bid the merchant and his helper good day, but did not speak to the two Kiowa women.

No one spoke until she was out of earshot.

The merchant waved a railroad spike of a finger in Daniel's face. "That tin shield don't give you no right to question me, boy. I might call you a white Comanch', but you ain't no white man. Best know your place, Killstraight. Don't get uppity like some Yankee nigger. I tol' that Bible-thumper I signed it, and I signed it. That's the end of the story, boy. End of the story."

Buck, the black man, no longer laughed.

Daniel met McEveety's glare for ten full seconds. No one spoke. Even the dogs had quit growling. Footsteps on the hardwood floors turned his attention to the doorway, and there stood Charles Flint, wearing sleeve garters and wiping ink off his fingers with a handkerchief.

Suddenly Daniel remembered, and he couldn't help but stare at the bookkeeper's hands. The ink, he found with relief, was black. Flint shoved the handkerchief into the pocket of his trousers, and said: "If it's referring to that letter my father signed,

Daniel, I can answer any questions."

"That's right," McEveety said. "You two bucks hash things out. I got a store to run." He spit between the cracks in the porch, and stormed inside.

The black man stepped off the porch, and walked around the post. The Kiowa women remained silent.

"You never mentioned this in Fort Worth," Daniel said after a long silence.

Flint sighed. "I did not think it was important. My father said he signed the paper. The rancher also said so." He shrugged, and leaned against the door frame. "I am sorry, *bávi*. I did not know this was important. I am no detective. I am a bookkeeper."

It was Daniel's turn to sigh. He crossed the porch until he found a comfortable, shadier spot on the wall to lean on. "It is not important," he told Flint. "I just wonder why he" — motioning inside the store toward McEveety — "would witness it."

"He is a white man. A man of property. People would not question his word."

Daniel wasn't quite so sure about that. George McEveety was not Lee Hall or Burk Burnett. Still, he nodded as if in agreement with Flint. "This Carmody," Daniel said. "I have not seen him on our land before. Did he know McEveety? Has he traded here before?"

Flint shook his head. "The only time I ever saw the *Tejano* was in Fort Worth at the restaurant. I swear this is true." His eyes said he wasn't lying, and Daniel felt remorse for having doubted another *Nermernuh,* no matter who his father happened to be.

"Your father signed the agreement?"

"*Haa.* This he has never denied. You know that as well as I do. When Agent Biggers brought the agreement to the post, Mister McEveety said he had signed it, and then we took it to my father. He said the words were what he and Carmody agreed to."

"The other witnesses," Daniel continued. "Vince Christensen works for Carmody. The other is someone named Tony Johnson. Do you know them? Have they ever . . . ?"

"Their names mean nothing, *bávi.* But that does not mean I have never seen them here or anywhere."

Hoofs clopped down the road, but Daniel ignored them. He stood there, staring at his moccasins, trying to decide where he should go next. Well, that seemed obvious.

"I must go back to Fort Sill," he said.

"Why?"

"To send a telegram to Hugh Gunter." Stupid. He should have thought about that before leaving the agency, after Biggers had shown him the wire from Kyne. It was out of the way, but Deputy Marshal Harvey Noble had taught Daniel not to believe everything you read. He would need to confirm with Gunter that Carmody did lease Cherokee range. "Then I must find this Vince Christensen. He was in Fort Worth, near the hotel, the night. . . ." He stopped short.

"I hope both help you better than I have done, *bávi*. I am sorry to have failed you."

Daniel looked up, started to tell Flint that he was not to blame, but the bookkeeper was gazing at the steps, a smile replacing his frown, and that's when Daniel heard the giggling of girls' voices. He straightened, turned, and saw Oajuicauojué's laughing face as she slid off her pony, and climbed the steps. Behind her strode her older sister, Rain Shower.

"We have come to trade," Oajuicauojué announced. She treated Daniel to a coquettish grin, and slipped inside the door.

"I must go," Flint said, and followed.

Rain Shower passed through the threshold without a word, without a glance at Daniel.

Angrily Daniel stormed off the porch, swung into the saddle, and kicked his buckskin mare into a gallop.

CHAPTER TWENTY

When he reached The Big Pasture the following morning, his heart felt lighter, and he regretted his jealousy. He should not be angry at Rain Shower, or at Tetecae. This land, perhaps the most holy that belonged to The People, often affected him so. It made him happy, let him forget whatever troubled him.

Surrounding The Big Pasture, the Wichita Mountains stood bold, powerful, the trees so verdant that even the rocks looked green. In the pasture, the tall grass was lush, almost reaching his saddle, waving in the refreshing breeze.

The mare's hoofs splashed across a creek, and, somewhere to the north, a longhorn bawled. Daniel couldn't see the cow, however, for the grass was too high.

What struck him as odd, though, was the fact that he couldn't see any cattle. Oh, he knew they were there, but finding three thousand head of dumb *Tejano* beef in three hundred thousand acres could take forever. Usually, at this time of year, it was impossible not to stumble over cattle the Pale Eyes shipped north to graze during the summer. Of course, Daniel didn't need to find the cattle. He just rode toward the smoke rising from the edge of the woods at the foot of a hill. The wind carried not only the smell of smoke, but the aroma of coffee, and bacon. That, he knew, would lead him to Vince Christensen.

The mare snorted, stopped, and Daniel heard the dung splatter beneath the grass. He waited, then let his mount graze on some of the grass. *Why let Carmody hog it all?* he asked himself.

Ahead of him, in the rocks above the smoke, sunlight glinted. Daniel leaned forward, wondering. The mare lifted her head — and saved Daniel's life.

He never heard the shot until the echo reached him after the mare lay in the grass, kicking spasmodically though already dead. He had pitched out of the saddle, rolled through the grass, and now started to push himself up. The second shot tore through the grass far from him. On his knees, Daniel reached for the revolver, spotted something brown through the tall grass, came to his feet, and sprinted toward it.

The second shot he heard, and felt, instantly. It dug a ditch across his left side, and knocked him into the mound of manure the buckskin had just deposited, ricocheting off the boulder in front of him. Rolling over, he felt tears stream down his face, and he cursed himself for crying, but, son-of-a-bitch, his side hurt. The next shot kicked up mud into his cheeks, and he raised the Remington, shakily, and snapped a shot.

"Damned *taibo* gun!" he said through clenched teeth. The percussion cap had misfired.

He turned over, crawled, leaped the final feet, and pulled himself into a ball behind the boulder a second before the next bullet clipped off the side of the big rock. Daniel moved to his right, aimed, pulled the trigger. This time the Remington bucked in his hand, and he slid back behind the boulder.

"Stupid." He lowered the smoking revolver. The shooter had to be a good two hundred yards, probably more, from where he squatted — far out of range for the antiquated cap-and-ball revolver the agency provided him with. From the thundering echo that bounced off the Wichitas, from how hard his horse had dropped, from the way his side bled and throbbed, he was up against one of those far-shooting Sharps rifles the *Tejanos* had used to whip The People at Adobe Walls.

Daniel had no chance, and he knew it. Now would be a good time to begin his death song.

A fly buzzed. Next came the sound of hoofs on hard rock. Daniel picked up the Remington, thumbed back the hammer, and leaned to his left. Cautiously he pushed back the grass with the long barrel. Sweat burned his eyes, clouded his vision, but he spotted a horse — brown, maybe a bay — trotting up the hill, away from the snaking smoke. He couldn't make out much about the rider, other than he wore a light-colored hat and a duster that billowed behind him in the wind. Still, he wasn't truly certain that he wasn't hallucinating. Horse and rider vanished behind the hill, and Daniel slid back behind the rock. He tore a strip of cloth from his calico shirt, pressed it against his side, and pulled himself up.

Dizziness and nausea almost knocked him onto his back, but somehow he managed to keep his feet. Salty sweat poured into the wound, and he bit his bottom lip. Cattle bawled, and more hoofs sounded, but these came from the east. Still, Daniel fumbled for his revolver, felt it slip from his fingers

271

and off the boulder, and felt himself sliding back to the ground.

"Vince! Vince!" A shot rang out.

"Get up!" Rough hands dragged Daniel to his feet. A hand slapped his face. Fingers gripped his black hair, and pulled it until Daniel screamed. His eyes opened.

Another shot roared. Daniel managed to glimpse a Pale Eyes cowboy on a side-stepping horse cock a Colt, send another bullet toward the sky. "Vince!" the rider yelled.

"Damn it, Joe," the man pulling Daniel's hair snapped, "lope over yonder. See what the hell's going on. See if Vince is wounded or what. Now! We'll bring this buck along."

"Bet these Comanch' was tryin' to steal our herd," another voice said. "And Vince stopped 'em."

He neither heard nor saw the rider leave. The next thing he knew, his face was mashed against the flank of a horse. He thought he saw the brand, †††, but wasn't sure. Someone jerked him by his vest into the saddle, and then the rider swung up behind him, the saddle's big horn jamming into Daniel's bleeding side. Spurs chimed, and the horse exploded.

Daniel vomited.

A sledge-hammer jarred his head. "Do that again . . . I kill you here."

Air rushed out of his lungs. The cowhand had thrown him to the ground. He reached for his bleeding side, but, before he made it, a boot rocked his ribs. What the buffalo gun's bullet had failed to do, the boot succeeded. Three ribs cracked, and Daniel felt his bladder release.

"Bastard. This red bastard. . . ."

"Put that gun away."

"But he murdered Vince. Slit his throat!"

"We ain't shootin' him."

"But. . . ."

"We're hangin' the red nigger."

Someone jerked his head off the gravel. Hemp slid over his head, tightened against his throat. They jerked him to his feet. The rope choked off his air. When he fell, they dragged him.

"To that blackjack yonder."

He wouldn't live to make it to the tree. He'd choke to death right here, or bleed to death.

Another cannon roared, and a *taibo* screamed.

A pistol roared over Daniel's face. He forced his eyes open, found out he could breathe again, saw a gloved hand cock a revolver. Another bullet screamed, and the man holding the gun fell back, crying out in pain.

"It's the whole damned Comanche nation!"

"Injuns! God A'mighty, they'll butcher us all!"

"Shut up, Joe!"

Then, guttural English: "Guns down! Now! Else die!"

Shadows crossed his face. How cool it suddenly felt, and he opened his eyes. Twice Bent Nose's ugly face hovered above him. His mangled hands reached down to Daniel's side, and Daniel flinched, tightened his eyes, remembered how he had wet himself, and felt shame. He was no warrior, but a frightened child.

"Just stand back there." This was in English. A voice he recognized.

"You speak English? This bastard killed our foreman. Slit his throat."

"Look at him. Look at him. Look at what he done to Vince!"

"Just shut up. Don't move. We don't want to kill anyone."

He turned his head. Did not believe what he saw. Charles Flint stood, rifle in both hands, standing in front of three or four *Te-*

274

janos, yelling at them. One more Pale Eyes sat against a rock, blood soaking through his blue shirt at the left shoulder.

Another voice reached his ears, this one speaking the language of The People, saying that coup had been counted, that now it was time to kill these thieves, or turn them over to The People's women for torture. Horses snorted all around him, and Daniel made his head turn the other way.

"No, Father!" Charles Flint's voice again. "We will not kill anyone!"

Daniel swallowed. Isa-tai swung around on his horse, face defiant, holding a rifle over his head. Then he began to sing. To Daniel's surprise, he did not argue with Flint or Twice Bent Nose. Instead, he sang a song of pride.

Look at my son
Look at my son
Look at my son
See how brave he is
See how brave he is
He has taken his first coup
He has saved the life of a warrior of The
    People
We will sing songs in his honor
Look at my son
Look at my son

Look at my son
Tetecae
Tetecae
Tetecae
See how brave he is

The words held no meaning for Daniel. Not now. What he wanted to focus on, what he had to remember, was the rifle Isa-tai held. It was a Sharps, one of those far-killing weapons of the buffalo hunters. And Isa-tai's face. He must remember that, too. Painted red.

CHAPTER TWENTY-ONE

He woke into a world of darkness.

Cold. Damp. The smell of rot.

As his eyes grew accustomed to the darkness, smoky gray light sneaked between iron bars on a window above him. Shivering, he brought his hand to his forehead. Even that slight exertion exhausted him, and his hand slid off his head and struck hard rock, wet rock, skinning his knuckles. His throat felt parched, and fire blazed across his side every time he drew a breath. He ran his tongue over cracked, bleeding lips. He touched his chest, realized he lay on a blanket, shirtless, though his ribs were bandaged. Turning his head, he could just barely make out the thick door. Dripping water was the only sound, almost deafening, maddening, until he began to make out voices carrying beyond the barred windows.

He called out, but no one could hear a whisper he barely heard himself. He was alone, but Daniel knew where he was. He had sent his share of men here himself.

Bluecoats called it the dungeon. The People knew it as The Lodges That Are Always In Darkness.

The post guardhouse at Fort Sill.

Daniel closed his eyes, letting sleep overtake him again.

The song brought him back to life. A gourd rattled over his head, then his chest, and he felt the cloth being pulled away, small fingers gently applying a salve to the wound in his side.

The rattling and the chant stopped, and a strong voice called out: "You are awake, my son!"

His eyes fluttered, focused, and a mostly toothless smile greeted him.

Tears filled his eyes, and he tried to reach up to Nagwee. The *puhakat*'s fat hand swallowed his, and pressed it against his cheek.

"We feared for you, He Whose Arrows Fly Straight Into The Hearts Of His Enemies. I wanted to perform another *pianahuwait,* but the Long Knives would not allow it. They will not even allow you into the big doctor house at the soldier fort. But my *puha* remains strong. You will live, and that is good for The People."

"Tsu Kuh Puah," Daniel whispered. "I shamed The People. I disgraced myself. When the Pale Eyes wounded me, I cried from the pain. When one kicked me in the ribs, I wet myself."

Nagwee lowered Daniel's hand, and patted his shoulder. "There is no disgrace. You performed bravely. The Pale Eyes say you killed a *taibo.* You would have killed the others, but there were too many. It is good that Twice Bent Nose arrived when he did, or we would speak your name no more. Instead, now, we will sing songs of your bravery, in your honor. For you. And for Twice Bent Nose, Tetecae, and Isa-tai, who stopped the other *Tejanos* from killing you."

Hands began wrapping a new bandage across his side and chest, but Daniel tried to comprehend what Nagwee had just told him. He wet his lips, blinked, shook his head slightly.

"Tsu Kuh Puah." Speaking hurt. He wanted to ask for water, but felt he needed to explain first. "I killed no one."

"Hush." The sharp, feminine voice brought his attention to his chest, and he flinched as those delicate, once gentle, hands tightened as they knotted the bandage. Daniel looked away from Nagwee and met Rain Shower's stare.

"Don't talk," she said. "You are still weak."

His lips parted, but she raised a warning right fist. His lips closed. His Adam's apple bobbed.

As Nagwee disappeared in a dark corner, Rain Shower suddenly broke out in laughter. Briefly Daniel joined her, but his ribs ached too much, and he shook his head, fighting off the pain. The medicine man returned, sat, gently lifted Daniel's head, and he tasted sweet, cool water. He drank greedily, wanted more, but this Nagwee would not allow.

The old holy man then gathered his belongings, and walked away. Daniel heard Nagwee's fist hitting the door. Keys rattled, metal turned, and the door dragged heavily against the rock floor as it opened.

"You done?" a bluecoat voice called out.

With a grunt, Nagwee stepped into the hall.

"Hey, woman. You done?"

"No!" Rain Shower answered in English.

Tobacco spit splattered into the slop bucket in the corner, and the door slowly shut.

"I did not kill that *taibo*," Daniel told her.

"This I know. The Pale Eyes are such fools. The agent, Biggers, he yelled at the big bluecoat chief, but they say you must stay here. For now. One *taibo* is dead. Another, in the soldier fort, might die."

She slid down the blanket, and touched his hand. Daniel shuddered.

"I hear Tetecae was very brave." He stumbled over the words.

"*Bah.* He is not as brave as you. Twice Bent Nose was even braver. He stopped them from. . . ." She couldn't finish, forced a smile, and tried again. "And Isa-tai, his *puha* was very strong. He shot the one the Pale Eyes say might die. But you were the bravest. One *Nermernuh* against a dozen Pale Eyes." She leaned forward, and pressed her lips to his.

"It was not that many," Daniel said after they had kissed. He knew he sounded un-convincing.

"Twice Bent Nose says there were even more Pale Eyes."

"He. . . ." Daniel shrugged, and gave up on trying to translate the pale-eyes phrase "stretches the truth" into the language of The People.

She kissed him again, though this time on his forehead, and stood. "I must go. The bluecoat will be impatient."

"I. . . ."

He didn't know what to say, so she said it for him: "I love you, He Whose Arrows Fly

Straight Into The Hearts Of His Enemies. I have always loved you. I will always love you."

He runs in the morning sun, side no longer throbbing, legs no longer weak, wearing not the uniform of a Metal Shirt, but buckskins and moccasins, no shirt, a lone hawk feather hanging behind his left ear. He carries a magnificent shield that would have impressed even old Isa Nanaka.

Stopping, he reaches down and plucks the leaves from a bush, crumpling them in his hand, bringing them to his nostrils. The scent is stimulating. It makes him free. Sage. Holy sage. He stands in a field of sage that stretches across the prairie. Nothing to see but blue sky and green sage.

The marsh hawk lands on a nearby clump.

Daniel sees it, and greets the raptor politely.

"This is holy land." The marsh hawk speaks in the voice Daniel remembers as his father's.

"It is." Daniel nods. "The People will always cherish it."

"No," the hawk tells him. "The People will not have it for long. That is to their disgrace."

"I do not understand."

"You will, my son. In time, you will."

Silence. The wind blows. Daniel and the hawk fill their lungs with sage-sweet air.

"Your side has healed?" the hawk asks.

"It hurts no more."

"Because of this holy ground."

"Haa. And because of Nagwee's puha."

"Haa. His puha has always been strong."

Another voice whispers behind him: "Should I bring up your disgrace, Isa-tai?"

"Yellow Bear?" he asks, whipping his head around, but discovers nothing but sage.

Daniel's head falls, and he cannot look back at the marsh hawk. Tears stream down his cheeks.

"What is the matter, Oá?"

He looks up. The hawk called him Horn, the name Daniel had been given before his father presented him with his own name, He Whose Arrows Fly Straight Into The Hearts Of His Enemies.

"I spoke the name of a brave Nermernuh who has traveled to The Land Beyond The Sun." Daniel's voice cracks as he confesses, and bitter tears flood the ground.

The hawk shakes his head. "He was not dead when you spoke his name."

He forces his head up, sniffs, wipes the last tears from his eyes, and says: "I do not understand."

The hawk spreads its wings. "This is holy land."

Silence. The wind still blows.

"What else troubles you?" the hawk asks.

He touches his side. Now it hurts. "Father," Daniel says, "I disgraced myself. I cried when those Pale Eyes shot me. I wet myself when they broke my ribs."

"Nagwee said there was no shame, and I am not one who would argue with Nagwee. Pain is no disgrace, Oá. Nor is fear. Neither means cowardice, and you are no coward, my son. No, pain and fear are part of life. And death."

Yellow Bear's voice comes from another direction. "Should I bring up your disgrace, Isa-tai?"

When Daniel looks, however, again, he sees nothing but sage, so he turns back to his father.

"What does he mean?"

"Who?"

"The one who has traveled to The Land Beyond The Sun."

"I did not hear him, my son. He was speaking to you. Not to me."

"Why have you come?"

"Because I love you."

Tears well again. His voice chokes. "I love you, too, Father."

"The marsh hawk is your puha, as it was mine," his father says. "You will always find strength in the hawk. That is why you wear my feather on your hat."

He reaches up, surprised. He is wearing the battered, dusty black hat he had bought at McEveety's post a year earlier. But hadn't he been wearing just a ribbon and a lone feather dangling behind his ear? He turns the hat around by the brim, the feather floating in the breeze.

Sage remains pungent.

When he hears Yellow Bear's voice again, now coming from the north, he does not bother to look. His tears stain the sage leaves, which turn into blood.

"It is hard for you, Daniel," the marsh hawk says. "It will always be hard for you."

"I am not Daniel," he says.

"You are Daniel. And you are Killstraight. And you are Sergeant. And you are He Whose Arrows Fly Straight Into The Hearts Of His Enemies. You are Oá."

Adds a feminine voice: "And you are Huuma."

He pivots, heart aching, and gazes at his mother, the way she looked before the Kwahadis surrendered. Young, beautiful. She has not come to him in the form of an animal, but as a Mescalero captive who became one of The People.

Smiling, he asks: "I am With The Stick? This I do not understand."

"When you were but a child, just learning to walk, wherever you went, you would be carrying a twig." His mother's voice is musical, relaxing, as refreshing as the sage. *"Perhaps it gave you balance. Perhaps you just wanted it to chew on, for often that is what you did. Always, however, you grasped a stick. So your father and I called you With The Stick."*

"I do not remember this."

"Of course not," the hawk tells him, *"for you were too young."*

He closes his eyes, trying to summon the memory of this childhood story, but can't. When he opens his eyes, his mother has gone.

"Mother!" He turns, desperate. The hawk has flown away. Daniel stands alone in a wilderness of sage. His side begins to throb. He wears the uniform of a Metal Shirt.

"One thing lasts forever," the familiar voice says, and, when he turns to the west, he knows he will see Yellow Bear this time.

Sitting cross-legged, the old man prepares a pipe, which he offers to the directions before breathing fire into the bowl. Yellow Bear smokes, then offers the pipe to Daniel.

"What lasts forever, *Tsu Kuh Puah?*" Daniel asks. *He smokes, and passes the pipe back to the elder.*

"Not you," Yellow Bear replies. *"Nor I.*

286

Certainly not the buffalo. Sadly not even this."
He gestures toward the sage. "Perhaps not
The People as we know The People. Certainly
not the taibos, ignorant and as unclean as
they are. Not the Mescalero. Not the marsh
hawks."

"Then what?"

"Love." Yellow Bear nods. "Some day, the
taibos, especially the Tejanos, will say that
The People fought them the hardest, and why
did we do this? For the love of our family. Our
ways. Our land. Love endures."

"I do not understand."

"I think you do." The pipe has disappeared.
"Isa Nanaka remains with you. As does Marsh
Hawk. And your mother. I will always be here
for you, my son. Quanah and Nagwee will
always be here for you. Rain Shower will
always be here for you. Don't forget us. We
shall not forget you. For we love you. And we
know that you love us. You love all The
People. That is why you are a Metal Shirt."

Yellow Bear's body is becoming translucent.

Desperation fills Daniel's voice. "Don't leave
me! Tsu Kuh Puah!"

The old man smiles. "I said I will never leave
you, my son."

"But there is something you said." Yellow
Bear is fading into the sage. " 'Should I bring
up your disgrace, Isa-tai?' You said that. But

what does it mean?" He shouts to only sage. "What does it mean? Please, Tsu Kuh Puah. What does that mean?"

From the east echoes Yellow Bear's fading voice. "I think you know the answer to that question, too."

Alone, sweating, he closes his eyes, trying to dam back the tears. When his eyes open, he no longer sees a never-ending field of sage. Something flaps above his head, and he looks up, finds the bluecoat flag of red and white stripes, of stars in a night sky, flapping in the wind.

Daniel stands in the center of the parade ground at Fort Sill.

CHAPTER TWENTY-TWO

Now he knew how Quanah had felt when the Fort Worth doctor insisted he take a wheelchair to the T&P depot. Defiantly pushing aside the curved walnut cane Major Becker had offered him, Daniel stood, taking a deep breath. That was a mistake. Pain rifled up his side, making him grimace, but Daniel tried not to show how much he hurt.

"Are you ready?" Rain Shower asked.

"I am ready." He took a tentative step toward the open door.

"You're as mule-headed as Quanah Parker," Major Becker said, causing Daniel to smile.

Light almost blinded him when he stepped into the tiny hallway, and he was still inside the guardhouse. He fumbled along, feeling Rain Shower beside him, hearing the footsteps of Major Becker, the post surgeon, behind him. From outside, came angry voices, muffled by the prison's thick stone walls. A bluecoat snapped to attention, and pulled open the outer door.

Even more light. Daniel had to stop, squeeze his eyelids closed.

"Are you sure you don't want this cane, Daniel?" Major Becker asked.

He wasn't quite sure of anything, but he forced his eyes open, waited for the dots to disappear, and stepped into clean air for the first time in a week.

"There's the murderin' savage!"

"We should have lynched that sum-bitch when we had the chance!"

"What kind a law is this, Marshal?" a voice thundered. "Lettin' a murderin' red devil out?"

"Reckon that's the kind of law a Texian should expect from a damyankee."

"Carmody." The drawl eased Daniel's tension just a tad. "You're the biggest damned fool I've had the displeasure of meetin' in a month of Sundays."

The big *Tejano* rancher straightened, face turning scarlet, and started to raise a fist, but Deputy U.S. Marshal Harvey P. Noble stopped him with words.

"That's right, Carmody. Add assaultin' a federal peace officer to the charges I might file against your ornery hide. Hell, I might even call it attempted murder." Noble's big, gloved hand rested on the butt of his revolver. "Or maybe, with my luck, I won't have to file no charges, just a report on how come I killed a worthless cur at Fort Sill."

Another cowhand said: "Why aren't you chargin' that buck with murder? He killed Vince Christensen. Slit his throat like you'd do a deer."

"Daniel Killstraight didn't kill anyone." That was another familiar voice. Turning, Daniel spotted the Cherokee policeman, Hugh Gunter, sitting at the edge of the guardhouse's porch, his long legs dangling toward the ground. Gunter was whittling a stick, but now he stopped and pointed the blade of a Barlow knife at one of Carmody's cowhands.

Daniel looked around. Carmody stood in front of the steps to the guardhouse, facing Harvey Noble. Behind the big rancher waited four cowhands, holding the reins to their mounts in their left hands, their right palms balancing precariously over the butts of their own weapons. Carmody's big dun grazed on Army grass. A buckboard was parked beside the dun. In the back, Daniel saw, were two pine coffins.

Hugh Gunter was still speaking. "Your man got his throat slit. Daniel yonder didn't even have a knife on him. Plus, you idiots yourselves said you found Daniel shot in the side, his horse killed, three hundred yards from where your ramrod's body was found. Now how in the hell do you figure Daniel killed him?"

Before one of the cowhands could speak, Gunter cut him off: "Maybe you reckon that Daniel is a big medicine man among the Comanches. Maybe he used some redskin magic to slit this Christensen gent's throat. Then changed that knife into a Forty-Four Remington. Then managed to shoot his own horse in the head. 'Course, that must have been more Comanche magic 'cause the bullet we dug out of that horse's head was a chunk of lead that had to be Fifty caliber. About the same caliber that likely cut Daniel's side."

"Who the hell are you?" another cowboy demanded.

Gunter closed the blade. "I'm your better."

The reins dropped to the grass. The cowhand made a beeline, but stopped at the click of the hammer of a Colt now held in Harvey Noble's right hand.

"How many bodies you want to haul back to Texas, Carmody?"

"Whit," Carmody said, "let it lie."

The cowboy's fist clenched. His body

shook. But he stayed put.

A blond-haired cowboy with a freckled face — likely still in his teens — cleared his throat. "Well, Vince sure didn't shoot this Indian, neither. Not if you say it was a Fifty caliber. Vince had a Forty-caliber Bullard."

Another cowboy snickered. "And he couldn't hit the backside of a barn, let alone a movin' target three hundred yards away."

"We never said your cowhand shot anybody, either," Hugh Gunter said. "Hard to shoot anybody, with your throat slit ear to ear. But you Texians'll believe anything."

"Hugh. . . ." Noble's voice revealed tension. "Let's behave like gentlemen."

"Gentlemen!" Carmody spat. "Damyankees. Damned prairie niggers."

"I didn't come here to start a ruction, Carmody," Noble said, his voice powerful and steady once again. "Came this way to stop one. And I'm no Yank. Born, bred, and baptized in Arkansas." He reached into his jacket, and pulled out a folded set of papers. "This here is a court order that says you are to get your Texas longhorns off The Big Pasture. Forthwith. That means no dilly-dallyin'. If you don't, Carmody, I'll just say it's ration day and the Comanches, Kiowas, and Apaches'll have three thousand head to slaughter."

Carmody made a start for the marshal, but the Colt stopped him, too. "I got it legal," Carmody stammered. "Isa-tai . . . he signed."

"Carmody" — Noble shook his head pathetically — "you must be an idiot. After you come up here and got an ignorant Comanche to sign three copies of a letter you wrote out, Quanah Parker and the Northern Texas Stock Growers' Association were having their lawyers file writs in courts. You gave one copy of that thing you wrote to your cowhands to give to any Indian or agent, kept the other to yourself, gave another one to Dan Waggoner. Figured that made everything legal, especially since you had witnesses sign it, too."

"Witnesses." Hugh Gunter chuckled.

"Yeah." Noble's head shook. "Vince Christensen served time in Huntsville for manslaughter. He also rode for you. So did that other cowhand, can't rightly recollect his name. And then you got George McEveety. He left two wives behind in Mississippi. A bigamist. Also, the way I understand it, a liar, cheat, whoremonger, whiskey peddler, and genuine rapscallion. Yes, sir, that's a fine band of witnesses you got."

Sol Carmody stood, flexing his fingers. Noble paused to give him time to speak, but, when the rancher said nothing, Noble kept talking. "You didn't even file the *agreement* you got with any court. Didn't have it notarized. This ain't the old days, Carmody. It's Eighteen Eighty-Eight. We're civilized. Mostly."

"That paper. . . ."

"Is as worthless as you are, Carmody. Hell, you might be facin' criminal charges of extortion. Judge Parker and me'll have to talk that over with the commissioner. You didn't need that grass. You got plenty in the Cherokee Nation. Ain't that right, Hugh?"

Gunter nodded. "He did. But that agreement is being reconsidered after what all's come up hereabouts. Sol Carmody ain't the type any of us Five Civilized Tribes want to associate with."

The rancher's mouth hung open.

"You just thought you could take advantage of these poor Indians and make a handsome profit for yourself," Noble told him. "What was that we figured he'd make out with, Hugh?"

Gunter answered: "Nineteen thousand two hundred and fifty dollars."

Noble smiled. "Sounds like grand larceny. Yes, sir, a real handsome profit . . . if it worked."

"It didn't," Gunter said. "Stupid Texians."

Daniel fought off dizziness. Comprehending all this was proving too hard.

"A Comanch' killed Tony Johnson, Marshal," another cowboy said. "Witnesses will swear to that."

"And I got witnesses who'll say they was part of a tribal police posse stoppin' a bunch of trespassin' Texians from lynchin' a Comanche peace officer." Noble shook his head in disgust.

"That's for a jury to decide, ain't it?" yelled another cowboy, his head bandaged, left eye blackened. Apparently he was the one upon whom Charles Flint had counted coup.

"I ain't wastin' Judge Parker's time on something as picayune as this." Noble waved his Colt at all the cowhands. "Your Johnson boy was killed by Isa-tai, but that was self-defense. Criminy, I should run the lot of you in for tryin' to lynch a bona-fide peace officer. But then them ticky mossyhorns would still be eatin' Comanche grass that rightfully belongs to Capt'n Hall and his outfit."

Noble's tone changed. "The other one, your top hand, well, you're damned right. That was murder. Cold-blooded. But Killstraight didn't do it. I'm certain sure of that. You rest easy, Carmody. All of you Texas

296

brush poppers. I'll find the son-of-a-bitch, and that son-of-a-bitch'll hang."

"Even if it was an Injun?" the man named Whit asked. " 'Cause you seem to like a lot of Injuns, Marshal." The cowboy glared at Gunter, who pushed his silk top hat back with the stick he had been whittling, and smiled.

Another rider came loping toward the guardhouse.

"It was not an Indian," said Daniel, who suddenly faced better than a half-dozen stunned men.

He took a step down. Gently. Another. His side seared, but he made it to the bottom without falling. Rain Shower stood behind him, her face worried. He wet his lips and said: "I saw a man. White man. On a dark horse. He rode over the hill, away from camp. He must have seen your riders coming across The Big Pasture."

"Could you recognize him, Daniel?" Gunter asked.

His head shook. "Too far away. He wore a hat. Tan, I think, but it could have been covered with dirt. And. . . ."

The rider reined in on a blood bay gelding. Daniel swallowed. The man slid off the saddle, grabbing his back with one hand, while fetching a note pad with the other.

"Damnation," he said. "Looks like I've got another story that'll get me a job back in the East. Showdown at Fort Sill! What's going on here? I'm Billy Kyne. Dallas *Herald*."

The ends of Kyne's duster flapped in the wind.

"So, Marshal, let me get all this down straight. Factual, for once in the *Herald*'s short, fruitless life." Billy Kyne took a swig from his flask, which he passed to the federal deputy.

They sat in Noble's and Gunter's camp in the sage west of Fort Sill near Cache Creek, the Cherokee poking the fire under the coffee pot, and Noble, looking worn out and pale, rubbing a foot with one hand while sitting on a rock.

Daniel sat beside Rain Shower. She held his hand.

"You read the *Herald* story. We telegraphed that to all the Fort Worth papers, even to the federal marshal. I'm sure you saw it. Heard about it in the dram shops and all."

"All I saw was the writ the marshal give me. All I heard was what he told me." Noble took a drink, and passed the flask to Gunter, who pitched it back to Kyne without taking a sip.

"Well, the *Herald* . . . well, actually me . . .

broke the story. It'll be in *Harper's Weekly* soon, I assure you. Don't know how many papers in the East. Carmody's scheme has been foiled. He attempted to blackmail the Northern Texas Stock Growers' Association, wanted to deprive the great Comanche nation" — winking at Daniel and Rain Shower — "of wealth the tribe desperately needs. But justice, thanks to the Dallas *Herald,* prevails. Can I quote you, Marshal?"

Noble drank again from the flask Kyne had tossed him. "All I saw was the writ the marshal give me," the deputy repeated. "All I heard was what he told me."

"Excellent. This case is closed." Kyne waited for the flask to come back his way.

It was Gunter who spoke. "Hell, it ain't over. Who the hell killed that Texas waddie? Who the hell shot Daniel?"

Kyne looked perplexed. "I thought the cowhand shot Daniel."

"Uhn-huh." Gunter flung the stick into the sage. "Then cut his own throat out of remorse."

The end of the pencil went into Kyne's mouth. He turned it, biting, several rotations before removing it and writing something in his tablet. "Well, this is excellent to be sure. Another mystery. Another article for the *Herald,* or better yet, the New York

Tribune." He wrote again, then looked at Daniel. "And who tried to murder Quanah? Right, Daniel?"

That got both Noble's and Gunter's attention.

"What are you talkin' about?" Noble asked. "From what I read, that was an accident."

The eyes bore into Daniel, who took a deep breath, slowly exhaled and said: "It was no accident."

They waited for his explanation.

"You say it was a white man, eh, Killstraight?" Kyne was talking again, talking and scribbling, scribbling and talking. "The one who shot you? The one who slit the cowboy's throat?"

Instead of answering, Daniel asked: "When did you get here, Mister Kyne?"

"I arrived at Fort Sill when they carried you into. . . ." He dropped the pencil, and smiled weakly. "Killstraight. Surely. . . ." His eyes darted to Noble's, then Gunter's, to Rain Shower's, and back to Daniel's. "Killstraight. We're pards. You don't think I'd. . . ." He wet his lips.

Undeterred, Kyne scooped up his pencil, slid it over his ear, and thumbed back several pages in his tablet. "This is interesting, gentlemen. Most interesting. Three men witnessed the document Carmody signed with Isa-tai. Two of those are dead. The third is George McEveety, a wretched man who runs the foul trading post in these godless parts. I think it's time for me to interview that cad and get to the bottom of this. If you'll excuse me, gentlemen." He tipped his hat at Rain Shower. "And you, dear squaw, as beautiful and as lovely as Hera, daughter of Kronos, wife of Zeus, I bid *adieu*."

Even before Billy Kyne was on his horse, Gunter had filled a tin mug with coffee. "Daniel," the Cherokee asked angrily, "how in hell did you hook up with that insufferable son-of-a-bitch?"

Daniel smiled. "Actually," he said, "he reminded me of you."

CHAPTER TWENTY-THREE

In the cabin the Pale Eyes had built for Ben Buffalo Bone's father, Daniel ducked under the pinto's neck, his right hand gently rubbing the coarse hair. He came up on the other side of the horse, walking over straw, speaking softly, his hand never leaving the pinto's body. The stallion's tail swished. "Good boy," Daniel said, and stepped away, admiring the animal.

"Cuhtz Bávi is too generous," Daniel said. "I should not accept such a gift, for I have nothing of value to return to your uncle."

Rain Shower grabbed Daniel's hand and squeezed it. "Cuhtz Bávi," she said, "thinks he will get the horse back."

She giggled.

It was a Mexican Hat pinto, and Daniel knew what The People said of a horse like this: ride it, and you are invincible. That Rain Shower's uncle, the head of the household since her father's death, would give such a gift overwhelmed him.

"Do you . . . ?" He stopped. Saying — *Do you think you would be worth such a pony?* — did not strike him as a smart thing to say, especially considering how much he enjoyed her hand in his.

"What will you call him?" she asked.

He shrugged. "What would you?"

She held her chin, considering. The white cotton dress she wore highlighted her round face and raven hair. Ben Buffalo Bone, Daniel decided, was wrong. Rain Shower was far more beautiful than her younger sister. She would be worth twenty horses like the Mexican Hat pinto.

"I would call him Kwihnai."

"Eagle." Daniel nodded. "It is a good name. I will call him that."

Leaving the horse to graze on hay, Daniel led Rain Shower around the makeshift stall and into the portion of the house where Daniel lived. Gingerly Daniel bent down and picked up the saddle, a wood and deer-horn frame covered with rawhide and a Navajo saddle blanket.

"You are leaving?" Rain Shower sounded hurt.

"I must try out my new pony," he said lightly, forcing a smile.

"Your wounds have not completely healed.

You should not ride hard."

"I will go no faster than a trot."

"You should not go far."

"I won't go far."

"How far?"

He stopped his work, and grinned at her. "Crater Creek."

After gathering his hackamore along with the saddle, Daniel went back to Eagle. Rain Shower followed him.

"That is where Nagwee has his lodge," she said.

"That is who I must see."

She did not speak again until Daniel had saddled his new horse, and returned to his living area to gather his holster and revolver. Her face turned hard as her frown.

"I am not going there to arrest Nagwee," he said lightly.

Silence. Then: "You think Isa-tai is responsible for all of this."

He did not answer. Instead, he checked the caps on the Remington.

"Isa-tai would not. . . ."

"Isa-tai despises Quanah," he said. The jovial banter was gone, and he regretted that, but he knew what he had to do. "He would have given away The Big Pasture and The People would have nothing."

"He did not shoot you."

304

Daniel holstered the Remington. "He carries a rifle like the one the Pale Eyes used to hunt buffalo with."

"Which he took off a Pale Eyes he himself killed." She raised a finger. "You said it was a *taibo* who shot you."

"I saw a man in *taibo* clothes riding over the hill. Having thought more of this, I now realize that person did not have to be the one who shot me." It could have been Billy Kyne, riding away upon hearing the shots for the reporter was, at heart, a coward. It could have been anyone. Hell, it could have been Isa-tai, dressed up in pale-eyes clothes. Even had Daniel been able to identify the man, he could never prove that rider had shot at him. Not in a *taibo* courtroom.

"Isa-tai saved Quanah's life," Rain Shower argued. "He and Nagwee performed the Big Doctoring."

"And Isa-tai painted his face red."

"That is his *puha*. And what does it mean? The paint he wears does not make him a murderer."

Sighing, Daniel explained the red prints that had been found on the windowpane and lamp globes at the room above the Fort Worth mercantile. "Billy Kyne said it was red ink."

"Ink." Rain Shower shook her head. "A

Nermernuh uses vermillion, not ink."

"Perhaps it was vermillion." He led Eagle out of the cabin and into the sunlight.

"If he had meant to kill you," Rain Shower said, "you would be dead. Isa-tai has the best eyes of any of The People when it comes to shooting a long gun. Tetecae told me that himself."

Daniel swung into the saddle.

"He saved your life," Rain Shower said. "He killed one of the Pale Eyes who was trying to kill you. He saved the life of Quanah."

He wanted to explain, but found no words. Rain Shower started to argue more, but her expression changed, and she stiffened.

"I must see Nagwee," he said. "I will speak to you later."

"I must see someone, too," she said.

He pressed the paint horse's sides with his moccasins, and felt Eagle take flight.

In the blistering heat of the day, with no clouds to block the sun's rays, Daniel found Nagwee sitting in his brush arbor. Three dogs barked as he rode Eagle across Crater Creek, and Daniel greeted the old *puhakat,* and swung from the saddle.

"*Maruaweeka!*" Nagwee called out, and

306

began gathering his pipe and tobacco. "That is a fine horse you ride, my son."

"Thank you. It was a gift from Cuhtz Bávi."

The old man laughed. "You should be giving Cuhtz Bávi horses, not the other way around."

Daniel stepped inside the arbor, and Nagwee motioned for him to sit. Hot as the afternoon was, Nagwee had a small fire going in the brush arbor, as if he had expected someone would join him for a smoke.

"What do you call that horse?" the old man said as his thick fingers and thumb packed the bowl with tobacco.

"Kwihnai."

"A good name. You want to trade?"

Smiling, Daniel shook his head.

"I could run him in many races against the Long Knives. I could win much money."

"I could race him myself."

"Then I will bet on you. Let us smoke."

"Two nights ago," Daniel said carefully, "I had a . . . dream."

Nagwee lowered the pipe. "A vision?"

He shook his head. "I said a dream, *Tsu Kuh Puah.*"

The old man's belly bounced as he laughed. "Sum-bitch," he said, using one of the few pale-eyes words he knew and liked, "He Whose Arrows Fly Straight Into The Hearts Of His Enemies had a vision."

Again Daniel started to protest, but Nagwee held up his thick right hand. "Tell me of this dream."

They smoked again after Daniel had told the *puhakat* all he could remember of the dream, or vision, or whatever one called it. One of the dogs had fallen asleep in front of Nagwee's teepee, and snored. This was the only sound.

"Why do you come to me?" Nagwee asked.

"You are a man of great *puha.* You are the wisest *puhakat* among The People. My father once went to you when he had a . . . dream. You explained to him his purpose, you told him what he needed to do, what the vis- . . . what the spirits told him he should do. You have helped Quanah. You have helped many. I hoped that you might help me."

Nagwee looked up. His smile became lost in the crevasses of his large face.

"You don't need me, my son. You already know."

"I. . . ."

"Tell me. Tell Nagwee what you think this vision means."

Daniel swallowed, looked away. After inhaling deeply, he faced the *puhakat* again. "First, will you tell me about Medicine Bluff Creek?" he asked.

Nagwee grunted. "The People knew it to have much healing powers. It was the most priceless thing The People had."

"Sage grows there," Daniel said.

The old man nodded. "Where sage grows, the land is holy."

Daniel waited, trying to find the right words, and finally said: "Major Becker. He is the doctor at the soldier fort where the Long Knives stay. He tells me that Fort Sill was established in Eighteen Sixty-Nine. Um . . . nineteen winters ago."

Nagwee looked at the roof of the arbor, chewing on his lips, tapping his fingers, then faced Daniel again. "That would be just about right."

"The People were powerful then, stronger than we are now. We would not have let the Pale Eyes just take this land from us. We would have fought them."

Nagwee's thick fingers began tamping the pipe bowl again. "We are lucky," he said. "Many of the Apaches, they were sent from their homeland to Florida, as were many of our own warriors. But now our men . . . those who have not traveled to The Land

Beyond The Sun . . . have returned to this country. The Apaches stay here, too, far from their home. The Cherokees, the Creeks, those other inferior Indian peoples who live toward the rising sun, they are many miles . . . too many for an old man like me to count . . . from their homes. The Pale Eyes drove them out. We live near Medicine Bluff Creek. That is good."

Daniel made his voice stern as he repeated: "Fort Sill stands on The People's holiest ground. That soldier fort has stood there almost as long as I have breathed. We would not have let the Pale Eyes just take this land from us. We would have fought them."

Setting the pipe down, Nagwee looked solemn. A tear fell down his cheek. "We could not fight them," he said. "They did not steal the land. It was given to them."

Tears welled in Daniel's own eyes, and he looked away, shaking his head, mumbling: "And that is Isa-tai's disgrace."

Nagwee cleared his throat. "Isa-tai was a young *puhakat* then. He trusted the Pale Eyes. He loved them. When the bluecoats came, it was Isa-tai who led them to Medicine Bluff Creek. He thought if he gave the Long Knives The People's most precious thing, they would love The People. They would let us alone. He did not know or understand the true nature of all Pale Eyes. Later" — Nagwee had to stop to wipe away the tears, to swallow down the bile — "later . . . when he saw what was in the pale-eyes hearts, he became bitter. That is why he wanted to wipe out the killers of the buffalo. Maybe he would have, had not the Cheyenne brave destroyed his *puha*."

Daniel tried to shake his head clear. "Did Quanah know this?"

"I think not. When Isa-tai gave the Long Knives our land, Quanah would not have been much older than you are now. He was a warrior, a fine, brave warrior, but he was not the great leader of The People that he has become. Besides, Quanah, your family, and most of the Kwahadis lived in the land of the *Tejanos,* on the Staked Plains, not along Medicine Bluff Creek. Quanah would not come here until more than a handful of winters later."

Daniel stared at Nagwee. "Who knew what Isa-tai had done?"

Nagwee shrugged. "Most are names we must never speak again."

"But the father of Quanah's favorite wife. The one who traveled to The Land Beyond The Sun when we were in the *Tejano* town called Fort Worth . . . he knew."

The nod was solemn, final. "Yes, he knew."

He had been awake for more than an hour, but still lay on the blanket, one arm over his head, the other gently holding his aching side. Cuhtz Bávi's dogs barked in the morning light, and Eagle stamped his hoofs, demanding breakfast. Daniel tried to block all of that out. The dogs barked louder. Ben Buffalo Bone yelled.

A horse snorted, and Daniel realized someone had ridden to Cuhtz Bávi's lodge.

Back in Fort Worth, Tetecae had said Yellow Bear's death had been an accident, and Daniel had believed that. Quanah had been the intended victim. Why would anyone want an old *puhakat* like Yellow Bear dead? Now, Daniel realized how wrong he had been. If Quanah had died, Isa-tai would not have grieved, but it was Yellow Bear who he had to silence.

Yellow Bear.

A piercing wail, almost inhuman, lifted Daniel out of his bed. Next came shrieks. Shouts. The sound of confused dogs running away. Cuhtz Bávi's voice began a death song, and Daniel was up, holding his ribs, running through the door.

He saw the horse, a blue roan pulling a travois, recognizing the rider as an Apache named Netdahe, head hanging down. Sitting beside the travois, Ben Buffalo Bone's mother lifted her head to the sky, and screamed.

"No!" Daniel yelled.

Tears blinding him, he stumbled, falling to his knees beside the travois. His vision returned, though he wished it hadn't, and he reached down, and lifted Rain Shower into his arms. He hugged her tightly, kissed her cold forehead, rocked her, rocked her.

Ben Buffalo Bone was sawing off his braids. Cuhtz Bávi mourned his niece and adopted daughter in song. Daniel felt as if he had been kicked in the stomach. He laid Rain Shower's head back on the travois, kissed her lips, stroked her hair, saw the bruises around her throat.

He also spotted a smudge of red ink on the collar of her new white dress.

Savagely he shot to his feet, found the Apache, and demanded: "Where did you find her?"

Netdahe did not understand the language of The People. Daniel had to sign his question, and the Apache answered. Netdahe had not been in this country long, but Daniel knew where he meant.

Blue Beaver Creek. Along the sage. Where Isa-tai lived.

He headed toward his lodge, which seemed to become farther from him, not closer, weaving now, heart shattered, trying to find a way to make it to Eagle.

Then he was lying on the ground, curling up like an infant, crying . . . wishing he were dead . . . wondering how he could ever go on . . . alone.

CHAPTER TWENTY-FOUR

"Daniel. . . ." Closing his Bible, Agent Joshua Biggers pushed himself to his feet. His mouth opened, and his face showed shock and repulsion, which the young minister tried to hide.

His hair had been shorn, shorter now than even the Pale Eyes had cut it at Carlisle. He had carved gashes on both forearms, his calves, thighs. The arm wounds had clotted, but the legs bled again after his ride to the agency headquarters. Biggers would likely never understand how The People grieved. Ben Buffalo Bone had chopped off not only his braids, but his left pinky. Daniel had considered removing fingers himself, but then he remembered how Rain Shower had held his hands, and he could not bring himself to do that.

Standing in front of Biggers's desk, he looked at the ring he had braided from Rain Shower's black hair. He tried to find courage, tried to stop the tears from overflowing again.

"Daniel," Biggers tried again. "I know this is hard. But you must believe me, my son, when I say that she's in a far better place now. Matthew said blessed are they that mourn, blessed are the meek, blessed are the merciful, blessed are the peacemakers, blessed are the pure in heart. Rain Shower was all of those, and much, much more."

Daniel looked at the wall. " 'Blessed are they which are persecuted for righteousness's sake,' " he said, " 'for theirs is the kingdom of heaven.' "

"That's right." Biggers followed Daniel's gaze. He tapped on the drawing tacked to the wall. "A Kiowa girl drew this. I just think it's beautiful. Because of what happened at Calvary, Daniel, Rain Shower won't really die. She lives now, with Jesus. She'll be there waiting for you. But she'll also always be with you."

Daniel stepped around the desk. He studied the picture. Reached up, touched it, and with a curse, snatched it from the wall, and stormed outside.

"Jesus, look what the cats drug up." George McEveety laughed as he pushed himself off the overturned keg, and blocked the doorway to the entrance path. He was alone outside this day. The Negro named Buck was nowhere to be seen. Nor were the two silent Kiowa women. "Hold on, Killstraight. You ain't bleedin' all over my merchandise, boy. You just turn. . . ."

Daniel hit him, feeling the pain shoot through his ribs, feeling the gashes in his arms open again. From underneath the porch, the dogs barked. McEveety bounced into the wall, and Daniel struck him again, again, once more as the trader slid to the porch. Then he kicked McEveety in the head, and moved to the counter.

Dogs growled, but none dared climb the steps.

"My God, Daniel!" Charles Flint said. "What . . . ?"

"I was at the agency just now," Daniel said. Somehow he reached the counter, and leaned against it. He had to catch his breath. Blood ran down his arms and into his fingers, dripping onto the dust that coated the store's floor. His side screamed in pain. His legs ached, throbbed, bled.

Flint remained quiet. When Daniel could breathe again, he said: "I was requesting permission to arrest your father."

The bookkeeper straightened. "Daniel, my father did not kill anyone . . . except the *Te-*

jano who he shot to save your life."

Daniel reached to the ledger. He turned a page.

"He gave away Medicine Bluff Creek," he said, and turned another page, then looked at Tetecae to see his expression. "The People's land. Holy land. Gave it to the bluecoats." He turned another page. "Just as he would have given away The Big Pasture." Another page. "For nothing."

"You're wrong, Daniel. My father saved Quanah's life. Your life. My father is a great man. A powerful *puhakat*."

"He shoots a big buffalo rifle."

"Which he took from a dead *taibo*. Along with the scalp he also took from that Pale Eyes when we were children. Look!" He pointed to the rack of weapons, most of them worthless old muskets, chained behind the counter. "Even on the reservation, it is easy to find a rifle."

Turning another page in the ledger, Daniel said: "Isa-tai wears red paint."

"For his *puha*."

Daniel looked up. "Why was he wearing red paint when he saved me?"

Flint shook his head. "He didn't go there to save you. We . . . Twice Bent Nose and I . . . we ran into him and a party of young braves he was leading. He was planning on stealing cattle from the *Tejanos,* as he said he would."

Daniel flipped the page.

"My father did not kill Yellow Bear," Flint said. "He did not kill the *Tejano* cowboy. He did not try to kill Quanah. He would never have harmed. . . ." He looked down.

"Can you say her name?" Daniel asked.

Flint's head shook.

"I know your father is innocent," Daniel said, his heart breaking as he tapped on the page of the ledger. "You did it."

Flint's head jerked up, and he took a step back. His eyes fell to the ledger.

"Bávi. . . ."

Flint rocked back, his lips bleeding. Daniel didn't even realize he had backhanded the bookkeeper until he saw the blood, saw his own hand shaking over the counter.

"Don't call me brother!" Daniel roared. "I saw the Kiowa girl's drawing on ledger paper on Agent Biggers's wall. Red ink. Black ink. I remember the phrases now from Carlisle. 'In the red' and 'in the black.' Never did understand what they really meant."

Daniel's breath had the taste of gall. He shook his head with disgust. "The girl I loved once said Isa-tai was a great shot with a rifle, and she spoke the truth. Your father taught you how to shoot. I had forgotten that. You obviously hadn't and, as you say, finding a weapon was easy."

Before Flint could protest, Daniel added: "I thought I saw a *taibo* riding away after I was shot. But it was you . . . wearing your pale-eyes clothes."

"I rode there with Twice Bent Nose. . . ."

"You rode into Twice Bent Nose. He told me that at the agency. You had no choice but to ride back with him. And then your father and his raiding party joined up. Saving my life was an accident, Tetecae."

Flint shook his head, touching his lips with trembling fingers.

"And here's something else," Daniel said. "The only person who knew I was going to see the pale-eyes cowboy was you. I told you that right here. You weren't sure what Vince Christensen had seen in the alley in Fort Worth, so you rode there, slit his throat, and tried to kill me."

Flint shook his head, tried to laugh, and said: "Daniel, you are way, way. . . ." But Daniel's eyes told the bookkeeper something else, and Flint threw the inkwell into Daniel's face.

Turning, trying to shield his eyes, Daniel slipped, hit the floor hard. His chest cried out in pain. He saw Flint leap over the

320

counter, saw something flash in his hand. As Flint ran for the door, Daniel drew his Remington.

Hearing the hammer click, Flint turned quickly, bringing up his arm, a pepperbox pistol in his right hand. Daniel's Remington roared first. The bullet smashed the wall, startling Flint. He never fired his pistol. Instead, he turned away, ran for the door.

Daniel's second shot struck Flint in the back, and the bookkeeper tripped over George McEveety's boots, crashed onto the porch, tumbled down the steps.

The dogs wailed, yipped, barked, but remained hiding under the porch.

Stepping over the unconscious trader, Daniel had to lean against the warped column for support. He still held the pistol, but hadn't cocked it. Charles Flint was sitting, one hand stanching the flow of blood from his lower back, not looking at Daniel, but at a *puhakat* mounted on a fine buckskin stallion.

Isa-tai frowned at his son.

"Father," Flint groaned. "You have to understand. . . . Father . . . I did it for you . . . Yellow Bear . . . he would have told everyone about Medicine Bluff Creek. You remember? The cowboy . . . he might . . . I don't know . . . I had to make sure. . . ."

"And what of her?" Daniel barely recognized his own voice.

Flint shook his head. "She . . . saw. . . ." Speaking in English now, pleading to Daniel: "I didn't mean to hurt her, Daniel. I swear to God I didn't mean it."

He flung his head back to Isa-tai. "Father," he said in the language of The People. "I had to protect you. You remember, Father. You said giving away our most precious land was your biggest disgrace . . . *until they sent me to Carlisle!*"

Isa-tai said nothing. Straightening his shoulders, he spit, turned the buckskin away, and eased the horse down the trail, back toward Blue Beaver Creek.

"Father!"

Daniel came down the steps.

"Father!"

He didn't remember walking, but now he stood over Flint. Daniel cocked the .44's hammer.

Flint turned, face streaked with tears, with pain. "Kill me, Daniel!" he begged. "For God's sake, kill me. Kill me. Kill me. Please, please, please, just kill me."

Daniel raised the revolver.

CHAPTER TWENTY-FIVE

He remembered Isa-tai's song.

My son is dead to me
My son is dead to me
My son is dead to me
He is dead to all The People
Hear me now
Tetecae
It is the last time
You will hear his name
He is dead
Speak his name no more
He is dead to me
He is dead to me
He is dead to me
He is dead to us all
He forgot the ways of The People
The People's ways are good
The People's ways are good
The People's ways are good
I have no son

Do not mourn him
Do not speak his name
He is not worthy
My son is dead to me
My son is dead to me
My son is dead to me
He is dead to all The People
Hear me now

Then the rest of Isa-tai's song haunted Daniel as the song had done for the past eight months.

I am dead to The People
I am dead to The People
I am dead to The People
I am dead to all The People
Hear me now
Isa-tai
Do not speak my name
You will not hear my name
I am dead
Speak my name no more
I am dead to you
I am dead to you
I am dead to you
I am dead to you all
I forgot the ways of The People
The People's ways are good
The People's ways are good

The People's ways are good
I gave away our most holy land
Do not mourn me
Do not speak my name
I am not worthy
I am dead to you
I am dead to you
I am dead to you
I am dead to all The People
Hear me now

He hadn't planned on being here, yet here he stood on a cool spring morning in Fort Smith, Arkansas, having delivered seven prisoners to the cold, dark dungeon to await their trial. Most of his wounds had healed, and his hair was growing back, but now those wounds felt raw again, and he thought that maybe he should just leave. Turn back.

Deputy U.S. Marshal Harvey P. Noble, dressed in the uniform Judge Parker made all his volunteers wear for this special duty, put a hand on Daniel's shoulder. "You sure you're all right, Daniel?"

He nodded.

"All right. If you need anything, I'll be" — Noble frowned — "up there."

Daniel watched the tall, aging deputy climb the steps, and take his place beside George Maledon.

"Here he comes!" a reporter called out, and a melody of voices rang out.

Two, almost three years earlier, Daniel had watched three men hanged on these same gallows, but on this April morning, Charles Flint, also wearing a new suit, stepped onto the platform to die alone. A man in a dark suit began reading from a paper, but Daniel did not care to listen to the words.

"Hello, Killstraight," a voice sounded behind him. Daniel glanced over his shoulder, then turned away from the gallows.

William J. Kyne had lost weight. His clothes looked more expensive, and he sported a well-groomed beard. His breath smelled of coffee, not rye. The reporter even looked sober.

"The *Herald* send you up here?" Daniel asked.

With a wry smile, Kyne reached into his vest pocket and withdrew a card, which he passed on to Daniel. "The Cincinnati *Commercial.* It isn't the *Tribune,* isn't New York, isn't even the East Coast. But it's a start."

Daniel returned the card, and started to look back. Off in a shady corner, six elderly women began singing as a Black Robe prayed for Charles Flint's soul.

"I hate to do this, partner," Kyne said,

"but it's my job."

Daniel looked back. Kyne withdrew a folded piece of paper from his pocket. "Captain Pratt wired this to the newspaper reporters here. Wonder if you'd care to comment?"

Daniel took the paper, unfolded it, read:

FIRST, I WISH TO EXPRESS MY DEEPEST SYMPATHY TO THE PARENTS, FAMILY, AND FRIENDS OF VINCE CHRISTENSEN STOP

Only the Pale Eyes, Daniel thought bitterly. *Not Yellow Bear. Not Rain Shower. But, then, Charles Flint wouldn't be hanging if he had killed only an old Comanche man and a young Comanche girl.*

JUSTICE HAS BEEN SERVED AND I HOPE THIS ENDS THE UNCALLED FOR ASSAULT THAT HAS BOMBARDED THE CARLISLE INDUSTRIAL SCHOOL STOP WE DO NOT TEACH MURDER STOP FOR ALL THOSE NAYSAYERS I AGAIN POINT OUT THAT IT WAS A COMANCHE INDIAN AND A FORMER STUDENT AT THIS SAME SCHOOL WHO SOLVED THIS EVIL CRIME AND BROUGHT THE PERPETRATOR TO JUSTICE STOP I

HAVE ALWAYS PREACHED THAT WE MUST KILL THE INDIAN AND NOT THE MAN BUT IN THIS CASE WE MUST EXECUTE BOTH MAN AND INDIAN STOP MAY OUR LORD IN HEAVEN HAVE MERCY ON CHARLES FLINT'S SOUL

Behind him, the trap door thudded, the choir gasped. Daniel heard everything — and felt relief that he had not seen Charles Flint die.

Daniel returned the telegram to Kyne, who wrote something in his notebook, then asked: "Well?"

Daniel shook his head. "I have nothing to say."

Kyne's smile was truly sad, but not from disappointment. "That's what I figured. Don't worry. I won't make up something and attribute it to you. Unlike the Dallas *Herald,* the *Commercial* has real journalistic standards." He offered his hand. "I am sorry, Killstraight, about that girl. Can't remember her name, but I know she was sweet on you, and I reckon you liked her a lot, too." He shook his head. "She was pretty. It was a damned shame, Killstraight. I mean that."

To his surprise, Daniel accepted the handshake, then watched Billy Kyne excuse himself, and hurry over with the rest of the newspaper reporters to talk to the marshals, Flint's court-appointed attorney, and the hangman, Maledon.

Daniel stared at the ring he had made from Rain Shower's hair. Birds began to sing again.

He had wanted to say something, to let Billy Kyne quote him, but knew he couldn't. Kyne couldn't have understood. Nor would have School Father Pratt. Even the agent, Joshua Biggers, who tried to understand, couldn't. Without glancing back at the gallows, Daniel stepped with the crowd through the gates and into the throng of curious Pale Eyes waiting outside the execution yard's walls.

As he walked to Eagle, he thought again of what he had wanted to tell Kyne, but what no Pale Eyes could ever comprehend.

When you kill the Indian, you kill the man.

AUTHOR'S NOTE

Most biographies of Quanah Parker mention his near-death escape from asphyxiation in Fort Worth, Texas. He was sharing a room with Yellow Bear, his father-in-law or uncle (depending on which account) at the Pickwick Hotel or, as Richard F. Selcer notes in *Fort Worth Characters,* in the second-floor apartment of an adjacent building. In all accounts, a gas lamp was left on, Yellow Bear died, and Quanah barely escaped with his own life.

Murder conspiracy? Highly unlikely, but the story seemed too good an opportunity to pass up, so I turned it into a murder mystery. The incident happened in December 1885, but I moved it to the summer of 1888.

Sources for Fort Worth included the aforementioned *Fort Worth Characters* by Richard F. Selcer (University of North Texas Press, 2009) as well as Selcer's *Hell's*

Half Acre (Texas Christian University Press, 1991) and Oliver Knight's *Fort Worth: Outpost on the Trinity* (Texas Christian University Press, 1990).

For the Comanche language, I relied on *Comanche Vocabulary: Trilingual Edition,* compiled by Manuel García Rejón and translated and edited by Daniel J. Gelo (University of Texas Press, 1995), *Comanche Dictionary and Grammar* by Lila Wistrand-Robinson and James Armagost (SIL International, 1990), and the Comanche National Museum & Cultural Center in Lawton, Oklahoma.

As always with my Killstraight novels, William T. Hagan's *Indian Police and Judges* (Yale University Press, 1966) and *United States-Comanche Relations: The Reservation Years* (University of Oklahoma Press, 1990) proved valuable, as did *The Comanches: Lords of the South Plains* by Ernest Wallace and E. Adamson Hoebel (University of Oklahoma Press, 1952, 1986). Other sources include *The Comanches* by Joseph H. Cash and Gerald W. Wolff (Indian Tribal Series, 1974); *Comanches: The Destruction of a People* by T.R. Fehrenbach (Alfred A. Knopf, 1974); *Los Comanches: The Horse People, 1751–1845* (University of New

Mexico Press, 1993); *Encyclopedia of Religion and Ethics, Part 22* by James Hastings and John A. Selbie (Kessinger Publishing, 2003); and *The Comanches: A History, 1706–1875* by Thomas W. Kavanagh (University of Nebraska Press, 1996).

I also made a new friend in fellow Comanche enthusiast and historian, S.C. Gwynne, whose *Empire of the Summer Moon: Quanah Parker and the Rise and Fall of the Comanches, the Most Powerful Indian Tribe in American History* (Scribner, 2010) was a *New York Times* bestseller. I gathered a lot of new information and ideas from Gwynne's powerful book. And, no, Gwynne, a reporter for the Dallas *Morning News,* wasn't the inspiration for Billy Kyne.

Richard Henry Pratt's autobiography *Battlefield & Classroom,* edited by Robert M. Utley (University of Oklahoma Press, 2003), provided background on the Carlisle boarding school, as did *The Indian Industrial School: Carlisle, Pennsylvania 1879–1918* by Linda F. Witmer (Cumberland County Historical Society, 1993). *Quanah Parker, Comanche Chief* by William T. Hagan (University of Oklahoma Press, 1993), and *The Last Comanche Chief: The Life and Times of Quanah Parker* by Bill Neeley (John

Wiley & Sons, 1995) were also frequently consulted.

The Eagle Park Trading Post near Cache, Oklahoma gave me an extended tour of Quanah's Star House and the Wichita Mountains, and an excellent history lesson. The Star House could definitely use some restoration work, but it's still standing, and the post deserves much praise for doing its best to keep this part of Comanche history alive.

Finally I owe my Comanche friends (and Quanah Parker descendants) Nocona and Quanah Burgess, their father, Ronald "Chief Tachaco", and their families many thanks for their help, support, friendship — and their amazing art.

Johnny D. Boggs
Santa Fe, New Mexico

ABOUT THE AUTHOR

Johnny D. Boggs has worked cattle, shot rapids in a canoe, hiked across mountains and deserts, traipsed around ghost towns, and spent hours poring over microfilm in library archives — all in the name of finding a good story. He's also one of the few Western writers to have won four Spur Awards from Western Writers of America (for his novels, *Camp Ford,* in 2006, *Doubtful Cañon,* in 2008, and *Hard Winter* in 2010, and his short story, "A Piano at Dead Man's Crossing", in 2002) and the Western Heritage Wrangler Award from the National Cowboy and Western Heritage Museum (for his novel, *Spark on the Prairie: The Trial of the Kiowa Chiefs,* in 2004). A native of South Carolina, Boggs spent almost fifteen years in Texas as a journalist at the Dallas *Times Herald* and Fort Worth *Star-Telegram* before moving to New Mexico in 1998 to concentrate full time on his novels. Author of dozens of published short stories, he has also written for more than fifty newspapers and magazines, and is a frequent contributor to *Boys' Life, New Mexico Magazine, Persimmon Hill,* and *True West.* His Western novels cover a wide range. *The Lonesome Chisholm Trail* (Five Star Westerns, 2000) is an authentic cattle-drive story, while *Lonely Trumpet* (Five Star Westerns, 2002) is an historical novel about the first black graduate of West Point. *The Despoilers* (Five Star Westerns, 2002) and *Ghost Legion* (Five Star Westerns, 2005) are set in the Carolina backcountry during the Revolutionary War. *The Big Fifty* (Five Star Westerns, 2003) chronicles the slaughter of buffalo on the southern plains in the 1870s, while *East of the Border* (Five Star Westerns, 2004) is a comedy about the theatrical offerings of Buffalo Bill Cody, Wild Bill Hickok, and Texas Jack Omohundro, and *Camp Ford* (Five Star Westerns, 2005) tells about a Civil War baseball game between Union prisoners of war and Confederate guards. "Boggs's narrative voice captures the old-fashioned style of the past," *Publishers Weekly* said, and *Booklist* called him "among the best Western writers at work today." Boggs lives with his wife Lisa and son Jack

in Santa Fe. His website is www.johnnyd
boggs.com.